Killing
Harry Bones

Jonathan Harries

INFINITY
PUBLISHING

ISBN 978-1-4958-1482-2
eISBN 978-1-4958-1483-9

Published July 2017

INFINITY PUBLISHING
1094 New DeHaven Street, Suite 100
West Conshohocken, PA 19428-2713
Toll-free (877) BUY BOOK
Local Phone (610) 941-9999
Fax (610) 941-9959
Info@buybooksontheweb.com
www.buybooksontheweb.com

DEDICATION

To two of the greatest friends ever. Separated perhaps by time and space, but always with me.

Do you know which way the wind will blow?
The sands of time will run?
Be prepared for judgment day for it will surely come.

CONTENTS

Chapter 1..**1**
In which a nasty person gets his comeuppance

Chapter 2..**5**
In which two policemen discuss some grotesque
murders

Chapter 3..**13**
In which Roger Storm contemplates ending his
pointless existence.

Chapter 4..**17**
In which Roger sees a ghost

Chapter 5..**41**
In which Roger meets Freddy for the first time

Chapter 6..**53**
In which Roger hears about a mind-boggling plan

Chapter 7..**67**
In which Roger reflects on another Freddy-fueled
incident during their school days

Chapter 8..**79**
In which Freddy and the *sexy assassin* explain
more of their plan to Roger

Chapter 9..**83**
In which Inspector Bunter visits his colleague,
Inspector Darmstaedter with more bad news

Chapter 10.................................89
In which Freddy and Conchita get even deeper
into their incredible scheme to save Africa

Chapter 11.................................101
In which Roger recalls another of Freddy's crazy
capers

Chapter 12.................................121
In which Roger gets some time to consider his
situation

Chapter 13.................................123
In which Inspectors Bunter and Darmstaedter
hear a rather racy story from the widow
Heidenreich

Chapter 14.................................129
In which an elephant is saved from slaughter

Chapter 15.................................135
In which some really nasty people begin to hatch
a plan of their own

Chapter 16.................................141
In which Roger gets to meet another ghost from
his past

Chapter 17.................................145
In which Roger thinks back to the last time he
saw Jamie alive

Chapter 18.................................163
In which Roger enjoys a delicious meal with the
rest of the team

Chapter 19.................................169
In which Inspectors Bunter and Darmstaedter
come to an interesting conclusion

Harry Bones sat back in the plump, black leather armchair, one of four that surrounded the glass coffee table in his large office overlooking Michigan Avenue in Chicago. Next to two plates of uneaten sushi was an open file with a stack of emails he'd printed earlier that morning. He smiled to himself as he delicately picked up a piece of spicy California role with his well-manicured fingers and dipped it into a little plastic cup of soy sauce. As he bent forward he re-read the top email. "I've never wanted to fuck a dwarf, but if I did, I think I've just seen the perfect one." The email had been written by Roger Storm, the man he'd forced to resign from the company just minutes before.

Harry felt very pleased with himself. He looked at his reflection in the small mirror his therapist had advised him to keep discreetly positioned on the coffee table. There was not a blemish on his recently whitened teeth. Not a strand out of place on his exquisitely-styled grey mane.

Then to his horror he noticed a hair protruding from his left nostril. He gave a shudder of disgust, then deftly plucked the offending follicle with a small tweezer he kept in his coat pocket for just such emergencies. He looked in the mirror once again and breathed a sigh of contentment. All was right with the world. He took one more deep breath and recited the mantra his therapist had given him: "'I am myself. I love myself. I respect myself'."

"I love," myself," he repeated. Because he really did.

He'd finally eliminated all of the people who'd stood to get a lot of money at the end of the year from the extremely profitable advertising agency he owned. It hadn't been easy and it had required a great deal of planning and underhanded sophistry. It might, he realized, force him to dole out a few thousand dollars to some of the sycophants who'd helped him arrange the whole sordid affair. But in the end he would be left with the entire bonus pool. At least three times what he would have taken if he hadn't found a way to eradicate some of his most senior people.

The only thing that had made him slightly uncomfortable about the morning's events was when he'd generously asked Roger what he intended to do now that he'd joined the legion of the unemployed.

"I'm going to think of a way to kill you, Harry."

Harry Bones laughed. He was not in the least bit worried. Roger Storm was a non-confrontational wimp.

He thought about inviting his latest mistress in to share the sushi, but decided against it.

Harry Bones was a very greedy man.

Chapter 1

IN WHICH A NASTY PERSON
GETS HIS COMEUPPANCE

The Okavango Swamps, Botswana
About a year ago

By 8:30 in the morning it was warm enough for the five tourists to strip off the jackets and sweat tops they'd put on to guard against the chill that envelops the bush early in the morning, when sleepy visitors are driven from the various safari lodges around the great Okavango Delta in search of the local wildlife. The open Land Rover carrying Marty and Kitty Nussbaum of Montgomery Alabama, Odile and Benoit DuPlessis, from the 16th arrondissement of Paris and the lately widowed Bernadette Liddesdale from Haltwhistle, Northumberland, had finally stopped for the elderly safari goers to take a much needed pee break. While the women squatted behind a nearby bush to perform their toilette, Peacock, the guide from the local BaTawana tribe, pointed out the male hippo making his way through the clear water of the river towards what appeared to be, from the frantic movement and high pitched squealing, a female hippo partially hidden in the reeds.

"He is in great heat," said Peacock to Marty and Benoit, pointing out the bull's enormous and decidedly tumescent penis.

"Good God," observed Bernadette Liddesdale who, with the other two ablutionists, had rejoined the group. "He's flinging shit around with his tail"

"Yes," said Peacock. "It is a part of the mating ritual. It is how he attracts the woman hippo."

"It would not work for me," snorted Odile.

"I'm not sure anything would," whispered Benoit to Marty.

"You like jig-a-jig?" asked Peacock, who was observing the proceedings with a level of ennui found only in twenty-three-year-olds who are fucking their brains out on a regular basis. "Well that woman hippo she is going to get jig-a-jigged like nothing you can imagine."

"Where exactly is the female," asked Marty. "I can't see her."

"Mostly under the water," replied Peacock. "But she will stick her head up to breathe in a minute."

"I am astonished she can survive," observed the Frenchman as the bull hippo grunted and attempted to mount his submerged mate. The more she struggled to escape from what in more enlightened society would be classified as violent rape, the more determined the bull became.

"There are times when they do not survive," Peacock told them. "Oh yes, there are times when the male will jig-a-jig the female to death."

At that very moment there was a shrill scream. So loud in fact that a group of yellow-billed hornbills flew shrieking into the sky from a Jackalberry tree. The female hippo raised her head from the water.

Except it wasn't a female hippo head that appeared, its features frozen in horror. It was that of a short, fat German trophy hunter whose buttocks had been smeared with pheromones extracted from the vagina of the female hippo he'd shot the day before.

Chapter 2

IN WHICH TWO POLICEMAN DISCUSS SOME GROTESQUE MURDERS

Wiesbaden, Germany
A few weeks later

Chief Inspector Constantin Darmstaedter stared at his phone, hoping to hell it wouldn't ring. It was Friday afternoon, a normally quiet time in the Federal Criminal Investigation Office – the Bundeskriminalamt - and he was looking forward to an early start to the weekend. His in-laws were in town and his extremely wealthy father-in-law had booked at table at M-Restaurant, a trendy place that the good chief inspector couldn't have afforded even if he'd taken that bribe from Elif Bayrak, the Turkish madam of Wiesbaden's most exclusive brothel. Darmstaedter's reverie, which involved a glimpse of the thigh of an Ethiopian woman reclining on Madam Bayrak's chaise, was interrupted by the shrill radar ringtone on his iPhone.

The incoming call flashed up as "private" but he knew immediately it was from his friend,

Senior Inspector Matthew Bunter at Interpol Headquarters in Lyon, France.

For a minute he considered ignoring the call. He knew if he took it he'd have to follow up. And follow-up required effort and effort was not something the Chief Inspector felt like expending just then. He decided that his wife was right about how annoying that particular ringtone was and, more to shut it off than anything else, he answered.

"Matthew?"

"Hello, Constantin, old chap. I'm surprised you're still at the office and not off somewhere drinking a cold pint." Bunter's voice was cheery for a man with three of the most bizarre murders on his plate.

"I was waiting for your call", Darmstaedter lied, "and then I am going to have not one beer, my friend, but several to wash down a splendid meal."

"Don't blame you, mate. Well we can make this quick. Did you manage to find out anything at all about who may have wanted Heidenreich killed?"

Darmstaedter put his feet up on his desk and fumbled in his jacket pocket for his cigarettes, forgetting for a moment he'd given up smoking a few days ago. He looked at his notepad and shook his head.

"It's not an easy question to answer, Matthew. For a start, the list of people who would have liked to see him dead is almost endless. He was a not a jolly good fellow, as you Brits would say."

"In my opinion people who get pleasure from blowing the hell out of defenseless animals seldom are. What other sorts of beastly things did he get up to?"

"The answer to that depends on how long you have to listen."

"Unlike you, Constantin I have a pretty empty evening. So tell me all you can."

"Well, he was a ruthless man in his business dealings. His staff at his various companies hated him – I couldn't find one person who had a nice thing to say about him – and even his wife and son, from the report, didn't seem too upset by the fact that he was dead. Not that I'd suspect them. As nasty a pair of people as they may be, I cannot imagine they could have engineered Heidenreich's death in that particular manner. My God, I think hippos must have enormous penises, no?"

"Up to sixty centimeters," the Interpol man who'd already looked it up on Wikipedia said quite nonchalantly. "Split him like a ripe fig. Horrible, just horrible. No, no, my mind isn't going to his wife or son at all. Even if they could have arranged for him to be shagged to death, they couldn't possibly have had anything to do with the two other murders that I haven't even told you about. But if you can give me a few more minutes I could use that big brain of yours."

Darmstaedter stood up slowly. He liked the idea that Bunter thought his brain was big. He felt it justified the size of his head which, while not out of proportion to his six-foot-five body, had always made him self-conscious when trying to find a bike helmet. He looked at his watch. In truth he had plenty of time before dinner and he'd come to appreciate Bunter a great deal over the past five years. They'd collaborated on numerous cases and established more than just a routine working relationship.

"Whatever you're working on is probably far preferable to seeing my mother-in-law eating beef tartar or listening to my father-in-law going on and on about his irritable bowel syndrome. So yes, Matthew, I am attentive."

"Good man. So look, a month ago some game scouts in a large private game reserve in South Africa found three bodies next to a dead elephant whose tusks had been hacked from its head with a chainsaw. Two were local poachers, but the third was a wealthy Hong Kong businessman named James Chan. His teeth had been ripped from his mouth with a pair of pliers. He either succumbed to shock or choked on his own blood. I don't imagine it was a very pleasant way to die."

"Holy Christ!" Darmstaedter said, feeling dinner with the in-laws might actually be preferable to what Bunter had to say. "What about the third?"

"An American fast-food billionaire named David Lontard who'd been bow-hunting giraffe up in northern Tanzania. His companions found him naked, tied to a wooden post and shot full of arrows."

"Ah, like Saint Sebastian, "Darmstaedter said picturing the early Christian's martyrdom.

"Exactly, except this individual was no saint I can promise you." Bunter laughed at his own questionable wit, but when Darmstaedter didn't respond he carried on in his usual flat tone. "He was a big game hunter who claimed he'd killed one of just about every endangered species there is."

"And you suspect that all of these people are connected somehow?"

"I do. Though other than the fact that they were all rich and ruthless and enjoyed hunting I can't really put my finger on how. It's rather frustrating and, as you can imagine, the top brass are putting pressure on me."

"Did these men have business dealings perhaps?" Darmstaedter asked sensing his friend's frustration.

"I can't be sure of course, but we haven't been able to dig up any. Heidenreich was in chemicals, Lontard had a chain of disgusting sandwich stores and James Chan I guess was an antiques dealer who made millions selling 'ancient' ivory artifacts and ground up tiger balls or whatever, to some pathetic old men who haven't heard of Viagra. I have to admit Constantin I'm trying to be objective but I don't have much sympathy for any of them."

"Of course, I hear you Matthew. But we must be objective if we are to solve this. I will keep looking into Heidenreich's business connections here in Germany and I believe I will make a trip to

Botswana next week to discuss the matter with the police and game scouts who recovered the body. My report says no one saw anything unusual before the attack and if there were traces of human misconduct they were covered by the devastation caused by the male hippo. But of course I don't believe this. It is impossible for such a crime to happen without witnesses."

"Unfortunately the same's true for the other murders. No one heard or saw anything unusual and there wasn't a hint of any strange vehicles, or anything else for that matter, in the vicinity. That's the weird party Constantin, no witnesses at all. And that's what keeps me up at night. All of their guides say they saw the three victims safely to private airstrips, at which point all of the parties seemed to have mysteriously vanished until their bodies showed up. It doesn't make sense."

"No, it doesn't," agreed Darmstaedter. "Too many coincidences for them not to be related. Perhaps if we can understand the timeline precisely, between when they were last seen alive and when the bodies were found, we may be able to crack this thing."

"Know what, Constantin? I may join you in Botswana next week. Perhaps the two of us asking the right questions may bring something to light. In any case, it'll be good to work with you again."

Ten days later as they nursed cold beers on the veranda of the Duck Inn in Maun, the iconic town from where many of the safaris in Botswana begin, they realized they were up against a very dangerous individual or a very powerful organization that defied the most advanced investigation techniques available. The two policemen had discovered nothing at all. It was, Darmstaedter observed, lighting up yet another cigarette, "Der Sheisst."

Chapter 3

IN WHICH ROGER STORM CONTEMPLATES ENDING HIS POINTLESS EXISTENCE

Chicago
About the same time

R oger Storm swallowed the dregs of his vodka and realized that every second thought he'd had over the past few months had been about death and dying. It was almost twenty-five years ago to the day that he'd emigrated from South Africa, and the great American dream he'd had, that had been so close to reality he could taste it, was now in tatters. And he blamed it all on his ex-boss, the miserable and despicable, but unfortunately unforgettable, Harry Bones.

While he understood the self-fulfilling prophecy of being preoccupied with sadness and the intense and inherent dangers of wearing one's heart on one's sleeve, he couldn't shake the feeling that he was about to self-destruct. His doctor had prescribed antidepressants but, worrying about the potential side effects of erectile dysfunction and hoping by some miracle he'd get laid, he kept faith that he could get over both the loss of his job and subsequent divorce by himself. He desperately needed another drink.

He stood up and shuffled to the little galley kitchen with the intention of pouring himself a large vodka, forgetting for a moment the bottle was long empty. He looked around the kitchen for anything else that could serve as medication, but all he found in the fridge was a bottle of red wine that had been open for about a month. It smelt awful and tasted like someone had washed their socks in it, but such was his desperation that instead of pouring it down the drain, he decided to add a few ice cube to make it slightly palatable.

As he returned to his sitting room his email pinged. Most of the email he got these days was the usual spam from political parties asking for money or special offers from Amazon. He stared at it more out of boredom than anything else. His finger hovered over the delete button but he stopped himself mid-click. This email was indeed different, an invitation to speak at a conference put together by an organization that hosted one of the major European advertising award festivals. He contemplated it for a while, his mind going through the endless possibilities an excess of alcohol presents. It was a mistake or a cruel joke. No one wanted a washed up old creative guy. Yet, as the old adage goes, beneath the veil of sadness there is always the mirage of hope.

As it turned out when he called the organizers the next day, he found out it wasn't a mistake at all. Someone had dropped out of the conference at the last minute and they were desperate for a replacement. As he'd spoken at a number of their events in years past they'd decided to give him a call. The conference was set to begin in just over a week in Paris. Which meant they needed a commitment then and there. Knowing, if he procrastinated, he would find a million reasons not to go, he decided to say "yes".

And so it was that, on a rainy day in October, less than six days after getting the email, he found himself in Paris.

Chapter 4

In which Roger sees a ghost

Paris, France
Two days after his arrival

His speech, "If we did advertising like Antonio Stradivari made violins," had met with a tepid reaction, and he walked off the stage at the convention hall feeling like a fifty-six-year-old relic of the analog age with the nerve to lecture people who'd grown up not knowing anything but digital technology. A few of them smiled politely, but no one shook his hand or attempted to engage him in conversation. He looked at his watch and saw that it was 5:30. His presentation had been the last of the day and the crowds were drifting off to their hotels, no doubt to prepare themselves for drinks and dinner and whatever debauchery young people on company expense accounts get up to when they're away from home. He waited for a while to see if he'd bump into anyone he knew who might invite him to join them for dinner but the only person he saw was Rob, the big Australian who'd organized the event and who was clearly in a hurry.

"Nice job, mate. Interesting premise."

"Do you think so?" Roger asked hopefully.

"Yeah. Well you know," said Rob who clearly didn't. "I don't believe those youngsters even have the foggiest idea who Stradivarius was. They've all grown up on Guitar Hero. Now there's a really interesting premise for a speech by the way."

"His real name was Stradivari, Antonio Stradivari. He only used Stradivarius to sign his violins," Roger corrected him. "And I think Guitar Hero is a totally different premise of which I know very little."

"There you go. Find out. Something to think about for next time. Well good on ya, Rog. Plans for this evening?"

"Um. No actually. Quite free," he said hopefully, instantly regretting his slightly terse correction to Rob's absurd suggestion.

"God, you're a lucky bastard. I've got dinner with a bunch of holding company execs at that new Guy Savoy place. Boring buggers. French-fucking-food, ugh. I'd invite you but you'd hate it. Gotta run, mate. Enjoy Paris. We put you up at the Lancaster, didn't we? Nice hotel."

With that he strode off leaving Roger to contemplate yet another lonely night eating dinner in his room and drinking far too much from the mini bar. Sighing deeply, as people who feel sorry for themselves invariably do, Roger walked out to the taxi stand and in his atrocious French told the cab driver to take him to the Lancaster. It had begun to drizzle which didn't seem to dampen the mood of the tourists on the Champs Elysees. They bustled along staring into the windows of stores that could be found in their own home cities but that clearly had a different feel and meaning to them in Europe's second most popular destination. Roger understood perfectly. It's hard to feel sad in Paris, even when it's raining. But that was what worried him. Here he was sadder than he'd ever been. The thought of speaking at the conference had given him some mild respite, but he knew the speech wasn't his best effort and the audience had seen that. Life had lost both reward and meaning. He had tumbled into the downward spiral that deprives all of hope equally, regardless of circumstance. No job, no ass (his ex-wife had pointed out that his butt was disappearing the day before she asked for the divorce) and no love. His two sons were both married and once they'd seen him settled into his apartment had found little or no time for him. It was, in his emotionally scrambled mind, a truly ghastly situation. He knew he couldn't go on like this.

He looked out the cab window and saw a short man whose perfectly-coiffed hair made him think suddenly of Harry Bones, and sadness gave way to anger. He thought of yet another horrendously dark way to kill him. This one involved a clamp, Harry's balls, a jar of treacle and a colony of red ants. But the man disappeared into a store and Roger's anger subsided as it did every time he had these thoughts since his dismissal. He returned to the reality of who he was. The whole idea of murdering his ex-boss was as ludicrous as the contemplation of his own suicide. He didn't have the nerve and never would.

Roger desperately needed something else to occupy his mind. He couldn't really do any work until his contract expired in eighteen months and he didn't have enough money to live for more than a year or two after that. He thought of what a friend had said about it being better to "kill someone in your mind" than in person. It would have no doubt been good therapy, but he could no sooner commit mental murder than he could physical. Roger made his mind up that he would seek out a psychiatrist as soon as he returned to Chicago the day after next.

It was in this mood that he arrived at the hotel on what he'd soon discover was to be the most extraordinary evening of his life thus far.

He paid the cab driver and scuttled through the rain to the entrance, where the pleasant woman behind the reception desk gave him the key to his room. He decided not to wait for the world's slowest elevator, and climbed the creaky stairs to the first floor.

Room 16 of the Lancaster Hotel on the Rue du Berri is small. Certainly comfortable, perhaps even elegant and assuredly Bel Epoque, though in the most liberal sense of the term. But small nonetheless. He took off his black sneakers and expensive, though ill-fitting, jeans and sprawled on the bed. He stared at the ceiling as if the cream-colored paint and chandelier might supply answers to the questions racing through his mind.

The laws of geometry are very clear on the subject of space; a small room cannot have a large ceiling. And so despite the fact that his brain, normally well focused on subjects relating to geometry (one of his best subjects in high school), was meandering from one abysmal thought to another, he soon found himself running out of ceiling at which to stare. He picked up his iPhone and spun through his emails. There wasn't one worth reading. He thought of calling his sons but decided they'd probably be busy and say something that would make him feel awkward.

The truth was Roger missed everything in his life that was gone. He missed his ex-wife and his kids and his job. He suddenly missed his long-deceased parents, and thought back to when he was about eight years old and his father who he later learned suffered from clinical depression, ended up at a mental hospital. He stayed in treatment for three months and Roger remembered going to visit him with his mother and sister without the faintest idea of what was wrong with him. Only that he cried a lot.

Roger's eyes moved down from the ceiling to the flat-screen TV that seemed slightly out of place amidst the heavy gold drapes and brocade. He picked up the remote and considered watching some porn. He wasn't a big porn watcher as such, especially in hotel rooms. It was never quite as satisfying as he wanted it to be. Perhaps this time the sight of nubile flesh bouncing around in the illusion of joy and fulfillment would lift his spirits. The lifting would need to be heavy. Paris might well be the City of Light but there was very little lightness about him.

"Shit!"

The remote was stuck. He tried to push the button harder but it wouldn't budge.

"What the hell," he cried in frustration, flinging it across the room into the walnut desk, dislodging the batteries onto the floor. "Why can't I get a goddam break?"

He looked at himself in the mirror and saw a pretty disheartening reflection. His face was puffy and his hair, usually slightly disheveled, looked like it had been the subject of a wind-tunnel exercise gone horribly awry. He didn't even attempt to look at the rest of his body; it was quite frankly too awful to contemplate. It was only 6:50 in the evening, but he was hungry and he needed a drink.

He picked up his jeans and searched in vain for his hairbrush. Even that seemed to have given up on him. He did the best he could with his fingers, and pulling on a grey cashmere cardigan that covered the creases in his shirt and gave him the appearance, he imagined, of an eccentric middle-aged gentleman, he made the decision to go out to eat dinner by himself.

Five minutes later he emerged into the lobby. The concierge, Mathieu, was on the phone trying to avoid the attentions of three women who, judging by their big bulky T. Anthony suitcases, had just arrived from the US. Roger stood politely behind them waiting his turn. Clearly Mathieu, who he had tipped, he felt, quite generously the night before, was determined to ignore the women. Mathieu put down the phone and smiled pleasantly at him.

"Monsieur Storm, how is your stay?"

"Excuse me," said one of the women, "but I believe we were here first."

"I don't believe so, madam," said Mathieu putting heavy emphasis on the *I*. "Monsieur Storm has been here for a few days." He looked through her as if she were invisible. "What can I do for you Monsieur?"

"Well, the menu button on the remote is stuck for a start," Roger said, trying to be nonchalant, "so I guess I'm just going to go out for a bite. Is there a place around here where I can get a really good roast chicken?"

"Hah," smiled Mathieu. "Have you been watching pornography, Monsieur Storm? We've found that semen is the worst thing for remote controllers. It clogs the buttons. I will have housekeeping clean it for you."

"Christ," Roger said turning bright red as he realized the three women had overheard everything. "I haven't been watching pornography. I never watch it. Don't need to". He said this to the women who were looking at him with abject disgust.

"Pervert," whispered one of them. "Just like my ex-husband."

"Jesus," said Roger perhaps a little too loudly, "I am not a pervert, and I said I was not watching pornography. I'm hungry. All I want to do is eat. And all I want to eat is chicken."

"I think chicken's his code word for cock," laughed the divorced woman to her companions. "I told you he was a pervert."

It wasn't anger or disdain that forced his retort, simply a slight stirring in his creative juices. He scowled at the woman whose features, after what must have been numerous plastic surgeries, had migrated towards the back of her head. "Madam, I'm certain your husband liked pornography because the thought of having sex with you was just too horrific. Now Mathieu, the restaurant, *please.*"

"Monsieur Storm, you are in Paris," laughed Mathieu as the three women stared back with angry disdain. "Surely you would rather taste some more interesting food. Roast chicken is so boring. It is a dish my grandmother would cook. And, I might add, that was even after her truffle-sniffing hog ripped a large piece of flesh off her arm when she tried to remove a giant black Perigord truffle from its mouth. She changed to dogs after that, you can be sure."

"Look," Roger said, getting slightly frustrated. "I am sorry for your grandmother and I'm sure her recipe is still magnificent despite her disability. But I love roast chicken. I want roast chicken. I would sincerely appreciate the name of a restaurant."

Mathieu, whom Roger imagined didn't care much for Americans in any case and seemed to - though he couldn't swear to this - have thoroughly enjoyed embarrassing him, pulled out a pen and wrote down the name of a restaurant.

"Here we are Monsieur Storm. Chez Daphne. It's a few minutes from here, where the old Rue Balzac used to be. They have an excellent rotisserie chicken and a good wine list. You will enjoy it."

"Can you make a reservation for me?"

"Of course Monsieur Storm. For what time?"

"Time? Now, I'm hungry."

"I think Monsieur Storm you will not need a reservation for this time. In Paris at this time only Americans and old people who suck potato soup through their false teeth eat."

"Well, call them anyway please. I'd prefer it."

"Fine," said Mathieu, picking up the phone and dialing the number on his card. "If you insist."

He spoke quickly in French which Roger failed to understand.

"They are expecting you", he smiled. "Bon appetite."

Roger thanked him and nodded to the ladies who glared back at him through their tightly pinched faces. Taking a proffered umbrella from the doorman he made my way onto Rue du Berri armed with all the information he needed for a thoroughly dull evening. He was actually feeling quite good about his comeback to the women. It gave him temporary confidence and with a hint of a purpose to his step, he strode off into the Paris evening and the event that would change his life.

A couple of things happened on the walk that Roger was not aware of at the time but heard about later. He did not notice the man getting out of the black Mercedes sedan across the street from the hotel who began to follow him. He did not notice the woman who got out of the small silver Citroen and began to follow the man following him. He certainly didn't hear what one or two passersby must have thought sounded like the backfiring of one of the many scooters that plowed in and out of the traffic on the Rue De Berri but what was in fact a subsonic bullet fired from a compact pistol fitted with a sound suppressor. He most assuredly didn't see the front of the first follower's head explode like a watermelon being hit with a baseball bat. He did, however, notice what looked like a splotch of thick red grape juice on the sleeve of his cardigan when he sat down at the bar at the restaurant.

Chez Daphne was a relatively modern, Hausemann-style establishment with large frescoes, mirrors and blends of brown, mauves and blue that contrasted with its starched white tablecloths. Not at all what Roger was hoping for. For some reason he assumed it would be more of a bistro with wooden floors and waiters in long white aprons, and he was feeling slightly annoyed until he saw the plump chickens turning slowly on the large rotisserie. They looked and smelled absolutely delicious. Though the restaurant was, as Mathieu had predicted, virtually empty, the maitre'd insisted he wait at the bar until a suitable table could be arranged. Roger pulled out one of the velvet bar stools and sat down, realizing he had absolutely no idea how the Gallic mind operated. How difficult was it to find an empty table in a restaurant of empty tables?

Just after his divorce, when he first moved into his apartment, he'd relished the idea of going to a restaurant by himself, ordering anything he felt like and then reading a book. Soon he came to understand that the tables he was being put at were always slightly out the way, towards the kitchen or the bathroom, because no one really wanted to see the lonely guy. It made the restaurant seem dull. So after a while he began to order dinner at the bar. Sitting with other people, even though most of them were couples talking to each other, made him feel a little less out of place. He managed to develop a technique where he'd turn his head and smile so that to anyone perusing the bar it would look as if he were part of the group. Not that anyone was actually looking. Sitting at the bar had its drawbacks in that he invariably ended up drinking too much. Like most people with a serious drinking problem he didn't think he was an alcoholic. But he had to admit that if he wasn't he was certainly pretty damn close.

He looked up at the array of brightly lit bottles behind the bar and sighed. Two nights ago he'd woken up with a terrible headache and worried that he'd have to face the fact he did indeed have alcohol dependency. When the aspirin kicked in he decided he didn't really care so long as it killed him quickly. Alcohol was self-medication and it worked perfectly.

Roger glanced at the bartender and wondered if she'd speak to him.

She was an attractive young woman with short blond hair, a ring in her nose and angry tattoos that ran up her arms and disappeared into a tight white tank top that itself hid little from his sex-deprived eyes. She smiled at him as she finished arranging some Calla lilies in a beautiful Lalique vase.

"What can I get for you Monsieur?"

"I'd like a Johnny Walker Black straight up," he replied having no clue whatsoever as to why he'd ordered a substance he had very little taste for, other than he felt it might impress her. It clearly didn't.

"You are not a whisky man, monsieur," she said as he tried to down it in one shot and nearly choked. "In fact you look more like a vodka or white wine person. Here let me pour you a glass of my favorite white wine."

Before he could reply she had pulled out a bottle from among many in an ice bucket and poured him a glass.

"The 2011 Ganevat Les Chamois du Paradis from the Jura region. You will find it fascinating, I promise."

"Jesus," he said almost spitting it back in the glass. "The damn thing's off."

"No, no," she said. "It is oxidated, not oxidized. This is the unique characteristic of many Jura white wines. Take another sip and role it around your mouth. Interesting, no?"

Roger took another small sip. "Well, it's certainly interesting, I'll give you that but I'm not sure in a good way."

He took another sip and suddenly it seemed very familiar. "I've had this before somewhere. Why did you think I'd like it, by the way?"

She didn't answer and Roger looked up to see that she'd turned away to deal with another customer at the other end of the bar. As hard as he tried to focus on his drink and not stare at the stunning woman who had just sat down to order a glass of champagne, it was hard not to stare.

She was dressed in black leather leggings and a light Montcler jacket with a fur collar. Slim, he thought, but not skinny. Defined but not muscular. Definitely European but with a hint of added exoticism. In a word he decided, perfect. She looked to be in her forties; though he was normally useless at guessing people's ages. She had silver-blond hair that fell over her shoulders and large eyes. Roger couldn't quite sense their color from where he sat but it didn't matter; he was in love.

The woman glanced over at him, smiled and said something to the bartender who nodded in agreement. Roger had the crazy thought of offering to buy her a drink, then felt that might be a little presumptuous. She was clearly waiting for someone. Or was she? The debate raged in his head and he knew he was overthinking the situation. He took another sip of the wine and once again got the impression that he'd had it somewhere before. Eventually he gave up and feeling both hungry and ignored looked around for the maitre'd to find out what the hold up with his table was all about. He found him at the rear of the restaurant saying something to a single diner who sat in a booth with his back towards the bar. For an instant the diner turned his head towards the Maitre'd and asked a question. At that point Roger's world exploded.

There is a defining moment in life when things suddenly begin to move in slow motion. The blood drains from one's upper extremities. One's breathing stops. The sounds outside one's head fade to a dull hollow thump. When that moment comes, one instinctively realizes that everything that takes place from that point in time onwards will somehow be different; and all the things one believes, that have made life up until then somewhat understandable, will vanish like mist before the sun.

This was that moment for Roger. The nerve endings in his body suddenly went numb. The glass of wine slipped through his fingers and crashed to the floor. The blood rushed from his head. He could feel his eyes begin to blink at a dangerously rapid rate and for a second he thought he was having a stroke. Instead he realized he was seeing a ghost, because at that precise moment, on that seemingly pre-ordained day, he saw his dead friend, Freddy Blank, eating, no, positively devouring, in clearly un-corpse-like fashion, a large plate of roast chicken and mashed potatoes. The moment that was to change his life had arrived.

Without knowing quite what he was doing, Roger stood up, and like a condemned prisoner walking towards a noose, stumbled towards the table at which Freddy Blank, confirmed suicide victim and now potential zombie, was eating his chicken.

Suddenly the blood that had vacated his brain for more southern regions returned. He stopped to consider the possibility that he might be mistaken and was about to make a complete fool out of himself But it was too late. The chicken-eating apparition turned towards him and a big grin lit up its face.

"Roger, you're early. I wasn't expecting you for another thirty minutes. Here sit down man. You look like you're about to faint."

All Roger could do was gape. He tried to speak but nothing came out. He stood staring for a second and then opened his mouth again. But he was totally speechless and so he simply slumped into the bench opposite his old friend. There was no mistaking Freddy. The giant of his childhood and nemesis of every authority figure. Two hundred and eighty pounds, wavy blond hair, dancing blue eyes and the complexion of a pomegranate. Freddy, his friend who had died from a drug overdose in a flat in Kensington ten years before.

"Garçon, more Ganevat for my friend please before his heart gives way. You remember this wine. Don't you Roger? I once gave you a bottle and you loathed it."

All Roger could do was nod. Somewhere in the back of his mind he remembered Freddy bringing him a bottle of his favorite wine but he couldn't recall when or where.

The waiter, sensing an event had occurred perhaps just slightly less cataclysmic than a star being sucked into a black hole, rushed over with a full glass of wine. His face betrayed both horror and disgust as Roger swallowed it in one gulp and held his glass up for a refill. The waiter snatched it out his quivering hand, muttering something under his breath about Americans and binge drinking.

"Freddy," Roger said in a very quiet voice, "you're dead. I saw the headline in the paper and talked to your mom. You died from an overdose of heroin"

"Ah well, and everyone believed it except for the Duke. The bastard is still after me but he's getting old and I'm not that worried anymore."

"The Duke? What do you mean the Duke?

"The Duke is a nasty man with a gun."

"Like John Wayne?" Roger's mind was decidedly fuzzy from both the wine and the shock.

"For Christ's sake, not John Wayne. What the hell are you talking about Roger? Get a grip on yourself man. There's a lot to digest here. No, the Duke is a hit man hired by a group of people who thought I'd stolen a large sum of money from them. Well, I guess you couldn't possibly know that. But I like to think my colleagues and I are a little smarter than my enemies, and so they arranged my suicide. But don't worry, Roger. The guy who died of the overdose and who enough people thought was me, really did die of an overdose. Administered by himself, I might add. But he was a terrible person who'd been responsible for a lot of awful things, so he deserved it.

"Now I'd tell you more, my boy, but then as the old saying goes, I'd probably have to kill you. I'm kidding of course. I am going to tell you everything. Including why you're here. I'm sorry Roger. I hated doing that suicide thingy to you and Brian. But I didn't have a choice. Now, don't look so damn self-righteous. I promise you I didn't. You clearly didn't know it but I've been following both your lives since I disappeared. I know about your divorce and I know about your job - or lack thereof - and I know you are seriously depressed. I have some great pills for that by the way. And I am going to help you, because I owe that to you. You and Brian were always my best friends."

He paused, sensing Roger had recovered somewhat, though he hadn't by a long shot

"Does Brian know about you?" Roger asked wondering how Brian, whom he considered his closest friend, would have taken the news. Brian lived in Australia and if he and Roger were lucky they saw each other every second year for a few days.

"No, he doesn't and you and I will tell him at the right time and the right place. Trust me, he can't really help with what you and I and some others are going to do this time. As you will soon find out, this is neither the right time nor the place to tell Brian."

"Freddy," Roger said, as soon as the wine had slowed down those organs vital to communication. "This is pretty fucked up. Things like this don't happen. People do not return from the dead."

"Yes, Roger. I understand your feelings perfectly. You are confused and angry. This isn't going to be easy for you to comprehend, but as I said, I've been watching you for a while - I liked your speech by the way - and I think the timing is right. That's why I got Mathieu to send you here."

"That's bullshit. How could you have seen my speech or got Mathieu to send me here? That makes no sense. Not that any of this does."

"Oh, but it very much does. I was standing at the back of the conference hall this afternoon, and I pay Mathieu enough every month for him to tell me everything I need to know and do exactly what I tell him to do. Anyway, the point is no matter what you wanted to eat he would have told you that this restaurant serves a sublime something or other. Which it does by the way. The chicken is delicious, best in Paris in my opinion. I'm ordering one for you and another for myself. Don't sit there like a herring, man. All will become clear. I am simply waiting for my colleague. And if I'm not mistaken, here she is now."

Roger looked up to see the silver blonde from the bar sauntering over to the table. From the way she walked he knew he'd been right in thinking she was athletic. Her body rippled like licorice in the tight black outfit. She scooted into the booth next to Freddy and took his arm.

"Roger, I want you to meet Conchita Palomino. She is trained in at least three martial arts including Krag Maga, served in the Israeli Special Forces and the FARC terrorist organization. So don't mess with her." He laughed.

"The FARC were not terrorists," she said in a strangely mixed accent, punching Freddy quite hard on the arm. "They were agrarian freedom fighters. My father died for them."

"Her mom was Israeli and her dad Colombian," explained Freddy. "A wacky combination for sure, but my dear Conchita is absolutely sweet and quite invaluable. She takes adequate care of anyone who tries to do me some harm."

"I could take care of you, Roger, "she said, smiling coyly at him.

"Now, now my dear. Don't get any ideas about him. You have to worry about me."

"You two aren't..."

"Don't be silly," said Conchita. "Freddy is gay. He is committed to Jamie."

"Jamie? Not *that* Jamie? Don't tell me he came back to life, too."

"Of course *that* Jamie. If I'm alive then I can very much promise you so is Jamie...yes, yes, whom I know supposedly drowned in Johannesburg, but didn't, and will no doubt be meeting us shortly when we put the team together. Again, I will reveal everything in due course. You will have plenty of time to tell Conchita all about the stupid things that you and I got up to when we were kids. And we did get up to some nutty stuff."

Roger nodded without really knowing what he was nodding at.

"Don't worry too much right now Roger. You're shocked and confused and the answers will only serve to make you more so. Trust me you will be perfect for this.

Roger desperately wanted to ask questions but didn't know where to start or what to say. His bowels started to gurgle and his mouth went dry. He took another huge sip of his wine and stood up. And suddenly everything came out in a way that would have shocked his ex-wife who, like Harry Bones, was convinced that Roger was the least confrontational person on the planet.

"Freddy, if that's who you really are, because you could be anyone, you know, although I don't know anyone else who could be you - you were involved in some really insane stuff growing up. Things that you started and I was caught up in. Now you are clearly involved in something that I probably cannot comprehend, and I have to say I want nothing to do with it. I am going to walk out of here quite slowly. I am going back to my hotel and then I am flying back to Chicago tomorrow. That's it. Yes I am depressed, pretty badly I would imagine. And chances are I am going to drink myself to death pretty soon". Roger underscored this by taking a massive sip of his wine.

"And while I would love a reason to live and feel needed, this doesn't seem to be it. Goodbye Conchita, very nice to meet you.. Goodbye Freddy. I guess nice to see you again."

To Roger's surprise Freddy jumped up and grabbed him in a bear hug. "Too late for that Rog. I'm sure they've seen us together already and from now on they'll be after you, too. In fact Conchita already had to take care of one fellow who was following you. The problem is once they heard what I had in mind, they decided to take out our entire organization and anyone associated with it. And unfortunately that now includes you. They really are desperate for my plan to fail."

"Roger sat down and rubbed his forehead. Partial confusion had given way to total confusion. "Who is they and who was following me?

Before Freddy could answer, Conchita grabbed Roger's sleeve.

"A very nasty Serbian," she said, dipping the edge of a napkin in a glass of Volvic. "And here's piece of his brain on your nice Cashmere cardigan. But this should get it out; it hasn't dried."

Roger stared down as elegant fingers rubbed the wet napkin on a plum colored spot on the sleeve of his sweater. Conchita clucked her tongue as if cleaning up ketchup off a careless ten-year-old. Bile rose into his mouth and he felt himself begin to heave. Freddy patted him on the back none too gently.

"Don't throw up for Christ's sake. They'll never allow me back into this restaurant. Here, stop rolling your eyes and have a sip of water."

At that moment the waiter arrived with two plates of the roast chicken. Roger stared down at his and once again felt vomit rise.

"Here old boy," said Freddy." Eat your chicken and then we'll go over to my place. We checked you out the hotel, by the way. And don't worry about the umbrella. Mathieu said to keep it as a souvenir. You can get a good night's sleep and we'll start first thing in the morning. Oh my Lord, he's fainted. Poor guy. Probably shouldn't have told him that someone tried to pop him. Here Conchita, help me get him to the car."

The last thing Roger thought as the blood, which had traveled up and down his body quite intensely that evening, rushed once more from his brain, was "Freddy, you bastard what the hell else have you gotten me into now? You were always getting me into trouble."

That was when he passed out.

Chapter 5

IN WHICH ROGER MEETS FREDDY FOR THE FIRST TIME

Johannesburg, South Africa
In the mid 1960's

T he classroom had eighteen old wooden desks. Each, with the exception of one right in the back, was occupied by a pair of fifth grade boys and girls. The teacher's name was Dunden. A fat balding middle-aged man of Irish extraction dressed in grey flannel slacks and a tweed jacket that had perhaps in the past fit him, but now seemed to have given up in light of the expansion policy of his stomach and surrounding regions. Next to him stood a skinny boy in navy pants and a blue shirt named Roger Storm, whose first day at Saxonwold Primary School was clearly not destined to be a pleasant one. Roger was twelve years old, the new boy in a classroom made up of children who had been together since kindergarten. He felt awkward. He looked awkward. And though he was too terrified to speak, had he, he was sure he would have sounded awkward.

"Before you sit yourself down, Roger," said Mr. Dunden, "tell the class where you are from."

Roger tried desperately to speak. He looked at the faces of his new class mates. While the girls seemed bored, most of the boys were relishing his embarrassment. All except one. A boy at the back of the classroom with wavy blond hair and a huge grin. He was the only single occupant of a double desk and it was clear to Roger precisely why. He was enormous. His head was large and his hands, which he now held up in apparent encouragement, were the size of coconuts. For some unknown reason the large boy's smile and hand gestures gave Roger a sense of the courage he knew he didn't actually have.

In a voice that could well have come from the larynx of a large mouse he said, "I'm from Walvis Bay. My parents and my sister and I just moved here."

"Walvis Bay?" yelled the blond-haired boy. "What kind of a stupid name is that?"

"Freddy Blank," said Mr. Dunden with an angry look, "no one asked you to speak. However, since you asked, Walvis Bay means Whale Bay in English. It was a whaling station a long time back and is now the only harbor in Namibia. Now that we have established that geography is another subject that you are weak in, Freddy and seeing as you seem to have opened a rapport with Freddy, Roger, you can sit next to him. I'm sure it won't be for long, as he is usually in the headmaster's office most mornings."

Roger gingerly made his way back to Freddy's desk and tried to squeeze in. He couldn't be sure whether the large boy had been making fun of him, but had a feeling nonetheless that Freddy and he would get on. Freddy appeared to scoot over to give him what little space he could. Then, as Roger tried to sit, Freddy moved back over to his original position and Roger fell to the floor. The whole class turned round to stare. Roger was red faced as he stood up. Freddy was almost crying with laughter.

"Sorry," said Freddy through his tears. "I didn't mean to do that. Here, sit down."

Roger tried again and Freddy executed the exact same maneuver, sending Roger once again spilling onto the floor. It was at that moment that Mr. Dunden let fly the heavy wooden eraser he had been holding in his hand. His intended target was the head of Freddy Blank but his aim was off and the eraser caught Roger a glancing blow on the ear, causing him to shriek out in shock and agony and stumble back into the wall. Freddy, laughing harder than ever, jumped up to help him, at which point, Mr Dunden, enraged like a wounded buffalo, charged down the aisle swinging a heavy dictionary. The book took Freddy on the side of his head and even his two hundred pounds were no match for the one thousand six hundred and ninety-six page Concise Oxford English Dictionary. He went down yelling, taking the desk with him.

"You," screamed Mr. Dunden pointing at Roger, "pick the desk up and sit down and I'd better not hear a peep out of you the entire day. And you," he added turning to Freddy, "you bastard, get out of my classroom."

Both Freddy and Roger stood up, the latter trying desperately to hold back his tears. Freddy said nothing. He helped Roger right the desk and then walked slowly to the front of the classroom. His mirth had given way to a frightening anger. He turned to Mr Dunden who stood at the back of the room still clutching the heavy book.

"You have no right to do that. You can't treat children like that. And someone is going to teach you that one day." He opened the door and, smiling back at the rest of the class, walked out into the warm Johannesburg sunshine.

At precisely 7:35 pm the fire alarm went off at Saxonwold Primary School. By the time the fire brigade arrived, an entire classroom had been destroyed. A huge group of white home owners had gathered at the school. They were joined by their black servants, who stood at the back. Apartheid was in full swing in South Africa and no members of the black community who weren't employed as servants in the area would have dared to be seen at such a public gathering for fear of being arrested by the large contingent of police who'd arrived with the fire brigade.

"Do you think this is the work of terrorists?" asked the headmaster who was standing next to a police sergeant.

"Ja," replied the policemen in his heavy Afrikaans accent. "Probably some bloody black ANC bastard. But don't worry we'll find them." He scowled at the black servants who scowled back at him. "And then they will wish they had never been born."

The police force had already started moving amongst the black on-lookers, demanding to see their 'passes', the much despised identity documents that allowed their movement through restricted areas only. The police jostled and threatened them but none of them said a word.

No one apparently noticed the big twelve-year-old who stood at the back of the crowd, grinning and rubbing his pudgy hands in glee. It was only the next day when detectives were moving through the charred remains, that they discovered the note pinned to a nearby tree that led them directly to the house of Max Goldman and Betty Blank-Goldman, stepfather and mother of Freddy Blank.

The problem - as Freddy was soon to discover - with notes written by twelve-year-old boys, is that the grammar stinks, the spelling is awful and they're usually scribbled on a page torn from an exercise book. The note which read, *The next time you hit me you fat fart I will burn up your stupid dilapidated old house,* was on the back of an old homework assignment entitled "My Awful Summer' by Freddy Blank".

"Freddy," screamed Betty Blank-Goldman when the police captain appeared at the door and showed her the note.

Freddy, who had been lying on his bed playing with his ginger cat, heard his mom screaming but took no notice. His mom, a woman who had clearly suffered at the hands of two unruly sons and an ex-husband who was not only as odd as his boys but had had several affairs with women more impressed by money than charm or looks, usually screamed for him a dozen times a day. He knew she usually gave up after a few minutes.

Then the door to his room burst open and Mrs. Blank-Goldman entered. She rushed up to the bed and grabbed her son by the shoulders. She was not a large woman, and the effect was that of a small angry baboon grabbing an elephant. Freddy just stared up at her, only then realizing that she was quite serious.

"Mom, what's wrong?"

"Freddy Blank, have you done something terribly bad?

"Like what?" he asked in apparent innocence.

"You have to come with me. There's a policeman in the sitting room. He says you burned down the school. He can't be right, can he? Freddy you wouldn't have done that would you?"

When Roger learned of the scene, he could only imagine Freddy's reaction. While this may have been the most serious trouble Freddy had been in the twelve years since his thirteen pound body nearly killed his mother exiting the womb, Roger imagined he'd probably tried to brush it off with the same nonchalance he would brush off all the incidents that Roger and the third member of their small circle of friendship, Brian Morris, would be witness to in the years ahead.

However, the policeman, whose name was van der Westhuizen, was slightly less sympathetic than Mrs. Blank-Goldman. He sat on the sofa his eyebrows crossed in frustration and his hand on the butt of his pistol as if waiting for any excuse to pull it out. His frustration increased as the twelve-year-old boy patiently explained to him that he hadn't meant to burn down the whole classroom, just a small portion of it.

"Do you know what kind of trouble you are in?" asked the captain.

Van der Westhuizen had never met anyone like Freddy before. He thought of Jews as devious Christ killers, and he was disappointed that during the second World War South Africa had chosen to side with the British over the Germans who would have taken care of South Africa's Jewish problems. He wasn't sure exactly what those were, but he trusted the word of the priest at the Dutch Reformed Church who hated Jews almost as much as he hated black people. Clearly this horrible bastard of a child went beyond anything the priest droned on about every Sunday. He seemed positively evil. He sat on the chair opposite the captain and answered every question as if he was being asked what he'd eaten for breakfast.

"I'm sure I can make it up to the school," said Freddy. "I will gladly spend the weekend painting or cleaning. My teacher hit me on the head with a dictionary. He shouldn't have done that. I was only trying to send him a message. If you feel I sent the wrong message then I will make up for it."

"Painting or cleaning? Are you fucking - I am sorry Mrs Blank-Goldman, I did not mean to swear - insane? You could go to a juvenile jail for ten years. And I promise you a dictionary on the side of your fat head would be the nicest thing you get there. You could get stabbed. Or raped."

"What does 'raped' mean?" asked Freddy.

"It means that some other boy will stick his..."

"Enough, Captain van der Westhuizen," interrupted a now thoroughly pissed off Mrs. Blank-Goldman who had plonked herself next to Freddy. "That seems quite disgusting and, if you don't mind me saying so, very mean. He is only a high spirited boy who stood up for himself. And rightfully so. The things some teachers in our schools are allowed to get up to is beyond tolerable."

Captain van der Westhuizen just stared at her. Clearly the boy came from a family that was certifiably mad. He could only imagine what he would have done to his son had he been in the same position. But of course his son wouldn't have been in the same position. His son knew the difference between right and wrong. A sound beating every Friday evening had ensured that.

"High spirited? You call burning down half a school high spirited? If the teacher were smart he would have hit him on the head with a cricket bat. Your son is a criminal. A bloody arsonist."

At that moment Freddy began to laugh.

"What are you laughing at?" yelled van der Westhuizen. "You think this is funny? You think arson is a joke?"

"I don't know what arson is," said Freddy through his giggles, "it sounds like arse, and that's funny." With that he started convulsing again in laughter.

"That's very rude darling. You can see that Captain van der Westhuizen is really upset, "said Mrs Blank-Goldman. "Now go back to your room and I'll bring you a nice sandwich."

Upset may not have been a word that an independent observer would have used to describe the police captain. Enraged, possibly? Frustrated, certainly. Combustible? Most definitely.

"Mrs. Blank-Goldman am I not completely clear here?" said van der Westhuizen, his voice trembling in anger and his face going a dangerous purple, indicating a high-blood pressure problem that would no doubt kill him at some point. "Your son is going to juvenile jail. He is a bloody criminal."

"Oh please captain. Don't be so melodramatic. You have enough issues in this country, what with the way you treat black people, without having to worry about the antics of a twelve year old."

"Antics? Antics?" This time van der Westhuizen almost pulled his gun out its holster. "A school was nearly burned down, people could have been killed. This is not antics. This is the behavior of someone who should have been locked up in a loony bin a long time ago. You should get him a psychiatrist, and while you're at it get yourself checked out as well.

"How dare you insinuate anything about either my son's or my mental state? You who was about to discuss rape with a twelve-year-old boy. I'm quite shocked Captain."

"Shocked? You should be shocked...with electro-shock therapy in a mental institution. Maybe you'll understand me better," spluttered the captain. "Now, Mrs. Blank-Goldman, I have no recourse but to take your son into custody for the crime of arson. You may call your lawyer and you may accompany him down to the police station."

In the end though, Freddy's father's money worked hard to right the situation. As hard as it could to right the future and frequent hairbrained antics of his son. So hard in fact as to leave him penniless fifteen years later at the time of his death, convinced his son had been switched at birth with a descendant of Attila the Hun. Abe Blank paid not just for a new classroom, but also a swimming pool, and the school in consideration dropped all charges. The police reluctantly let Freddy go when they learned he would be sent to a special boarding school run by nuns in France. A country from which many of their ancestors had fled but for which they had as much loathing and distrust as they did for that evil, godless country called Russia.

"Serve that little rooinek right," said Captain van der Westhuizen as he sat at his desk a few weeks later enjoying a coffee with his friend, Col. Pienaar of the Security Police. "Let him go and live with those fucking frogs. They hate us South Africans. They'll probably kick his fat arse around and then perhaps he'll burn their school down and they can send him to Devil's Island. I just don't want to see him ever again. I cannot tell you what restraint I had to use not to leap over the table and strangle that twelve-year-old demon. There was mischief and mayhem in his eyes. The mind of a master criminal in the making."

"I don't think they use Devil's Island anymore, said Pienaar lighting an unfiltered Lucky Strike. "I think we are the only people who still use an island as a prison. Ja, maybe we should have sent him to Robben Island. Although from what you say about him, even we couldn't have stood to inflict someone like him on the political prisoners. They'd all be begging to be hanged instead." He laughed so hard at the thought that he nearly spilled his coffee. "I'm telling you man, I'm not sure you should have let him go like that. That boy is most definitely trouble, and trouble when it's not taken care of, has a bad habit of coming back. You mark my words: you will see him again."

"You're probably right, but let him be someone else's fucking trouble. We got enough of our own with those bloody black terrorist bastards and communist Jews. I don't need to worry about one kid."

"I don't know man," said Pienaar thoughtfully as he lit up another cigarette. "I just have a bad feeling about him."

The funny part was that nine years later Freddy did pop up again, much to the policeman's amazement. When Colonel van der Westhuizen, having been promoted to the title when Colonel Pienaar was caught having sex with one of the black prisoners, saw Freddy, he nearly fell out of his chair. The amazement lasted only long enough for him to jump up and aim a kick to Freddy's stomach. Not a hard thing to do as Freddy was lying on the ground handcuffed and chained.

Van der Westhuizen leaned over him. "I should have done that when I first saw you in your mother's house. But now we have plenty of time to make up for all that."

Chapter 6

IN WHICH ROGER HEARS ABOUT A MIND-BOGGLING PLAN

London, England
The morning after Roger passed out in the restaurant in Paris

What little morning sun there was in October made its way into the bedroom of the large cream-colored house. It crept over the pillow of the luxurious four-poster bed and settled on Roger's horrifically disheveled and hungover face. He opened his eyes slowly and, after brushing aside his hair, found himself once again staring at a ceiling. He was wide awake. That much he knew. But exactly where he was, was as yet a mystery. The ceiling for one was a good deal bigger than that at the Lancaster Hotel. He pondered his location for a moment, his brows knit, contributing even further to his awful appearance. He sat up suddenly, sending a paroxysm of intense pain to his head that served only to confuse him even more. When the room finally stopped spinning the events of the night before began to filter back to him. The bartender at Chez Daphne, his friend the apparently ex-deceased Freddy, and the vision in tight black pants with silver-blond hair named Conchita Palomino. After that his mind was blank. He had no idea how he'd gotten to wherever he was.

As the pain in his head began to redistribute itself across his body like a coat of nails, he almost threw up again. There was a metallic flotsam swirling about in his mouth, different from the rancid, morning-after taste he had grown accustomed to. He pulled off the thick down comforter and saw that he was dressed only in his boxers. He couldn't see any of his other clothes lying around the large and well-appointed bedroom. This was a problem. He did not want Conchita, whom he fantasized might glide through the door at any minute, seeing his flabby torso. Despite his total confusion as to where he was or what he was doing in wherever it was, he couldn't stop thinking about her. He closed his eyes and began to see the ridiculousness of his train of thought. What the hell was wrong with him? What did it matter who saw him? He didn't even know if Freddy and Conchita were real. Maybe everything he remembered was an hallucination. Just a bad booze-induced nightmare. He was not exactly *non compos mentis* but neither was he entirely *compos mentis*. Had he been kidnapped and if so, why?

He gingerly made his way over to the sash window and squinted out. All he could see were big cream colored houses and cobbled lanes. It felt more like London than Paris.

His train of logic was interrupted by the urgent physical need to take a shit. Putting his current state of puzzlement aside, he headed for the en-suite bathroom.

It was an equally elaborate affair, done out in green marble and dark wood. While the size of the bathtub was impressive, the object that caught his eye was the toilet. It had a control panel that boasted a heated seat, air-freshener and a cleaning and drying system that eliminated the need for toilet paper.

He'd just finished having his undercarriage sprayed clean and dried when his first pleasant reverie in a while was interrupted by a familiar voice.

"Roger old boy...you up?"

Roger washed his hands and walked back into the bedroom to see Freddy, dressed in jeans and a button down shirt, perched on the bed holding a copy of *The Independent*.

"Do you ever read this?" asked Freddy, waving the paper at Roger. "It's my favorite paper. Doesn't tell you how to think."

Roger's first reaction was unusually controlled. The incongruity of the situation, tempered by his toilet experience, allowed him to take a deep breath before replying.

"I do like *The Independent*, Freddy. I like to read it and the *The Guardian* when I'm in London." But even the most luxurious elimination experience in the world couldn't hold back the panic that began to well up in him. The floodgates opened. His emotions gave in and even to his own ears, his voice sounded as if it had gone up an octave to the register of a mezzosoprano or possibly a castrato. "London, Freddy? Why are we in London?"

"Why are we in London? Seems pretty obvious if you don't mind me saying, Roger. We couldn't stay in Paris now, could we. Those buggers had my house under surveillance. If they'd seen us bringing you in I'm afraid it would have been curtains old chap. So we made a quick decision to fly to London. And here we are: my London house, which is quite safe by the way. Had to give you a shot of something to knock you out again. You were quite hysterical. Do you need another one, by the way? You seem quite tense."

The sheer ridiculousness of Freddy's demeanor pulled Roger off the edge "Freddy, please," he said more calmly, sitting down on the bed next to his friend and holding his aching head in my hands. "Just stop for a minute. I don't know what's going on. I honestly don't."

Freddy began to say something but Roger stopped him.

"No, please just let me finish. A week ago I was suicidal. My life, as I had planned it, is finished as far as I'm concerned. My marriage, over after twenty-seven years. My ex-partner or boss or whatever the fuck he was, that son-of-a-bitch

Harry Bones, fired me after twenty-four years for some bullshit reason, so he could get his hands on the money that would have taken care of my retirement. My kids are off and doing their own thing and don't need me. Honestly, I was hoping to be hit with a massive stroke or heart-attack. I'd jump off a building if I had the guts. I have no reason in my own mind to want to live. Do you understand that?"

"I do Roger, and by the way we should talk about Harry Bones. I can have him taken care of tomorrow if you'd like."

Roger put his hand on Freddy's arm to stop him again. "My life is over, but then suddenly out of the blue dead people start popping up. Hit men start popping up. Unbelievably sexy assassins in black leather pants start popping up. I don't know what the hell is going on. I have no idea where I am or what I'm doing. I have been shot at and drugged. Seeing you doesn't make me less depressed, it just makes me more confused. So if you want me to do anything but run screaming out the door in my underwear you have to help me understand exactly what it is happening."

"All good points and fair questions Roger," Freddy replied standing up and folding the paper. "And, I think Conchita would like the idea of being referred to as a 'sexy assassin,' but why don't you do this first. Take a shower, shave...from the smell in the bathroom you've already shitted...and then come downstairs. We'll have some breakfast and Conchita and I will try to answer as much as possible and tell you exactly where we see you fitting in. And here, take two of these tablets, they'll fix the pain"

"Fine," said Roger taking the pills, "but I'm not coming down in these old boxers. Do you have my clothes?"

"Yes, in the closet over there. By the way, have you ever heard of an ironing board? We had to wash and press everything. So get in the shower old boy and by the time you're done the butler will have laid everything out for you on the bed. Do you still like kippers? We get the best kippers from the Isle of Man. Manx kippers are far superior to Scottish Kippers. So hurry up, I'm starving."

With that Freddy headed for the door, a big grin on his face. "God, Roger, it really is good to see you."

Fifteen minutes later, looking and feeling better than he had just a short while before, Roger emerged from his room dressed in a light blue shirt and jeans, both still warm from being freshly pressed.

His room was at the top of a rather grand winding staircase and he stopped for a moment to look around. There were at least eight other doors along the passageway that stretched from one end of the house to the other. Two of the doors were open and Roger was tempted to take a look inside one of them. As he slunk up the passage, the thick ginger-colored carpet deadened the sound of his shoes. Just before the first open door he stopped to take a look at a surprisingly modern painting on the wall. It looked like a Modigliani. He studied it for a minute and realized that it wasn't a print. The painting on the opposite wall was most definitely a Gerhard Richter and that looked like an original as well. Suddenly Roger recalled the clipping from the *London Evening Standard* his ex-father-in-law had sent him reporting Freddy's demise. "Cat-Loving Conman Dies in Mysterious Suicide" had been the headline of the article that told of Freddy dying from a heroine overdose and the accusations that he'd smuggled hundreds of original artworks out of South Africa. This, according to the article, had earned him the wrath of extremely wealthy people who used him to take valuable art to the UK during the waning years of Apartheid when it was illegal to take any currency or valuables out of South Africa. The brilliant part of Freddy's scheme was that he kept some of the art, sold the rest and pocketed most of the proceeds and there wasn't a damn thing the suckers who entrusted him with their art could do about it legally, without exposing themselves. Roger was wondering if the paintings on the wall were some of the purloined art when a man emerged from the second open doorway towards which he was headed, causing him to stop guiltily in mid-stride.

"Good morning, sir. May I help you?"

The man was enormous. Bigger than Freddy, but in a way that said he could break a large branch off a tree, or the leg of an overweight and out of shape middle-aged man, using only his bare hands. He was dressed in black pants, a white shirt and a grey vest that hugged his muscular torso.

"No, no," Roger replied rather too quickly. "Just going down. Just going to breakfast. Just stopped to look at the paintings. I'm Roger by the way."

He stuck out his hand towards the giant who turned around without taking it. It seemed both a rude and dismissive gesture.

"I know who you are, sir. My name is Corn, Zechariah Corn. Why don't you follow me? The staircase as you can see, is over here as opposed to over there. I will show you to the breakfast room where Mr. Blank and Miss Palomino are waiting for you. If you please."

Roger followed Corn down the stairs, his eyes focused on the back of his massive shaved head and neck. He wondered if the man had to have his shirts specially made. Then the delicious smell of freshly baked bread hit his nostrils and all thoughts of limb-breaking and oversize clothing issues vanished.

Like Roger's bedroom, the dining room had a charm and elegance that seemed to have come straight out of a P.G. Wodehouse novel. Dark wood paneling, a big crystal chandelier and thick velvet drapes that were pulled back to let in the pale morning light. Freddy and Conchita were seated at the top section of a long mahogany table with reed legs that could have seated eighteen people. Conchita, who was nibbling on a croissant, looked up and smiled at Roger. Freddy jumped up and pulled out a chair.

"Here sit down Roger and let's get you fed up - as my mom used to say. I see you've met Zechariah. Good, excellent. Zech why don't you tell Alfons that Mr. Storm will have his kippers and eggs now? And bring some more of that bread will you, with lashings of butter. I'm still starving."

Roger was about to tell Freddy that his accent and way of speaking was really affected for someone who'd grown up in Johannesburg, but decided to postpone any further criticism until he had a better understanding of what he'd actually gotten into. Or more importantly what he was going to get out of. He sat down in the proffered chair and smiled at Conchita. The morning light revealed that she was most definitely no longer in her twenties or thirties. Yet if anything he found her even more appealing than the night before. She smiled at him again and he felt himself blushing with embarrassment.

"Good morning, Roger." Her accent had a quirky lilt to it which only added to her appeal. "I hope you're feeling a little better, and I'm sorry we had to drug you, but the effects will wear off soon."

"I don't even know what happened last night. How did we get from Paris to London? The last thing I remember, probably, is passing out in the restaurant."

"Yes, you did..."

"And before you tasted the chicken, which is such a pity because it's so good," interrupted Freddy. "But all is not lost, here are your kippers and eggs, and Alfon's homemade bread".

Zechariah Corn placed a large plate in front of Roger. It contained a perfectly grilled kipper and two fried eggs done exactly the way he liked them. He inhaled deeply, realizing just how hungry he was. He took a piece of the bread which had been lightly toasted and slid it under the eggs. Then cutting into the still sizzling kipper with the skill of a surgeon, as Roger's cousin who actually was a surgeon had commented when he'd seen him fillet a trout, he scooped it into his mouth. Freddy was right, it was indeed delicious. Firm, fleshy with a very distinct oaky smokiness to it.

"My God, this is good."

"Knew you'd like them," said Freddy cheerfully. "They're positively the best you can get."

"May I continue?" asked Conchita. "Or are you two so enchanted with the food that you don't care to have questions answered?"

"Sorry, Conchita. Carry on, my dear," said Freddy as he spread butter and marmalade onto a piece of toast and popped it into his mouth.

"So, as I said, you did pass out and Freddy and I had to drag you out to the car. You were semi-awake on the back seat but babbling like an idiot when we arrived at the apartment in Saint Germain."

"Well," Roger said, fortified by the kipper and eggs, "I think 'idiot' maybe a little harsh. Even in my current state I'm hardly an 'idiot'."

"No," replied Conchita, "'idiot' would describe your condition perfectly. Don't be so sensitive. Anyway as we got to the apartment Zech noticed that there were two men at the entrance to the building. I recognized them immediately. Very bad men. They would have cut you to ribbons to get information and then they'd have killed you. And so we changed plans and drove to the airport and took the plane to Farnborough. That's why we're in the London house and not in Paris."

Roger didn't know where to start. So far, as he recalled, the number of people who had wanted to kill or torture him to death had risen to three. There were too many questions racing around his slowly recovering mind. He took another bite of kipper and egg and looked at Freddy. He couldn't think of anything to say, so he asked a totally irrelevant question instead..

"You have a plane?"

"Well, that's hardly the question I was expecting but maybe it's a good place to start. Actually we have two planes. A Citation X, which is really fast - it's the one we used last night - and a Falcon 7X, which we can fly from London to Tokyo if we need to. Though I can't imagine why we'd ever go to Tokyo again."

"Why wouldn't you go to Tokyo?" Roger asked not quite sure why he was asking a destination question when he had no idea what he was doing with someone whom he clearly didn't know anything about in a situation he didn't understand.

"No arms market in Japan to speak of," replied Freddy.

"Well there is the Yakuza," Conchita added. "You remember when the Yamaguchi-gumi family bought Berettas from us?"

"You're right, but how much money do we ever make on handguns? Hardly anything."

Roger felt himself slipping back into a state of disbelief. Not so much as to what was being said but as to what he was doing in a situation that couldn't have been much different than that of Gregor Samsa in Kafka's *Metamophosis* when he wakes up one morning to find that he's been turned into a giant insect.

"You're arms dealers?"

"Well yes we were, amongst other things. But we tried to sell to the right side."

"My God, who are you people? Right side, Japanese Mafia...Look, I have to get out of here." He said it but he wasn't sure he meant it. Outside had begun to sound worse than inside.

"If you are determined, then of course Roger you can go any time. But in all fairness please allow me to at least tell you what we are and what we're doing, and why we need you. You may end up wanting to be a part of it. It's really important, something that could save the wildlife in Africa.

And I know that's something you care very much about."

Roger nodded as if he had an inkling of what he was talking about, which he didn't.

"And in any case," said Conchita, you're likely to get killed if you simply decide to leave this house by yourself. I mean it. The people we are up against are ruthless."

"But I don't know anything. I don't know what you do, who they are or exactly where I am."

"I know my dear," said Conchita taking Roger's hand. "But they don't know that. They probably think we've already told you everything."

Roger stared at both of them. His head told him to run like hell and take his chances but his confusion was rapidly being replaced by fear and a sense of numbness in his legs. Then he noticed something that confused him even more. Conchita's squeezing of his hand was causing another part of his anatomy to stir. He hoped to hell she didn't notice.

Chapter 7

In which Roger reflects on another Freddy-fueled incident during their school days

Johannesburg, South Africa
The Mid 1960's

The little school for troubled children to which Freddy had been sent after the Incident of the Burned Down Classroom, was nestled comfortably into a pleasant valley near the French Alps. The nuns who ran it were of an old order, chosen not only for their teaching skills but also for their toughness and lack of empathy when it came to dealing with unruly children. As adept as they were with most of the children who these days would have no doubt been diagnosed with ADHD or some other learning disability, they were however no match for Frederick Blank. After a year that many of them felt foretold the coming of the biblical Beast, two of the oldest and most competent, decided to quit the order for a less stressful life and Freddy's mother was contacted and told to retrieve her son.

Freddy was ecstatic at the prospect of returning home to live with his family in South Africa. Mrs. Blank-Goldman was also delighted, as was the other Blank brother whose life had been decidedly dull since Freddy had been sent away. But when Max Goldman, Freddy's stepfather, heard about it, he went into severe depression and had to be hospitalized for a month. The hospital used shock treatment which later on Mr. Goldman described as less traumatic and indeed preferable to the time he was forced to spend with his stepsons.

It was at this time, a week after Freddy's return, that Roger and Brian Morris were reunited with their soon to be best friend. It was Saturday afternoon, the first weekend of the new school year. Roger and Brian, both aged thirteen, were spending the afternoon at Brian's house in Park Town, one of the oldest and most graceful northern suburbs of Johannesburg. The two boys were practicing chipping on the full green that Brian's father, a fanatical golfer, had constructed in their front yard when a loud "hey!" made them look up from their shots. A large red-faced boy with a thatch of blond hair, dressed in gym shorts and a t-shirt that was clearly too small for his extraordinary big frame, was wheeling a broken bicycle up the long drive.

"Hi guys," he yelled. "Can you help me here?" He was pushing the wobbling bike frame with one hand and carrying the handlebars in the other.

Roger immediately recognized him.

"You're Freddy Blank..?"

"How do you...oh, I remember you. You're the guy from Walvis Bay. What's your name again?"

"I'm Roger Storm and this is Brian Morris."

"Well it's good to see you again, and to meet you Brian. Look, the damn handlebars broke off while I was struggling up the hill."

"No wonder," exclaimed Brian grabbing the handlebars. "They're rusted through. You're lucky you didn't hurt yourself."

"Oh I hurt myself," said Freddy, showing a bloody elbow and torn knee. Brian and Roger looked at the wounds with a good deal of interest and admiration.

"Wow," said Brian. "There's a lot of blood. Maybe you should let my dad take a look. He's a doctor. C'mon I'll take you inside."

"Don't worry," said Freddy. "These are nothing. I've been in far worse situations." He lifted his shirt to show a large scar on his stomach and several on his legs and arms. "One of the nuns at the school I was at in France hit me with a scythe. I think she was trying to kill me though she told the doctor it was an accident. Those women were mad but I got my own back, don't worry. Let's just say they'll be using the lavender field as a toilet until they can raise enough money for repairs.

Call themselves the Brides of Christ...more like the Brides of Frankenstein. Anyway, all I need to do is call my mom and ask her to fetch me because I can't ride this busted thing home."

"Of course," said Brian. "Let's go inside and you can call. But I'm telling you, you should let my dad put something on those."

The three boys went in the back door where they were stopped by Brian's mom in the kitchen. She took one look at Freddy and almost recoiled in horror at the sight of his dripping wounds.

"You're bleeding all over the floor, young man. Just wait here and let me get a cloth."

Fifteen minutes later, after Freddy's elbow and knee were cleaned and bandaged and declared non life-threatening by Brian's father, the three boys sat round the table enjoying a slice of Mrs. Morris's famous chocolate cake.

"I'm starting at Park Town Boys High School on Monday by the way, that's why I was riding my bike. I wanted to see the place before next week."

"That's fantastic," said Roger. "That's where we go. It's an absolute shit hole."

"That doesn't worry me a bit," said Freddy spewing bits of cake from his mouth. "I'm probably not going to be there that long in any case. That's what my stepdad says."

"Why's that?" Roger and Brian leaned in closer.

"School isn't really my thing, you know, Roger. I usually get kicked out pretty quickly. Do you think I can have another piece of that cake?"

'What grade are you going to be in?" asked Brian passing the large boy an equally large slice.

As it turned out, despite the fact that Freddy was eight months older that Brian and Roger he would be in the same grade as them.

"Most of the teachers are bastards," explained Roger, "and the headmaster, Frik Marais, is supposed to be able to use a cane like you cannot imagine and I can assure you I am never going to be visiting him in his office."

But he was wrong on that count. Being friendly with Freddy, while having many positive advantages, invariably led to trouble, and both Brian and Roger, who would have been called nerds in today's schools found themselves at the receiving end of the headmaster's cane on numerous occasions.

Most white South Africans, especially the Afrikaans conservatives, were God-fearing people who took the bible literally. They justified mistreating black people by quoting the Book of Genesis and the Curse of Ham. They also justified corporal punishment of children with scripture: "spare the rod and spoil the child". In fact, corporal punishment was used liberally in all schools to keep discipline, and left most children cowering and terrified into cooperation. But the stick-wielding teachers of Park Town Boy's High School eventually conceded that there was one exception whom they could not beat into submission. No matter how many times Freddy was hit he never complained, and in fact would laugh through and after his punishments even though they were the most severe of any pupil.

It was almost as if he felt no pain nor had any conception of what was right or wrong, living in his own world where the general philosophy was to turn every situation into an opportunity to have fun. Being with Freddy was never dull. His legendary antics and misbehavior made him the hero of most of the younger boys in the lower grades, and because at fourteen he was already as large as the biggest boys in the senior class, he was never bullied. Everyone knew that Brian and Roger enjoyed a special relationship with Freddy, and so despite their nerdiness, neither were they.

Weekends were best of all. Freddy showed his friends how to sneak into movies without paying and revealed to them his elder brother's porn collection that he'd smuggled into the country from Denmark. Pornography, even *Playboy*, was banned in South Africa and had to be snuck in at great risk. If ever there was a case of a country where the dangers of not separating Church and State were on display, South Africa up until the late seventies would be it. Even television was thought of as godless entertainment, and only in 1978 did the government finally discover it was the perfect propaganda tool. Fear of a black uprising replaced the fear of God.

One of the places Freddy discovered and introduced to Brian and Roger was the so-called Indian Market. This mysterious place in downtown Johannesburg, while not off limits to whites (Indians and Asians being considered one class below whites but two above blacks), was almost a microcosm of what South Africa wasn't. Here whites, blacks and people of Asian descent seemed to mingle quite happily as they bargained for spices or clothing. Brian's and Roger's families were moderately liberal (which basically meant they didn't openly abuse black people) but Freddy's mother was extremely so and worked for an organization of women who protested against apartheid. Freddy treated black people the way he treated everyone and had taught himself Fanagalo. This was the lingua franca of the black miners of Johannesburg who came from many different tribes and spoke many different dialects. Very few whites bothered to learn any of the African languages, but because Freddy treated everyone equally, he developed a marvelous relationship with servants and their friends alike. Freddy talked to anyone and everyone and soon had Brian and Roger doing the same thing. It was during these conversations with ordinary black people that Roger came to see apartheid for what it really was and hate it with a passion that would only grow over the years. He always credited Freddy for first exposing him to the ridiculousness and stupidity of a cruel and arcane system.

While life at school was sometimes painful because of the trouble Freddy got them into, it was also fun and no doubt would have carried on that way for the entire five years, were it not for Freddy's expulsion during Standard 8, the equivalent of sophomore year in American schools

Freddy's final act of defiance at Park Town Boy's High School, came to be know as the Incidence of the Math Tin, a sequence of events that began in the geometry classroom of a particularly nasty and mean teacher named Barlow.

Barlow, who seemed to have only one outfit consisting of a brown tweed sports coat that was far too short for him and grey flannel pants that positively shone from his sedentary lifestyle, had a habit of punching the arms of any boy who earned his disfavor. Because he was large lout of a man with big fists and because most of the boys were a good deal smaller, those whom he punched could expect to not only suffer intense agony followed by awful numbness, but to have their arms remain black and blue for days. It so happened on this day that the class had been given an exceedingly difficult assignment. At least ten of the boys had failed it miserably.

"The following boys, or should I say the following stupid boys, will stand up," said Barlow holding a pile of papers.

As he read the names, the victims of a violence soon to be visited upon them, reluctantly stood up. Barlow read the names in alphabetical order.

"Aardman, Blank - what else is new, Gambol, Harper, Hendricks, Isaacson, Johaneddes, Rudge, Thomas and Zeeland."

Roger could hardly believe it. He knew, despite being good at geometry, he hadn't done well on the paper. He breathed a sigh of relief realizing that he must have done well enough not to fail. He felt terrible for those about to be punched but happy that he didn't number amongst them. He'd felt the effects of Barlow's punches before and knew he couldn't take another without embarrassing himself.

Barlow walked up to the first boy, Hendricks, who turned his head away. Barlow made a pineapple sized fist and then stopped.

"Hang on a second everyone, didn't I say ten stupid boys? Yes, I did and unless I'm very much mistaken, I only read out nine names. I'm sorry. Let me relook at my list."

He walked back to his desk and picked up the papers.

"Ah, yes. Storm, you may stand up too. I nearly forgot you and that would have been terrible. I'd hate you to feel you'd been left out."

By this time he was back in front of Hendricks. He pulled his fist back to his shoulder and punched the skinny frightened boy as hard as he could on the arm. Hendricks came from stouter stock than Roger, and while the punch clearly hurt, he simply bit his lip and sat down, his face the color of the chalk on the blackboard. With a grin usually reserved for the faces of true bullies, Barlow walked up to Roger.

"Stand up, boy."

Roger tried to stand, but his legs failed him. He knew he should be brave, but any ounce of bravery in his DNA, if any had indeed been present, vanished. He heard Barlow stomping towards him in his big brown clodhopper shoes. He felt Barlow's breath on the back of his neck and spittle on his ear. He crouched in horror, trying to disappear under his desk.

"Stand up, I said you miserable little coward and take your punishment."

Roger made one more feeble attempt to evaporate and failed. Barlow grabbed his hair and dragged the now quivering Roger to his feet. He pulled his arm back to deliver a vicious punch and then stopped. Roger opened his eyes and through his tears saw that Freddy was now standing next to him.

"Get the hell away, Blank," screamed Barlow.

"Wait Sir," said Freddy, grabbing his arm. "Why don't you punch me first. It'll loosen you up. You can even punch both my arms if you like." He turned his body sideways inviting Barlow to hit him.

Barlow let go of the cringing Roger and without a second thought swung at Freddy. The punch was hard. In a boxing match it probably would have drawn high praise from an experienced commentator. It snapped through the air and landed on Freddy's upper arm with the force of a charging bull.

There was a sound of bone breaking. A dull muffled crack and then a howl of pain unheard of in the class. This was immediately followed by a shriek of laughter.

Barlow's hand hung limply from his wrist. Even to the untrained eye it was clearly broken. Roger looked from Barlow's broken hand to Freddy's face, down which tears were streaming as Freddy fought to stop the convulsions of laughter that were threatening to envelop him. Freddy reached into his blazer sleeve and pulled out a math tin - those metallic boxes that contained dividers, compasses, rulers and other tools necessary for mastering geometry in the sixties. The tin was bent almost in half from the impact of Barlow's punch.

The awful sounds, in the meantime had drawn the attention of a neighboring teacher who, minutes later, rushed into the classroom and surveyed the scene. He ushered both Barlow, his face ashen and his eyes screwed up in pain, and Freddy out the class.

Barlow returned to school a week later his hand in a plaster cast and from that moment on never punched another boy. But Freddy did not return. When Roger called him at home that night Freddy told him that the school were not going to press assault charges but that Freddy could not return and that his parents were going to get him into what, in those days, was called a cram college, where he would finish his high school career.

Chapter 8

IN WHICH FREDDY AND THE
SEXY ASSASSIN EXPLAIN MORE
OF THEIR PLAN TO ROGER

London, England
About a year ago

F reddy and Conchita led Roger down a wide airy passage into a library. It was yet another magnificent room that matched the others in both grace, symmetry and warmth. The wooden floor-to-ceiling shelves were filled with books interspersed with the odd tribal artifact. While Freddy plonked himself down onto one of the chairs and Conchita sat at the leather topped desk and logged onto her computer, Roger took a few moments to examine some of the books. A complete leather-bound set of novels by Thackeray, clearly bought by the yard for show, stood side by side with hundreds of novels and current reference books. Many of them, he noticed, were on Africa and its wildlife. It was a room in which Roger felt, had he been alone and not in the company of madmen, he could have been unbelievably comfortable. He sat down in one of the big toffee-colored club chairs and immediately slid forward into an almost prone position. For some reason - perhaps the shrinkage in his buttock region as his ex-wife had so kindly pointed out - made sitting in big comfy chairs almost impossible. To add to his awkwardness, a large brown cat leaped onto where his lap would have been had he not been slumped. The cat had executed a perfect four point landing onto his groin and sensing potential slippage, dug in its claws. The pain was intense

"Jesus," Roger cried trying desperately to both sit up and dislodge the cat.

"Ah, Sebastian has discovered you," laughed Freddy trying to lift the cat whose claws were still firmly lodged in the skin of Roger's scrotum. "He normally only jumps on people he likes"

Roger pulled himself up as two more cats jumped up on him. One was a Manx and his mind went off on a tangent, as he wondered if it had enjoyed the remains of his kipper. He stroked the cats until they settled down purring gently on his lap, the touch of their fur making him feel less anxious and he recalled again the *London Evening Standard* headline about the cat-loving conman.

"Ugh," said Conchita as she watched the scene with feigned amusement, "I'm glad they chose you to jump up on. Personally I can't stand the beasts."

Freddy laughed. "Conchita's more of a dog person while I love cats. These three are a big part of my life..." He paused for a moment as if in thought. "Anyway, we don't have a lot of time today, so I'm going to start and Conchita can fill in when necessary. Obviously you will have questions, Roger, and feel free to ask. Just know this whole affair is hugely complex and delicate"

"Maybe I can make this easier for you," Roger said. Although he was feeling better after the breakfast, he still didn't feel one hundred percent and wasn't sure he could stomach long explanations. "Tell me exactly what you do now. What you are planning to do in the near future and what my part is expected to be in whatever it is you intend to do."

"That's good," said Conchita leaning forward. "I like that. I told you that's what we need Freddy. Articulated Simplicity."

"And that's why I told you we needed someone like Roger. You and I are not qualified in this area. We," said Freddy to Roger, gesturing at Conchita, "are the owners of what was one of the most successful global arms trading companies in the world. Still is, in a way. Even though we don't really sell weapons anymore or take on new clients. It's called PaloMar and we are registered in..."

Roger cut him off. "I just need enough to understand. I don't think I really want to know the details."

"Too late for that, old man. But fair enough, I will spare you all the details for now. You see Conchita and I and some of our associates have made an enormous amount of money...and I'm talking really, really a lot of money. I mean you can't imagine how much Roger, and we have decided to put that money..."

"Not all of it," Conchita interrupted, "but a good deal of it."

"Jesus," said Freddy, "will you two let me finish please. We have decided to put 'a good deal of it' towards saving Africa's displaced people and its dwindling wildlife from land encroachment, poachers and trophy hunters. What we need you to do is come up with something that will galvanize these poor people. Get them to sit up, listen and take action."

"That doesn't make any sense to me at this point. It sounds very honorable and I'm really glad you're thinking of doing good with all your money. Although without trying to be offensive it's slightly ironic, you being arms dealers and all that. But surely there's a ton of stuff being written and done already? I absolutely detest what's happening but what can you do that's different, that will make people 'sit up and listen' as you say?"

"What we do, that is different, is give the people and animals the advantage for a change. And this is where the idea gets really interesting, as I'm sure you'll agree."

Chapter 9

IN WHICH INSPECTOR BUNTER
VISITS HIS COLLEAGUE
INSPECTOR DARMSTAEDTER
WITH MORE BAD NEWS

Wisebaden, Germany
About the same time

"Matthew, how are you?" Darmstaedter said, standing up to greet Bunter as he walked into his office. Bunter was dressed formally in a blue serge suit with a crisp white shirt and his old regimental tie. Together with his perfectly combed ginger hair and trimmed mustache, he was, in Darmstaedter's opinion, the text-book picture of a stereotypical British detective.

"Please sit down, my dear friend. May I get you a coffee?"

"Thank you, Constantin. I had more than enough on the plane and I've been peeing like a mule. But I'd love a water if that's not too much trouble."

"None at all," replied Darmstatedter retrieving a bottle from the little fridge behind his desk.

"So you have your own fridge. Very fancy, I must say. At Interpol we're lucky to have a drinking fountain."

"I can see you are agitated. I assume from your coming here that you have some more information on the killings?"

"Agitated, may be the mild form of what I am going through right now. No, I don't have any real update on Heidenreich or the others, but I must tell you that it has happened again. And this time it's more than a single big game hunter or poacher."

Bunter reached into his worn leather briefcase and took out his laptop. "Take a look at this. It's an online article from the London *Daily Mail* from about a year ago."

Darmstaedter scanned the article which reported on the fact that the Tanzanian government had ordered forty-thousand Maasai tribesmen to be removed from part of their homeland after selling it from under their noses to a United Arab Emirate hunting outfit as a playground for Middle Eastern royalty.

"This is just disgusting," he snorted. "Haven't we done enough displacement of poor people in the past? Ach, I lose more and more faith in humanity every day. But I suspect that is not why you are showing me this. You think whoever is taking out the wildlife killers will strike here next?"

"I'm afraid I don't think, mate. I know. They struck yesterday and it's bloodier than all hell."

"I have seen nothing on the news…"

"And you won't just yet. Between the Dubai royals and the Tanzanians they've managed to keep it under wraps."

"Please," said Darmstaedter standing back up and walking to the large window that looked out on the park surrounding BKA, "tell me what happened."

"The hunting outfit is called Otterlo Business Corporation, headquartered in Dubai. Not an easy company to find out much about. On the surface it's run by a management board but as I discovered it's owned by the Royal Family and run by a Major General Mohammed Al Rahim, a close pal of the Emir. Or *was* a close pal but I will get to that in a moment.

"Eight days ago, a Boeing 737 specially fitted out for the royals landed at an airstrip in a place called Loliondo on the border of the Serengeti Game Reserve."

"That's the place that belonged to the Maasai?" asked Darmstaedter, his eyes narrowing in anticipation.

"Precisely. Well apparently OBC has been organizing, through some mysterious intermediary, massive hunts in the area for a few years. Their clients go in and slaughter hundreds of anything and everything. The Maasai have been driven off their grazing lands and most of the indigenous animals shot to hell. In fact according to the Maasai, the Arabs pay people to drive animals out of the Serengeti into the Loliondo these days. Of course the Tanzanians deny it..."

"That comes as no surprise," said Darmstaedter shaking his head sadly.

"After the hunts the meat and skins are shipped back to Dubai in a UAE air force cargo plane. The UAE royals have even invited one or two of our own royals in the past but luckily not on this trip...

"Anyway, as I said, the plane landed and was supposedly met by the Tanzanian representatives of OBC. Everything was going according to plan. The shooting party consisting of General Mohammed, two twenty-something-year-old sons of the Minister of Internal Affairs and their cousin Sheik Suhail, a son of one of the Emir's brothers and himself an heir to the throne. They got into four Range Rovers and were driven to the hunting camp. Now we don't know exactly what happened over the next two days in Loliondo..."

"My guess is not a picnic with cold beer and cake," laughed Darmstaedter grimly.

"I'd say that's a fair guess," Bunter did not see the humor. "What we do know is what happened in Dubai when the cargo plane carrying the usual freezers full of meat, skins and severed heads arrived back in Dubai."

"What are you saying?" asked Darmstaedter already suspecting the answer.

"What I'm saying,' replied Bunter standing up and joining his friend at the window, "is that OBC will have to find a new chairman, the Minister of

Internal Affairs may have to start indulging his daughters and the Emir will have to name a new heir. Though the previous one's head will probably look good over the mantelpiece."

Chapter 10

IN WHICH FREDDY AND CONCHITA GET EVEN DEEPER INTO THEIR INCREDIBLE SCHEME TO SAVE AFRICA
❦

London, England
Around the same time, give or take a few days.

"Sorry Freddy, but you have got be more explicit. What do you mean 'you give the animals the advantage'? Do you give the baboons AK47s and train them to shoot poachers?"

Freddy laughed. "Not exactly, but that's not a bad idea. Conchita, make a note to train the monkeys in the use of high-powered semi-automatic weapons."

"Please Freddy," said Conchita with the faint hint of a smile, "be serious, your friend thinks we are crazy enough."

That was true. Roger wasn't sure it would have sounded any less ridiculous if he were thinking clearly. He felt the bile rise in his throat once again. Kipper was not a good taste on the way up.

"Before you react," said Conchita, "although you look like you are about to vomit...Freddy, maybe bring that rubbish bin to him...let us give you a little background. Look Roger, you may not want to hear any of this but you do need to understand the enormity of what we are doing. I know it sounds incredible, but I can assure you we are very definitely not mad, as you are no doubt thinking."

Roger certainly was but he decided not to confirm it.

"Roger," said Freddy leaning forward in his chair. "Let me start by asking you a question. How many armed conflicts do you think are going on in the continent of Africa at any one time?"

"I don't know," Roger replied. "Do you mean full scale wars or internecine skirmishes?" He had absolutely no idea what he was asking but somehow interacting with the two lunatics – irrespective of how stunning one of them might be - made him feel slightly safer than sitting there with his mouth open.

"Oh I mean both and I mean much more." Freddy didn't wait for Roger to take a guess. "On average at any one moment, there is some form of fighting taking place in at least twenty-four of the fifty-three countries in Africa. Most of them without a clear purpose. Fighting and killing that is uncontrolled and opportunistic. Raping, maiming, kidnapping and in most cases on the surface at least, with no apparent rhyme or reason. And the worst part, the real horror, is that the evil is viral. It spreads across borders from one group to another like a disease carried on the wind.

"The minute this unhinged violence dies down or seems to be under control in one area, it flares up somewhere else. People like to think that much of it is religion-based because of the enormous concentration of Christianity and Islam in the north of the continent. And some of it is of course, Pentecostal Christians versus Islamists. But that doesn't hold true the more south you go. There is also a good deal that is tribal. One ethnic group killing another simply because they are different is nothing new. However, put belief and ethnicity aside for the moment. I am telling you that most of the violence, no matter how spontaneous it seems, is carefully controlled. And the reason behind it, is greed."

Freddy took a deep breath. "Greed for minerals, yes, and to a lesser extent, greed for oil. But the greatest greed of all, is for land. Land to grow crops. Land to house people. This insatiable desire is the main stimulus behind the fighting and genocide."

"That's a broad statement."

"Wrong," said Freddy. "Because we know who is behind it and who controls it."

Roger wanted to keep listening because there was a burning passion in Freddy's eyes. He'd only seen passion like that once before when he'd met Bill Clinton at an event he'd been invited to with a large donor to the Democratic Party in New York. It was the look of people who are so self-assured, so confident of their own moral righteousness that they become oblivious to anyone other than themselves. Quite frankly, Roger believed, it was something the average person should run away from as fast as possible. Advice he was seriously considering as the conversation went on.

"You're probably thinking that land is one thing Africa has in abundance," said Conchita. "And yes, there is enough land for different tribes to live on and make use of as they always have done. Even with the on-going ethnic disputes. What there isn't enough land for is the outsiders. People who've come in to exploit it for their own purposes."

"Do you know," said Freddy, "that by 2009, two-and-a-half millions hectares of land had been bought up in Africa?"

Roger turned around from staring out the window. "I don't doubt that at all but who's buying it? Surely it can't be only this one mysterious organization that you're hinting at."

"No, and that's what makes it difficult. China certainly is behind a lot of it. India, Saudi Arabia, Korea, they're there too. We cannot take on India or China or any country for that matter. That ultimately is a job for the United Nations. But we can take on this organization that serves as a front to buy up the land for oil companies, mineral companies, big US hedge funds and even unscrupulous individuals in Europe and Asia. This is an organization that not only facilitates a lot of what is going on, encouraging the wars and skirmishes by whatever means possible, but they also provide soldiers to move people off their lands. And its members are also some of the biggest and most despicable trophy hunters in the world. These are the same people who tried to kill you and destroy us."

"I was wondering when you were going to get back to the animals."

"I'll get there in a moment. I promise. But I have to give you a little more context.

"This overall issue is dispossession on a monumental scale. Because, before you interrupted, what I was about to say is that the figures are even worse and getting more so each day. The latest numbers show that to date, just six years later, fifty million hectares of land have been sold in Africa alone. Ethiopia with its thirteen million starving people has made three million hectares of its most fertile land available to rich countries and individuals to grow food for export. If you read articles on the land grab you will see that there are always promises that the locals will benefit but it's lies and deceit for the most part. They have created a displacement crisis and untold hunger in Nigeria Uganda, Tanzania, Congo, Malawi, Ethiopia and the Sudan. This is the virus that we have to stamp out.

Conchita was calmer but no less passionate. "Most people have no real idea about the refugee crisis in Africa. They're horrified about the Syrians flooding into Europe and the boat people but do not notice that within the absurdly defined borders of most African countries there are by current estimates nearly six million refugees."

"It's a little confusing," Roger said. "I mean, I sort of see the connection but the people and animal scenarios seem different. You started off talking about saving the wildlife but this issue seems even bigger than that. You're talking about destroying neocolonialism. The animals are just a side effect."

"You are right Roger and that is the danger: becoming unfocused," interjected Conchita. "But I truly believe if you have listened to what Freddy has been saying you will see that the two causes are very definitely related. Now, let your friend continue and hopefully the connection will become clearer."

"It's not either or, Roger. It's not people or animals. It's what and who is motivating the displacement and destruction of both."

Roger said nothing. Sunlight had flooded the room and he looked out the window onto the bricked alley that ran alongside the house. It was the first time he noticed how thick the glass was.

"Roger!" Freddy continued, becoming quite excited. "I believe, as do a lot of people, that this isn't really about numbers. It's partially about badly structured societies and poorly run economies. But good governments can change all that. The underlying issue is – and I will say it till you truly do get it - greed. An insatiable desire to profit from people who can't help themselves by stealing some of the cheapest land in the world. Land that is devoid of man and beast. And an organization that is taking full advantage of the situation by enabling its blood sucking members to go in and indulge their lust and barbarity by systematically killing the one thing that may save Africa from itself: the animals."

Conchita held up her hand for her partner to slow down. "The thing is Roger there is enough evidence to prove that wildlife preserves have enormous benefits to more people. Thirty people spending ten thousand dollars on a safari that directly benefits a local tribe is far better than one person paying fifty thousand dollars to shoot a lion that directly benefits a hunting company. Even two hundred people a year visiting a wildlife preserve that is owned by the local tribe is far more beneficial than the same size land being leased by a foreign country or a corrupt government."

"Okay, I get it but you keep talking about this organization? Who are they? How do they control things?" Roger felt ridiculous asking questions that made him sound like he was already intimately involved, because it was the last thing in the world he wanted to be. As much sympathy as he had for the people and the animals, he didn't feel he had enough energy to spend on any cause other than himself.

"At one point," Freddy answered," as we discovered later, they were a competitor of ours in the international arms trade. Then they started playing an even more deadly game."

"It's hard to imagine anything more deadly than selling weapons."

"That's a reasonable observation from your limited understanding of what we do. But there are things that you'll find out that may change what you're thinking We have two people who were operators in this organization until they decided to work for us. One you've met, Zecheriah, and the other you will meet a little later. He'll explain how the organization is made up of some of the most powerful and rich people on the planet. How they instigate uprisings and supply the mercenary forces that carry out the land grabs. Heavily armed mercenary forces that answer to no government, and are therefore free to do what they want. This organization, these people, are betting that rising populations around the world and climate change will make food even more valuable than oil."

"But wouldn't you have supplied the weapons to the people in the past?"

"Well yes, I already admitted we did at one point. But before you start getting all self righteous on me and Conchita, let me just explain. A few years ago we were contacted by an ex-CIA man we'd done business with before. He wanted us to supply weapons to a group that was supposed to be mounting a take-over attempt in Guinea Bissau. You may have read about it?"

"Not really. Not my type of reading."

"Well it was a pretty famous case with South African and British ex-special forces involved. Margaret Thatcher's son was named, as were some other well-known Brits. The money was big because the coup was supposedly being funded by the US and the UK. Or so the ex-CIA man told us.

"But no, we didn't sell the weapons. It was too complex and dirty. Then a few months later we found out who eventually organized the whole operation. It wasn't the CIA or Mi-6. It was a company registered in Lichtenstein. A rather mysterious organization - and I use the word mysterious with caution because evil is probably a better description - with ties to some of the most notorious thieves and villains imaginable. These people who belong to this organization are the ones I mentioned who finance half the wars in Africa, control some of the most powerful mercenary armies and kill more animals for their own pleasure than you can possibly imagine. And their ultimate goal is to own huge parts of Africa. Their aim was not to oust a corrupt government in Guinea Bissau. It was to put in an even more corrupt one."

"Ok, well I suppose now I know more about this 'mysterious organization'," Roger said, still not really wanting to know anything at all except how to get the hell out of there. "But I'm still a little unclear about the animal side. Why is that the focus of your fight?"

"As we said, Roger, animals are not the focus but the two causes are inseparable." Conchita sounded frustrated. "And the way we will take down this organization is to stop it from destroying both people and animals."

"Let me ask you a pointed question," said Freddy pouring himself a coffee from the pot that stood on the desk. "Do you really care about another hundred, two thousand, thirty thousand even, refugees from some country in Africa?"

Roger wanted to say 'yes' but the more he thought about every news report on refugees entering Europe illegally or crossing the borders into the USA, the more he realized that for most people the answer would be 'no'.

"We all feel sorry for them, Roger," said Conchita. "But we wish they'd go away. There are too many. It's a tsunami of desperation. Not just for the poor refugees but for the people who are forced to take them in. So ultimately – and this is important - helping these poor people is our goal. We wish to restore the status quo with people and the wildlife, the symbiotic relationship, that is critical to well-being of Africa."

"Let me ask you another question," said Freddy. "Do you recall the story of that lion called Cecil who was illegally shot by the big game hunting dentist from America?"

"Yes of course, I even signed a petition to get him extradited to Zimbabwe."

"Exactly. You and millions of people around the world wanted the dentist shot and skinned."

"I would have done it myself," Roger said remembering his anger.

"You should be beginning to understand where we are going with all of this. In our experience nothing brings out the inherent savagery in peace-loving people more than the senseless killing or cruelty to animals or defenseless children. You will also recall the picture of that three year old Kurdish boy washed up on the Turkish shore?"

"I certainly do understand that," Roger replied. "It's one of the oldest clichés in advertising. Put a baby or an animal in a commercial and everyone responds. I am, as you've probably gathered by now, not a violent person but when I do see these sorts of things posted on Facebook something happens to me and I just want to obliterate people who do that sort of thing."

"But you'd never go through with it would you? Like your desire to kill your ex-boss Harry Bones. Oh, I do get why you want to kill him. I did my own research on Harry Bones. He is a disgusting individual and in my opinion, and obviously yours, the world would be better without him. But Roger my friend, you will never be able to kill him. You and all the other people like you. The bleeding hearts. You cry, you write articles, you sign petitions but in the end you do nothing. But we do. We kill the killers."

Chapter 11

IN WHICH ROGER RECALLS ANOTHER OF FREDDY'S CRAZY CAPERS

Johannesburg, South Africa
The late '70s

It wasn't the headline in the morning paper that made Roger nearly choke on his muesli. It was the first three words of the article below the fold titled, "Judge gives Walter Mitty-type con artist R10 000 fine and ten year suspended sentence" that did the trick: "Horace Frederick Blank..."

The article told the incredible tale of how Freddy - Roger had no idea that Freddy's first name was actually Horace - had stolen over a million rands(the South African currency, at that time equal to about $1,400,000.00) worth of diamonds. The elaborate, and, once again hair-brained, scheme involved posing as both a bodyguard for the Queen Mother of Swaziland and an American Kentucky Fried Chicken franchisee.

Before he'd even finished the article the phone rang. It was Brian Morris. He'd also just read what came to be referred to as 'The Incident of the Fake Kentucky Fried Chicken Franchisee.'

"Well," said Freddy when the three of them got together later that week after he'd paid his fine and been released from the prison, "you know if I'd bought one extra day on the car rental I would have gotten away with it."

He took a sip of his beer and sat down in a big comfy armchair in Roger's apartment. Neither Brian nor Roger said anything. They knew Freddy would tell them everything in his own way.

"You guys will remember that about a year ago I bought up that old camp on the border of Bophutatswana..."

Bophutatswana was the first of ten "independent home-lands" that the South African government set up in order to create autonomous ethnic territories as part of the apartheid plan. The homelands consisted of thirteen percent of the entire country to house about seventy five percent of the population, and were a critical part of the government's policy to have no black African citizens of South Africa. The system collapsed with the dying gasps of apartheid.

Freddy, after working a number of years for a large hotel group had bought a run down summer camp for boys, and when Roger and Brian last spoke to him he was restoring it and turning it into a convention retreat.

"Well, when I got there and saw how desperately poor the people were, the ones who lived around the camp, I felt I had to do something for them. I tried to pay them decent salaries and I wanted to maybe build a school, but I'd bought that stupid second hand Rolls Royce as a convention car and I didn't have any extra money."

"Why didn't you just sell the car?" asked Brian. "You didn't really need it."

"I would have but I didn't think it was worth that much. Anyway I had another idea. I guess I must have seen something like it in a movie or read about it in a book."

Roger leaned forward. He knew what was coming would be entertaining.

"What I did was take the oldest woman on the property, one who didn't speak any English at all, and dress her as if she was the queen-mother of the King of Swaziland."

"Okay," said Roger sitting back and taking a long swallow of his beer. "That in itself is insane. First of all, Swaziland is a completely separate country where the inhabitants are Swazi and speak Swati as opposed to being Tswana and speaking Tswana. Second, how do you know the King even had a mother or how she dressed, and what the hell were you about to do?"

"Look I don't know whether he has a mother or not. And if I didn't know then I had little doubt that anyone else knew either. It's not important. What I did was make myself a card that read Swaziland Secret Service, put on a dark suit and drove the old lady into Johannesburg in the back of the Rolls. I pulled up outside Katz and Lourie Jewellers on Eloff Street, left the old lady in the back of the car and went in..."

"Why Katz and Lourie?" Roger asked. "I don't think a single black South African has ever set foot in that store."

"Exactly, that's why I chose it. It's so fucking old-school in terms of who they sell to and so secretive when it comes to their clients that I thought it would be perfect. I didn't want her to have to go in. My point was to get them to bring the jewelry out to her."

Brian, always the more logical of the three, rolled his eyes. "What was the plan?"

"I don't even know what the plan was. Maybe I was hoping they'd bring out a pile of jewelry and we could slip a piece into her blanket. Whatever was supposed to happen though happened and the manger allowed us to drive off with a diamond necklace worth a fortune on the pretense of getting the King's approval to buy. It was all so simple. The manager knew nothing of the Swazi royal family and believed everything I said."

"So actually, you stole the necklace?"

"No actually, I didn't. I returned the necklace a few days later telling them the King didn't like it. No one asked any questions, no one made any enquiries. And that was the end of that."

"Clearly not," said Roger.

"Correct. In fact, it was just the beginning," replied Freddy. "What it did was reinforce my belief that it is easy to fool people into giving you things, even very valuable things, when they think you're somebody important or rich. That is how I became Mr. A. P. Lowe, a wealthy Kentucky Fried Chicken franchisee from America."

Colonel van der Westhuizen, was speechless when he saw the half naked figure cuffed at the wrists and chained at the ankles lying on the floor of his office at John Vorster Square, Johannesburg's notorious police headquarters. The figure was bigger and fatter than he remembered, but nine years had gone by and the boy he knew as the jew-devil Freddy Blank was unmistakably the man now bleeding on his linoleum floor.

"Pull him up!" Van der Westhuizen yelled at the burly corporal who had dragged Freddy into his office.

The corporal put his hands under Freddy's armpits and attempted to lift. But when he felt the problematic disc in his back click, he let go of the three hundred and fifty pound man with a shriek. Freddy sank back onto the linoleum.

"I'm sorry, Colonel, he's too fucking heavy. My back, I think it's broken."

"Your back is not fucking broken and what the hell did you do to this bastard that he's half unconscious?"

The corporal staggered over to the Colonel's desk and attempted to push himself upright.

"Me and the sergeant were just trying to get him to confess. He just kept babbling on about some rubbish and then...and then he fell down the stairs."

"He fell down the stairs?" Van der Westhuizen was not so much speechless as he was furious. At least six prisoners had 'fallen down the stairs' in the last six weeks and the judges were starting to get suspicious. "You bloody idiot. I told you and that bird-brained sergeant that no one is to fall down the stairs again for at least three months. I said they can slip in the toilet. God dammit, man. Am I the only one with any sense around here? Now what did this bastard say?"

"He just told us the most ridiculous story you've ever heard, Colonel. I promise you a complete moron wouldn't believe it. It's all lies."

Van der Westhuizen knelt down on his carpet and grabbing Freddy's hair in his meaty fist, he brought his face within an inch of Freddy's rather mashed up nose..

"No, I know him. He may be the biggest criminal we have ever had in our clutches. The Moriarty of South Africa. I doubt what he told you is a lie."

The corporal blinked through his pain. He had no idea who Moriarty was but he was convinced the colonel had been nipping on the brandy he kept in one of his desk drawers.

"Oh yes," Colonel van der Westhuizen said, giving Freddy a kick in the ribs, "I knew I'd see you again you fat fucker."

He looked over at the corporal who was desperately trying to push himself upright on his desk.

"I have a good sense of these things you know Corporal. Some would call it criminal foresight. What the hell are you doing man?

"I'm in terrible pain sir," groaned the corporal as he slowly pushed himself up to a slight stoop and edged his way out of the office. He wasn't sure who was more insane, his colonel or Freddy Blank. Van der Westhuizen wouldn't have cared what the corporal thought. He was totally focused on the body on the floor that was slowly becoming less comatose.

"No, no Mr. Frederick Blank. No lawyer or bribe money is going to get you off this time. You will tell me how you stole those diamonds and then, then you will find yourself safely behind bars for a long time."

But even van der Westhuizen, as prepared as he was for the most fantastic of stories, found it hard to believe The Incident of the Fake Kentucky Fried Chicken Franchisee.

Horace Frederick Blank, brimming with confidence from very nearly walking away with a ridiculously expensive necklace from one of the most exclusive jewelers in South Africa, strolled into the headquarters of Kentucky Fried Chicken in Johannesburg.

He had set up a meeting with the head of franchise sales who, while off getting coffee for what he hoped would be his newest franchisee, didn't see Freddy steal a pile of letterhead from the stack on the side of his old Quiet Deluxe Model Royal typewriter and slip out down the fire escape. It was no matter thought the manager as he finished off both cups of coffee, the big fat guy looked like he preferred eating fried chicken to selling it. Not KFC material at all.

The manager of the Standard Bank in Rosebank, an affluent suburb just a few miles north of the city of Johannesburg, on the other hand was struck by the big blond American who strode into his office with what he thought of as a real wild west swagger.

"The name is Lowe, A.P. Lowe, from Louisville Kentucky," said Freddy in an accent that was somewhere between that of a Georgian peanut farmer and a Hassidic Jew from New York's garment district. The manager gave Mr. Lowe a big grin and winced slightly as the American grasped his outstretched hand. As South Africa still didn't have TV, his only exposure to American accents came from watching 16mm films of the Three Stooges on Saturday evenings. The guttural drawl didn't raise an iota of suspicion.

"Mr. Lowe," he said almost falling over his chair in excitement at having a genuine American in his bank. "What an absolute pleasure, sir."

In the mid-seventies many American companies operating in South Africa had begun to feel intense pressure from anti-apartheid groups to divest themselves of the country. This in turn made any American money coming into the country tantalizingly addictive to anyone and everyone who could get their hands on it.

"Here's the thing," said Mr. A. P Lowe handing over an official looking letter on Kentucky Fried Chicken letterhead and a picture of himself standing outside a KFC. "I am the first of a bunch of American franchisees who are going to be opening up multiple outlets in South Africa. I own about twenty in the States. Here's me in front of one of my smallest ones."

"Very impressive," said the bank manager taking a quick look at the picture and completely failing to notice that Lowe was standing next to a car with Johannesburg license plates. "Anything I can do to help, please let me know. We are as I am sure you've found out the premier bank in South Africa."

"No doubt about that," replied Lowe slapping the desk heartily. "That's why I came to you. I need a checkbook and I need to establish a line of credit pretty darn quickly. I'll have the money transferred to you on Monday but in good faith I'll deposit five hundred rands right now. I know it's only Thursday but it's a holiday in the US tomorrow."

"Not a problem Mr. Lowe. This is all very exciting and good for the country. I can definitely give you a checkbook but it will only have ten checks at this stage until I can get approval from the main branch."

"Perfect. That should be sufficient for now. Why don't you give me all the details and I'll send a telegram to my bank this afternoon to wire you six hundred thousand dollars on Monday."

The manager fairly danced his way out of his office promising himself he'd buy those new golf clubs he'd been dreaming about with his commission. Twenty minutes later Mr A.P. Lowe was shaking hands with the bank manager and putting his new checkbook in his briefcase. He snapped the briefcase closed quickly, and so the manager didn't notice the bank letterhead he'd purloined (just as he had at KFC) when the manager left his office to get the account started.

After a brief stop at his apartment, Freddy drove to the offices of a company that made rubber stamps for businesses, where he handed over an official letter from the Standard Bank, Rosebank branch, requesting a bank-guaranteed check stamp. He was assured it would be ready by noon on Friday. He drove his car to his brother's house, told his brother he was leaving for Switzerland for a short holiday the following evening and got a taxi to drop him off at Avis.

Once he'd procured a two day rental and arranged to drop the car off at the airport on Friday night, he drove back to his apartment, called up Swissair to book a one way ticket to Zurich, cancelled his phone service and utilities and told the building super that he wouldn't be returning. Then he checked himself into one of the better hotels in downtown Johannesburg, got the switchboard to connect him to three of the more renowned Johannesburg diamond dealers, made appointments for Friday afternoon, ordered room service and went to bed.

Both Roger and Brian had remained silent up to this point. The story had an almost unintelligible logic to it, but the elaborate plan seemed to be leading somewhere all the same.

"When did you work this out?" asked Brian. "I don't know where it's going, and I have to be honest, I have no idea how you managed to think this through."

Freddy looked carefully at his friends. "I don't really know either to be equally honest, Brian. Sometimes I'm not entirely sure how I do things. It's almost as if I can see things in my mind. It's all laid out for me. Like a game of Chutes and Ladders. But up until then, I'd landed on Ladders every time."

He sighed deeply and took a sip of his beer.

"The key to this plan was timing. I had to make sure that the bank manager couldn't check up on me till Monday because I had to visit the diamond dealers on Friday afternoon before they closed for the Sabbath. They're all religious Jews and I knew they wouldn't do anything on Saturday. Everything had to be done so I could fly out on Friday night. The problem with plans based on timing, though, is when something goes wrong. And in this case it did."

"Don't make it too easy Blank. Tell me you're not going to reveal anything else so I can kick you in the balls a few more times."

Van der Westhuizen wasn't joking. He was upset and confused. He had enjoyed torturing Freddy and he'd assumed he'd be continuing to do so for at least a week to get the whole story. He had a whole repertoire of things he wanted to try out.

"There's no point, Colonel," Freddy replied through his swollen mouth. "I'm tired. I don't have anything else to hide."

"So tell me again what you did on Friday afternoon after you got the 'Bank Guaranteed' rubber stamp?"

"I bought some dried prunes."

"Don't fuck with me, you bugger. What's dried prunes got to do with this whole mad plan?"

"I'm getting to it Colonel, just let me finish. I picked up the rubber stamp from the company and stamped every check. Each now guaranteed by the Rosebank branch of the Standard Bank for one hundred thousand rands

Colonel Van der Westhuizen got up from his chair and poured himself another cup of coffee. He was worried that his superiors wouldn't believe Freddy's confession. Freddy still hadn't told all and clearly the story, if it now involved dried prunes, could only go one way. And that way was not going to look good for van der Westhuizen when he stood up in court. Perhaps if he took a kinder approach.

"Would you like some coffee Blank?"

"Thank you Colonel," said Freddy. "I really am trying to tell you everything."

"I am sure you are Blank," replied van der Westhuizen, not believing a word of it.

He helped Freddy sit up, unlocked one of the handcuffs from the chair freeing Freddy's left arm and handed him a chipped mug of coffee. Freddy took a sip and winced as the lethal black substance flowed into a raw gap that had once been occupied by the molar now lying under the colonel's desk.

"So, as I was saying, after I had stamped each check guaranteed for one hundred thousand rands, I checked out of my hotel and drove to the first diamond dealer."

Freddy gave van der Westhuizen the name of a company run by two brothers who the colonel knew were involved in some extremely shady blood-diamond deals. They were also very involved with certain government officials. Van der Westhuizen listened with rapt attention.

"I walked in and told them I wanted to buy some special diamonds to take back to America."

"So you were again Mr. A.P. Lowe, not Mr. Blank."

"Yes, I showed them the Kentucky Fried Chicken franchisee letter with my photograph and that seemed to satisfy them. Of course I also showed them my bank guaranteed checks."

"No doubt the thought of all that money made them somewhat less interested in who you really were?"

"Well, they definitely didn't question me, but you know how everyone gets when there is money to be made."

"Everyone?" Van der Westhuizen was flabbergasted. "Not everyone. Don't give everyone a bad name. It's you bloody people. You Jesus-killing Jews are all the same. Greedy fucking bastards! Despicable heathens. Blood sucking cunts."

Van der Westhuiszen had forgotten his decision to try kindness as an alternative method of interrogation. The idea of wealthy conniving Jews oblivious to a clearly criminal action because of their money obsessed nature so incensed him that his rage took over. He smashed the coffee cup out of Freddy's hands and attempted to strangle him. But in the end Freddy's neck was too large for van der Westhuizen's hands and eventually he sent a now terrified Freddy down to a filthy cell. He was kept awake for days, his jailers throwing ice-cold water on him every time he closed his eyes.

"Jesus, Freddy," said Roger as Freddy's story and ordeal unfolded in his apartment. "Why didn't you just tell him the truth? That maniac could have killed you."

"It was the truth. It is the truth. It's just that no one ever believes my truth. Everything happened just the way I'm telling you now. I walked into their little office and told them who I was. I showed them the letter and my checkbook. That was all they needed to start the transactions. The older brother went to the safe and brought out some black velvet bags. They were full of cut stones that ranged from about one carat to nearly five. There were hundreds of them. Both brothers put in their jewelers' eyepieces and began picking each up to tell me everything about every one of those diamonds. They kept handing them to me to ask if I liked them. It was really amazing. I could have palmed any number and I don't think they would have noticed."

"So what were you going to do with the diamonds?" asked Brian.

"What do you think? I was going to sell them in Switzerland. I thought that was obvious."

"Nothing about the story is obvious Freddy," Roger said putting a comforting hand on his friend's shoulder.

"I know, I know. I really am sorry, but it's precisely what happened. They were relentless, you know, trying to push big diamonds on me. But in the end I decided that I didn't want to spend the money on one big diamond and so we settled on ten mid-sized, round cut, flawless, colorless diamonds. I haggled with them, simply for appearances' sake and at four o'clock, just before they closed for the Sabbath, we shook hands and I signed all of the checks over to them for a million rands."

"Just like that?"

"Yes, just like that."

"Okay," said Brian, "but we still don't know what the prunes were for and why the bad timing allowed you to get caught."

"My plan, just in case something went wrong and for some reason I was searched at the airport, was to put the diamonds into the prunes."

"If they'd searched you? Don't you think prunes would have been suspicious? I bet you fewer people leave South Africa with a bag of prunes than a bag of diamonds," said Brian.

"Maybe you're right, but it wasn't the prunes that got me caught. Everything at that point was going as planned. Nobody could do anything until Monday and by then I would be busy selling the diamonds in Switzerland and disappearing.

"I knew I had quite a window. It would take at least a day for everyone in Johannesburg to realize that something was horribly wrong, and all they would know is that an American Kentucky Fried Chicken franchisee named A.P. Lowe conned them and made them look pretty stupid. No one would have the name Freddy Blank."

"I suppose that's true," said Brian. "The bank manager, realizing he was going to get fired, would have played for time, and the diamond dealers, who no doubt have their own skeletons to hide, would have wanted to take care of you themselves. It is quite ingenious in a mentally retarded kind of way."

"My thoughts precisely," replied Freddy failing to pick up on the backhanded compliment. "So I went back to the hotel to get my bags, put the diamonds in the prunes, check out and drive to the airport. However, when I asked for my key, the desk clerk told me that Swiss Air had called to let me know that the Friday night plane had been cancelled and that I was now on the Saturday night flight."

"That's a problem," said Roger.

"I didn't think so at first," replied Freddy. "No one could do anything on Saturday either. I thought the worst that could happen was that I would perhaps have one day less in Zurich to find a buyer."

As Freddy had mentioned at the beginning of his story it was the car rental company that did him in. On his way to the airport on Saturday afternoon he was stopped by a police car looking for a red Toyota Corolla that had been reported stolen by Avis. Freddy had simply forgotten to tell them that he needed the car for an extra day. When Avis had telephoned his flat to ask him about it they found the service had been disconnected. So they sent someone round to his address and they were told by the super that Freddy had left the country. They had no alternative other than to call the police.

The two policemen who had stopped Freddy asked him for an explanation. When Freddy opened his briefcase to prove who he was and show them his ticket they saw the franchisee letter with the attached photograph introducing Freddy as A.P. Lowe. They decided this was evidence enough to take him in. When one of the policemen broke his tooth on a prune he'd eaten from Freddy's stockpile to ease his constipation, the game was up.

"It's amazing you got off with a suspended sentence and a fine," Brian said shaking his head at the peculiarities of a justice system that sentenced black people to years of detention and torture for trivial offenses but gave a self-confessed white criminal nothing but a slap on the wrist.

"It is," replied Freddy, "but as I said earlier, the more elaborate the proposition, the more fantastic the ruse, the more baffling the explanation, the less likely you are to be caught. In my case no one wanted to make too much out of it. It was just too fantastic. So I guess I got lucky."

"Who gave you the money to pay the fine?" asked Roger knowing Freddy's dad had died penniless a year earlier.

Freddy laughed.

"The diamond dealers, actually. While they were busy examining the diamonds, I simply palmed two of them and hid them at my brother's place before I left. I sold one to pay the fine and kept the other."

He pulled out a diamond as big as his thumbnail and showed it to his friends.

"I kept this one for luck. You never know when it will come in handy."

When Colonel van der Westhuizen heard the judge pass sentence on Freddy he almost fell out his chair. He had expected that Freddy would be serving at least fifteen years behind bars.

Later that day when he was called into the office of the chief of police, whom he knew resented him, he understood he was in trouble.

"Well, van der Westhuizen," said the chief as he lit up an unfiltered Lucky Strike, "you really fucked up this one."

"How so, sir?" asked van der Westhuizen, knowing full well how so.

The chief was unimpressed with van der Westhuizen's attempt at innocence.

"Let's get this straight, van der Westhuizen. You are the fool, not me. You claim to be the man who can get any information out of anyone. Well clearly that is no longer the case. You made a laughing stock out of the police. A big fat Englishman pulls off the biggest diamond robbery in our history and you can't produce anything but a cock-and-bull story that even the judge finds ludicrous?

"I am truly disappointed in you. I would dearly love to send you off to some God forsaken town like Poffadder. But I am a kind and generous person and so I will give you one last chance."

"Thank you Sir," van der Westhuizen said, knowing the chief to be anything but kind and generous. "This colonel will not let you down again."

"You mean 'this captain.' I am demoting you, van der Westhuizen and I cannot imagine what you will have to do to get your rank re-instated. These kinds of opportunities don't come around twice."

But the chief was wrong. An even bigger opportunity presented itself ten years later. It resulted, however, in van der Westhuizen being demoted to corporal and dying an awful death when a blood vessel exploded in his brain. The opportunity became known as the Incident of the Drowned Man.

Chapter 12

IN WHICH ROGER GETS SOME TIME
TO CONSIDER HIS SITUATION

London, England
Around a year ago

"Conchita and I have to go back to Paris for a few days to take care of some things, so you'll be on your own," Freddy said to Roger as he settled into the chair with one of the curmudgeonly cats purring softly on his lap. "You need to rest and relax. You can have the run of house. Do whatever you like. Eat whatever you like. Just tell Zechariah or Alfons what it is you want and they will see that you get it. But please, I'm begging you, do not try to leave or try to call or email anyone. We can't stop you of course, you are not a prisoner. But I can guarantee you, if they get the opportunity, they will take you and kill you. Please trust me, Roger."

Roger looked at Freddy and Conchita. Though he still believed they were both dangerous lunatics he could sense sincerity in Freddy's plea. Not being someone who ever took unnecessary chances he decided to take their word for it and enjoy the London house to the full. He still had no real idea what their plan was or what role he was supposed to play. All he knew was that it felt surprisingly good to have his friend back in his life and the thought of spending more time with Conchita was incredibly appealing.

It was the most relaxed he'd been in months. Alfons was a fine chef and he made Roger anything he wanted for breakfast, lunch and dinner. Zecheriah, while neither overly friendly nor talkative showed Roger the gym in the basement and even suggested a few exercises. He also opened up the liquor cabinet and poured Roger anything that took his fancy.

All Roger lacked was real conversation or communication with his sons. But there was plenty to read in the library and he'd made a promise to Freddy and Conchita to sit tight until their return. He tried a few times to get Zecheriah to open up about his previous life but the big man wasn't interested in talking and disappeared mysteriously every evening as soon as dinner was over.

Clearly, thought Roger, no one was going to attack him.

Chapter 13

In which Inspectors Bunter and Darmstaedter hear a rather racy story from the Widow Heidenreich

Leutstetten, Germany
Around the same time

Matthew Bunter and Constantin Darmstaedter were seated in big leather chairs in the baronial style reception room of the Heidenreich estate on the outskirts of the village of Leutstetten, about twenty-five kilometers from Munich. The towering walls of the room were covered with mounted heads from almost every known mammal, both large and small. Even a blue whale was represented by a three-and-a-half meter penis fixed to a dark wooden board.

"My God," exclaimed a shuddering Darmstaedter as he looked at what had once been a huge appendage. "I am glad Heidenreich wasn't fucked to death by a whale. There wouldn't have been much left of him to identify. This thing would have taken his head off from the inside."

"Christ," Bunter muttered, "I wonder how you shoot a whale? That prick must have harpooned it."

"While I appreciate the sentiment, I do not approve of such language in my house." The voice belonged to a tall, attractive middle-aged woman who had entered through a small door set just below the massive head of a bored looking Asian elephant. "I am Christina Heidenreich and I am assuming you are the two policemen who are investigating my husband's death?"

Both Bunter and Darmstaedter sprang up and Darmstaedter began to apologize profusely in German. He was interrupted by the elegant widow.

"Please, Inspector. We can speak in English. I am very comfortable in it and there is no need to apologize. The man who could kill all of these beautiful creatures deserves whatever happened to him, and any amount of derision you care to cast his way. He was, as the Americans say, a massive pain in the ass, and so being violated by a hippopotamus seems an appropriate death, don't you agree?"

Neither Bunter nor Darmstaedter dared move their heads.

"Maybe you don't, but I can think of no more fitting end to my husband. Now please sit and I will have some coffee brought in."

When the coffee and rather delicious apple strudel had been served, and after Mrs.

Heidenreich had explained that she planned to have the trophies removed and burned, she turned to the two policemen.

"From what I have been able to ascertain my late husband is not the only hunter to have met a rather sudden and appropriate end. Am I correct Inspector Bunter?"

Bunter's mustache bristled as he consulted his notebook. "I am not sure how you would know that Mrs. Heidenreich." He looked over at Darmstaedter who seemed equally puzzled, and then decided to let it go for the moment.

"Indeed you are correct though, ma'am, there have been a number of what seem to be revenge killings."

"You understand, Frau Heidenreich," said Darmstaedter, through a mouthful of strudel, "that it would not be appropriate to go into, should I say, the extremely gory details. But there are consistencies that lead us to believe that one organization is behind it."

"Perhaps an eco-terrorist group?" she asked.

"We can't rule anything out of course," said Bunter, "but in Inspector Darmstaedter's and my opinion, and it is merely an opinion mind you, no eco-terrorist group would have the funds or expertise to pull off deaths that are so extremely well planned and clearly cost an enormous sum of money. While we both feel we are close to discovering something that will bring these killers to justice, we are as of yet still in search of anything tangible."

"Which is why we have come to you, Frau Heidenreich. It is our aim to see if there is anything that connects all of the victims other than their love of murdering 'beautiful creatures,' as you put it." Darmstaedter placed his cup back on its saucer and looked at Mrs. Heidenreich with what he felt was his most sympathetic yet professional expression. He found her oddly erotic and he allowed his mind to wander for a second. He was picturing her on a horse, wearing nothing but a large sun hat, when a discreet cough by Bunter interrupted his reverie.

"Let me tell you about my husband Inspectors," said Mrs. Heidenreich, leaning forward so that Darmstaedter could see down the front of her dress, further throwing him into a spin. "He was not just an ass, he was an asshole!"

She said the word with such hatred that Bunter wondered precisely what it was about his and Constantin's whale-penis comments that she'd objected to.

"In what way Mrs. Heidenreich?"

"In every conceivable way. In every thing he did. With everyone he dealt with. Even his own family.

"Did he abuse you Frau Heidenreich?" Darmstaedter could not imagine anyone abusing this beautiful woman whom he now decided he was in love with.

"Oh, he raised his voice to me once when my little schnauzer defecated in his slipper, but I threatened to take a croquet mallet to his fat head if he ever did so again."

"I'm a little confused, Frau Heidenreich," said Darmstaedter leaning forward and getting an even better view of her décolletage. "You say your husband was not abusive and yet you saw the need to threaten him with a wooden hammer when he raised his voice to your dog?"

"There is nothing to be confused about Inspector. My husband was a bully. He used his big, disgusting body and his position and money to get anything he wanted from anyone and everyone. But like most bullies he was also a coward. He liked to hurt things that couldn't hurt him back. Which is why he hunted these poor animals."

"But *you* could hurt him back?" Bunter did his best impression of Basil Rathbone playing Sherlock Holmes, which he'd practiced in front of a mirror for hours. But this attempt to intimidate Mrs. Heidenreich was a total failure.

"Come, come, Inspector Bunter. I can tell by the way you ask that question that perhaps you believe I was in some way responsible?"

"Of course not, Mrs. Heidenreich. But it is my duty to ask those sort of questions. I certainly don't mean to offend you but Inspector Darmstaedter and I are trying to find some sort of connection and that unfortunately means eliminating all possibilities but one: the *truth*."

Darmstaedter looked over at his friend and scowled. He hated it when Matthew did his infuriatingly patronizing Sherlock Holmes routine. It made him feel like that hapless idiot Dr. Watson, and it never worked. In any case, hadn't this wonderful woman suffered enough?

"I do understand Inspector and I am going to reveal some facts that may help you," said Mrs. Heidenreich, remaining perfectly composed.

Both inspectors picked up their notebooks and pens while the widow Heidenreich poured herself another cup of coffee.

"My husband...my late husband... belonged to a secret club."

"A hunting club?" asked Bunter.

"Not as such Inspector, though I do know many of the members hunted. They were certainly all rich enough and powerful enough and arrogant enough to believe they could do anything they wanted. No, this was a very private sex club and it's how I know that there was more than one death. You see I had someone investigate this den of debauchery, this pleasure palace, where the very wealthy indulged in some of the most perverse acts imaginable."

Both detectives held their breath, their pens hovering above their notebooks like hummingbirds over honeysuckle.

"It is called 'The Naughty Schoolgirl Club,' and I have pictures."

Chapter 14

IN WHICH AN ELEPHANT IS SAVED FROM SLAUGHTER

The border of the Hwange National Park, Zambia
Around the same time

Saviour Mpariwa had been a guide and tracker
for Zimbabwe Big 5, one of the largest and
most successful trophy hunting companies in the
country, for over twenty-five years. Raised in the
village of Lubimbi, he'd learned his skills from
his father, who'd been a tracker for the white
Rhodesians in their battles with Robert Mugabe's
Zimbabwe African Liberation Army at the height
of the bush war. After his father had been killed by
a landmine disguised as a piece of buffalo dung,
Saviour had continued to hone his craft by first
becoming a poacher and then, after independence,
as a tracker guide for the hunting organization. The
job paid well and most of the American hunters
tipped huge sums whenever they brought down
some poor unsuspecting elephant, or leopard
lured into the open by a tethered goat.

Saviour was slight but wiry, especially compared to the professional hunter to whom he was now assigned. The hunter in question was Christoff Smit, a huge bull of a man who at one point before the end of apartheid had been with the South African Special Forces where the psychopathic behavior he displayed leading hunts had been perfectly suited to interrogating unfortunate members of South African liberation movements. His almost obese condition, fueled by copious amounts of beer and meat, meant that Saviour was always way ahead of him when they took clients into the bush.

Today Saviour was five hundred meters to the west of the hunting party which consisted of a prodigiously wealthy property developer from New York, Christoff Smit and a tracker in training who was lugging the American's heavy rifle.

"Where the hell is that tracker of yours Christoff?" asked the American whose name was Donald Brink Jr. "The heat and these damn flies are killing me. Let me remind you that I'm the one paying to do the killing. So let's find that elephant, goddammit."

"You have to be patient, please, Mr. Brink," replied Christoff, who thought the American was one of the most arrogant and stupid hunters he'd ever met. "Saviour knows what he is doing. As soon as he gets close to the elephant he will beep us." He indicated the two-way radio attached to the belt of his baggy cargo shorts. "Then - trust me - you will have plenty of fun shooting that old bull right between his eyes as he comes up to us, and that Rigby you have will bring him down like a sick old man with cancer of the balls."

"I'm not sure I get that analogy, Christoff, but I have to say," he took the rifle from the guide and chambered a round, "I'm looking forward to taking down that beast. His head's going to look great in my den."

Saviour on the other hand was not quite as enthusiastic. He'd come across the old elephant happily stripping the fruit off a Marula tree. He was staring at it silently, moving his hand down to the two-way receiver in his pants pocket to signal the location to Christoff and the idiotic American when he felt a tap on his shoulder.

He turned around slowly and his jaw dropped. To his credit, he froze rather than shrieked. Standing behind him was an enormous man dressed in camouflage pants and an olive green t-shirt. The man was at least six inches taller than Saviour and possibly the same weight as Christoff, but rippling with muscle rather than fat. The first thing Saviour noticed was that the man had no weapons, and the second thing he noticed was that as the man opened his lips to smile, he flashed the whitest teeth Saviour had ever seen.

"My name," said the big man, grasping Saviour's hand in his meaty paw, "is Ishea Payamps. And you, as I understand, are Saviour Mpariwa."

Saviour looked nervously at the elephant, who was still blissfully munching away.

"Oh don't worry about him," said Ishea wrapping his arm over Saviour's shoulder and leading him a little way into the bush. "That old boy is deaf as a doorpost. He won't spook easily."

Saviour was breathing heavily. Not out of fear he realized, but total surprise and confusion. He tried to pull away from Ishea, but the big man held him firmly.

"Now look, Saviour, I have no intention of harming you in any way. In fact, I am going to make your day and more likely your year."

Ishea reached into the side pocket of his pants and pulled out a thick wad of US hundred-dollar bills. "I am going to give you ten thousand dollars – which I think is more than you can earn in five years – to hand me that two-way radio and walk out of here and back to your village and forget you ever saw me and promise me you will never go back to that hunting organization. If you do as I ask, not only will you get this money but you will receive another ten thousand dollars in a month's time. If you don't however, then I will break your neck right now. And if you promise me to give up tracking and not breath a word of our little discussion but change your mind any time soon, I will send someone to your village who will kill you and your entire family."

Saviour was not someone who over-thought things, so he made a brief promise, took the money and disappeared into the thick bush in the exact opposite direction of Christoff and the American.

Ishea smiled to himself as he retrieved his machete, which he'd concealed in the undergrowth nearby, and started walking between the thorn bushes in the direction of the hunting party. He took one last look at the old elephant and smiled.

Two weeks later Donald's wife Missy, who had once been runner-up in the Miss Indiana beauty pageant, received a FedEx box. Inside, beautifully mounted on a hardwood base, was the grinning head of her husband.

Christoff Smit's wife, on the other hand, did not get anything quite as elaborate. Her package contained a boot that she immediately recognized as belonging to her husband. The severed foot inside the boot would not be quite as impressive as the umbrella stand next to the door made from the foot of an elephant her husband had killed a year earlier.

At this point Ishea Payamps was already back in London, sitting down to dinner in the big Georgian house.

Chapter 15

IN WHICH SOME REALLY NASTY
PEOPLE BEGIN TO HATCH A
PLAN OF THEIR OWN

Thuringia, Germany
Same time frame

There are over four hundred castles in in the state of Thuringia in central Germany. Most are open to the public. Burg Waldengraf was not. Its perch on a rocky crag high above a forested valley made it extremely tricky to reach by car, mountain bike or foot. Most visitors flew in by helicopter, passing over forests and fields that served as training grounds for mercenaries who used live ammunition in their mock attacks on structures that where built to look like villages in Africa. Even if tourists in the area had somehow managed to get to the castle and been invited in, they'd likely be extremely disappointed. It had been gutted completely on the inside and turned into an ultra high-tech headquarters for Der Felsen, one of the world's largest supplier of weapons, machinery and private military contractors. Over the past five years, it had also become the procuring front for over eighty billion dollars worth of land in Africa.

The current head of the organization was a Belgian named Geoffrey-Philippe van der Borrekens. At forty-two Geoffrey was the youngest person ever to run the seventy-year-old company. He had taken over from his uncle after working his way up through the ranks, starting as a mercenary in Liberia and eventually becoming Der Felsen's number one arms dealer in Asia.

At the moment he was extremely unhappy. He turned to his vice president of operations, a small bespectacled Austrian named Rudi Fleisser.

"I'm assuming you saw the news Rudi?"

"I did, Geoffrey, and once again we've succeeded in making this death as baffling to the authorities as the other four."

"Perhaps, Rudi. But the 'baffling' will not be for long. These people were some of our major shareholders. Their deaths have been carried out with unimaginable brutality and not every policeman is a complete idiot as you no doubt think. Sooner or later someone is going to put two and two together."

"And all they will get then, Geoffrey, is *five*."

Geoffrey appeared more puzzled than he normally did when Rudi tried to explain things.

"By that I mean we have made so mystifying it's almost impossible to trace anything back to us."

"Well, in future just say what you mean and don't muddle things with ridiculous statements that you just pull out of thin air. 'Two and two equals five'...hah, I'm surprised at you." Geoffrey had a very open face but his eyes were further apart than normal. His spiky blond hair and thick lips gave him a decidedly odd appearance, made even more peculiar by his lop-sided sneer.

Rudi smiled. He was not intimidated by his boss, and in fact considered Geoffrey a total nincompoop. The younger man was arrogant and ruthless, but he could not run Der Felsen without Rudi. Geoffrey was the muscle, but Rudi was the brains.

"What we need Geoffrey is proof that the party doing the killing is who you think it is. As yet, our man on the inside can't do that. For some reason that I cannot quite fathom, he has not been a part of those discussions, if indeed they took place. This alone makes me suspicious. And by the way, none of our other operatives managed to find out who that new person they've hired is or what they've employed him to do. We need..."

"I don't need proof," Geoffrey cut him off. It has to be that big fat fucker Freddy Blank who is behind this. It smells of him and Conchita. It stinks of them. We have observed them. We know!" He picked up his latest toy, a Smith & Wesson 460XVR revolver, and waved it about as if it was a salami.

Rudi watched warily. He hated the way Geoffrey played with weapons. "I agree with you Geoffrey, and I believe I raised that very possibility with you a few days ago when you were appraised of the letters. But we lack a flawless plan.Um, maybe you should put the gun down..."

Geoffrey brushed Rudi suggestion aside rather rudely. "I have a plan, Rudi, and it *is* flawless. It is also simple, which I realize may be hard for you to accept if you believe that two and two equals five. All we do is assemble a contingent of our best men, find Freddy and Conchita and kill them."

"What I was about to say before you cut me off, Geoffrey, was that if it is PaloMar - and let's say it is, for argument's sake - who in our organization is providing the information about the hunts? And second, why does our contact in PaloMar not know the full story? Are they on to him? Has he turned? These are important questions for your consideration."

As always, Rudi's logic had a way of calming Geoffrey, and he sat back behind his desk as he contemplated the questions. Yet there was a hit of petulance in Geoffrey's voice when he finally spoke. He was getting quite sick of Rudi and his patronizing ways.

"You're right, I suppose. And I have no doubt you have some thoughts on the subject."

"Yes, I have thoughts but no answers as yet. My suggestion is that we ask Demetri to look into it. Let him find out who amongst the men were closest to Ishea Payamps and Zecheriah Corn before they left us."

"Yes, we could start there." Geoffrey paused as he thought about the interrogation session. "In fact, I like it. No one can get people to talk quite like Demetri. And of course I will assist him."

He clapped his hands in sadistic glee.

"And when we find out..." He, pointed the Smith & Wesson at a wild boar's head mounted above the doorway and promptly blew it to pieces.

"Jesus Christ, Geoffrey! Must you keep doing that?" Rudi, his ears still ringing from the explosion of the .46 caliber bullet turned and walked out the room, leaving Geoffrey-Philippe pondering what he'd replace the boar's head with and what he'd do to the PaloMar group when he finally had them in his clutches.

Five very prominent shareholders, public figures in their respective countries, had been killed while hunting either on land that was temporarily owned by Der Felsen or on trips arranged as a courtesy by Geoffrey, against Rudi's council. What Geoffrey, Rudi and the other members of the operating council understood above all else, was that their deaths could in no way be tied to Der Felsen and a consequently huge amount of money had changed hands to get the local authorities to report the deaths as hunting accidents. As Geoffrey had pointed out to Rudi, that would not be possible much longer. Someone, somewhere would get to the bottom of it. Rudi may be smart, but no plan was completely fool-proof. Geoffrey knew Der Felsen's board was upset with him. They needed the shareholders to remain calm, and a number were already expressing doubts. This made the board nervous, and when its members were nervous, they questioned Geoffrey's authority.

Geoffrey had already sent Demetri Guria, the Bulgarian head of security for Der Felsen, to investigate each death. Using methods he'd learned under Colonel Petko Kovachef, who'd run a murder and kidnapping unit for the Bulgarian secret police known as Service 7, Guria had managed to extract some information from people who'd assisted on the hunts. The problem was none of them, despite undergoing the most horrific forms of torture, was able to provide any information beyond the fact that an unusually large person had given each of them enormous sums of money to just 'go home and forget everything'. While the description could have fit a number of individuals, Geoffrey was convinced it was Ishea Payamps, a man he'd once fought beside in West Africa, and then employed at Der Felsen, but who'd jumped ship rather suddenly to join PaloMar.

The very idea of PaloMar brought out a rage in the young Belgian, and he thought about the degrading meeting in which Freddy and Conchita had rejected Der Felsen's offer to buy them. He picked up the Smith & Wesson again, and picturing Freddy's head, inadvertently squeezed the trigger, blowing away a section of the door to his assistant's office, and the tip of her nose.

Chapter 16

IN WHICH ROGER GETS TO MEET ANOTHER GHOST FROM HIS PAST

❧

London, England
A day or so later

Zecheriah Corn, decked out in full butler regalia, was pouring Roger his second glass of Lagavulin thirty-seven year-old Single Malt when Freddy and Conchita walked into the drawing room.

"Aha," said Freddy when he saw the three quarters empty bottle. "I notice you've acquired a taste for the good stuff while we've been gone."

"Yes, I have," Roger replied taking a mouthful of the dark smoky liquid he'd been drinking steadily since they'd left him in London. "I've definitely got to like it. It's really good."

Freddy laughed. "Well don't get too attached, old boy. That's probably the last bottle in the world and at about two hundred pounds a glass it better be good."

"Good God, Freddy. Look, I'm terribly sorry. I honestly didn't know." Roger turned to look at

Zecheriah Corn as if trying to shift the blame, but he'd already left the room.

"Don't even think about it. I told Zecheriah to give you whatever you wanted while we were away."

Conchita kissed Roger on both cheeks. "You look so much better than you did a week ago."

"I have to say I feel a lot better." And he did feel remarkably better. He'd managed to sleep a lot, eat reasonably and work out every day – in a manner of speaking. He doubted his workouts would qualify as such to anyone with even a nominal level of fitness. Despite his recently acquired penchant for single-malt Scotch, Roger had actually cut down on drinking too. All of which contributed to a slight brightening in his outlook.

"Excellent. Because we're going to have dinner with the two other members of our little group who should be arriving any minute. Tonight I hope that everything will be made clear.

As if on cue Zecheriah walked back in and coughed politely.

"Jamie and Ishea have just arrived. Would you like me to tell the cook that you will be eating presently?"

Before Conchita could even answer, the door to the drawing room opened and in walked one of the biggest men Roger had ever seen. Not quite dwarfing Zecheriah, but certainly seeming as if you'd have a hard time deciding which of the two to bet on in a cage match. The giant stuck out a paw the size of the mutton chop Roger had once ordered at Keen's Steak House in New York.

"You must be Roger. Conchita and Freddy have told me a lot about you. I'm sorry you had to go through some of the stuff you did. Let's hope we can help each other from now on."

Roger wanted to ask Ishea to tell him how exactly they could help each other but his warm smile - and the fact that he turned to Conchita and grabbed her in a huge bear hug, causing her to giggle delightfully - threw him off his question completely. It also saddened Roger somewhat as he realized how pointless his infatuation with Conchita really was.

Then once again he was ripped from the emotional quicksand by the entrance of the fourth member of the group. He'd been preparing himself for seeing Jamie Bowes, but in truth nothing prepares one for meeting a person one last saw at his cremation.

Chapter 17

IN WHICH ROGER THINKS BACK TO THE LAST TIME HE SAW JAMIE ALIVE

Johannesburg, South Africa
25 years erstwhile

On a cool Sunday evening in July, Roger and his wife were sitting in front of the TV watching 'Police File,' the number-one show on the only network in a country still deprived of anything bearing any resemblance to entertainment on the box that was now in its fifth year of existence in the totalitarian state that was South Africa.

As Roger attempted to maneuver a large chunk of the chicken and cashew nut curry he'd made that morning into his mouth, his wife smacked him on the arm, dislodging the chicken from his fork and causing it to fall on his white jeans.

"Fucking hell!" he yelled.

"No, look at the TV quickly!"

Roger looked up to see a photo of Jamie Bowes next to a phone number.

"Anyone who saw or had contact with this individual on the night of February 3rd," said the announcer, "please contact Captain van der Westhuizen of the Johannesburg Central Intelligence Division at this number."

"What do we?" asked Carol.

"Oh Jesus," Roger replied. "I don't know. I guess we have to contact him and tell him we had dinner with Jamie that night. What in God's name has Freddy done this time?"

On Saturday February 3rd Roger had just returned home to Parktown North Johannesburg from his Saturday golf game when the phone rang. It was Freddy Blank.

"Freddy?" Roger was surprised to hear his friend's voice, as last he'd heard of Freddy, he'd been living in London, employed as the catering manager at one of the restaurants in Selfridges.

"Rog, old man. I just got in to Joburg this morning. Brought a really close friend of mine who's never been here before. His name is Jamie Bowes and I want you to meet him. Can you and Carol have dinner with us tonight?"
"Christ, Freddy. It's so good to hear from you and we'd love to meet Jamie. Look, we'll never get a babysitter tonight but if you and Jamie want to come here to eat we'd love to have you."

Carol, who'd overheard most of the conversation was slightly less enthusiastic.

"If you think I'm going grocery shopping right now you're mistaken. We have to bathe the kids and feed them and I don't have time to cook for your criminal friends."

"That's not fair. Freddy was never convicted and if you put the kids to bed I'll get take-outs. Freddy will be fine with that and I imagine his friend will too, whoever he may be."

"'Never convicted' is a pure technicality. He's a fucking lunatic and a criminal."

Carol was leering lasciviously at Jamie the entire evening and even Roger had to admit his guest was the most beautiful young man that he had ever seen. Extremely tall with curly blond hair that fell in a rakish wave to his shoulders. His eyes were a mesmerizing deep blue and he spoke with a languid confidence and lightheartedness that was both charming and disarming.

"So Jamie, explain to me what you do exactly?" asked Carol taking a sip of the peculiar white wine that Freddy and Jamie had brought.

"It's kind of complicated, but I'm a holographic photographer. It's quite a new field but I'm sure you've seen some photos in art galleries. It looks like you're seeing images in 3D."

"How fascinating and how brilliant you must be." Carol was almost licking her lips. Roger hadn't seen her like this before and while he felt jealous, he understood her fascination. Jamie had an almost otherworldly beauty.

"He is brilliant," said Freddy draping an arm over Jamie's shoulder. "He's shown me some amazing places in the UK, and I've met the most wonderful people through him. So now it's my turn to show him South Africa. We're off to the

Kruger National Park tomorrow, and after we're done here tonight I'm going to introduce him to some really fun people. It's a pity you can't come along but you've got the two little ones. I totally understand."

Freddy and Jamie didn't stay as long as Roger would have liked. He really did want to hear what his friend had been up to for the past few years but it was clear that the pair had other places to go that evening.

After Roger had cleared the plates and looked in on his two sleeping sons he joined Carol in bed. She was already fast asleep with a smile on her face. No doubt dreaming of Jamie, Roger thought.

Any idea he'd had of sleeping late erupted in the shrill ringing of the phone just after five. It was Freddy's mother. "Roger, you have to come quickly. There's been a terrible accident. Jamie's been killed and Freddy is hysterical. Come over now. I can't talk on the phone."

The line went dead.

"Who's that?" Carol half opened her eyes.

"It's Freddy's mom. She wants me to come over. Something's happened to Jamie but I don't know the details. I'll call you as soon as I know more."

Carol turned over and began to snore, her infatuation with Jamie clearly over.

Roger arrived at Mrs. Blank-Goldman's apartment just as the doctor was administering a shot of tranquilizar in to Freddy's arm. The syringe was the same size as the one vets fire into elephants to knock them out, and while Freddy walked around wailing pitifully for a few minutes, he soon collapsed into a chair and began to breathe heavily.

"I gave him a hell of a large dose so he should be ok for a while. If he wakes up within an hour give me a call and I'll come back and give him another shot. But I have to say Mrs. Blank-Goldman I've never experienced a reaction like that. Jamie must have meant a great deal to him."

"What are you implying Doctor?" she asked indignantly.

"Probably nothing. All I'm saying is that in all my years I haven't seen quite that reaction from any male his age. I've seen tears and I've seen utter sadness but raging hysteria is not common. It was almost theatrical. Anyway he's been through a lot. Let's see if the tranquilizer helps him"

Mrs. Blank-Goldman snorted and then seeing Roger for the first time, hugged him to her ample bosom.

"Roger, dear. Thanks for coming over. Oh my God, this is so awful. The police want you to go to the morgue and identify poor Jamie."

Before Roger could protest she had dragged him into another room where two policemen stood talking to Mr. Goldman.

"Officers, this is Roger Storm, Freddy's friend. He is willing to go to identify the body."

"Well, I'm not quite sure..." stammered Roger. "I mean I don't even know what happened. I uh..."

"No time for that now, you have to get a move on, man," the older of the two policemen said in his heavily accented English. He handed Roger a card with the address of the morgue. "Go immediately. There will be someone to meet you there. We can't start the autopsy before the corpse is identified."

"And then come back, dear. Freddy is going to need you when he wakes up," said Mrs. Blank-Goldman as she ushered the still clueless and bewildered Roger to the door.

Exiting the building, Roger ran into Freddy's brother Monty who was on his way in.

"Jesus, Roger, I heard what happened. How's Freddy?"

"Lights out for the moment. I still don't know exactly what happened but I'm supposed to go to the morgue to identify Jamie's body."

"That's ridiculous," replied Monty. "You know I'm a doctor?

"I thought you were a podiatrist?"

"That's still a doctor, for your information." Monty sounded offended.

"Well, maybe you'll come with me then? I don't have a clue where the morgue is."

"I'll do one better," said Monty, squeezing Roger's arm. "I'll go to the morgue. You go back up and just be there for him. I'll be back as soon as I'm done."

When Roger walked back into the apartment and told them of his fortuitous meeting with Monty everyone – other than the two policemen,

who weren't used to their orders being disobeyed
– seemed quite relieved. No one more so than
Roger who heard part of the story from Mrs. Blank-
Goldman and the rest from Freddy when he was
once again in a relatively calm and logical mood.

"When we left your place, Roger, I drove Jamie
to the Radium Hotel to meet some friends. Jamie
started talking to this girl and after about an hour
he asked me if I'd take a taxi because he wanted to
go home with her. I agreed, gave him the rental car
key and that was the last I heard from him until we
got a call from the cops at 3:30 this morning telling
me that Jamie had been killed when he drove his
car into a lake."

"Christ, Freddy. How did it happen?"

"I don't know. He must have driven her home
and was trying to find his way back here."

"How would he even have done that?" Roger
was totally confused. "I mean he just arrived
yesterday."

"I don't know Roger, the whole thing is a
nightmare."

Freddy began to sob quietly, and Roger decided
all his friend needed at that moment was to be
comforted. So he put his arm around him, as much
as an average person can put their arm around a
blimp, and just let his friend cry.

Later that morning a member of the city council
arrived to add his condolences and to apologize
for the condition of the road near the lake where a
school bus had had a similar but nonfatal accident

a month or two before. Numerous friends and family members of the Blank/Goldman clan popped in and out offering their thoughts and prayers and bringing vast amounts of cakes and sweets, as if any of those things mattered to an already obese man who didn't believe in any form of religion.

Monty got back to the apartment at lunchtime with the grim news that he'd identified the body, spoken with the pathologist, a friend of his, and arranged for the cremation to take place the next day.

In all the madness of the moment no one asked why the body wasn't being flown back to the UK to Jamie's parents or what had happened about the autopsy or any other of the numerous questions that should have come up at the time.

Of course they did come up like bad oysters, but only months later when Captain van der Westhuizen arrived at Roger and Carol's house at precisely five-thirty the day after they'd seen his plea for information about Jamie on Police File.

"So Mr. Storm how long have you known this this….this monst...uh, I mean this man, Frederick Blank?"

"Since grammer school, Captain. But Freddy's not in any trouble is he?

"Oh, Mr. Storm, I would not go so far as to say he is *not* in any trouble. In fact I would go so far to say he *is* in a great deal of trouble. Or..." and here van der Westhuizen rubbed his pudgy hands together, "he will be when I get to the bottom of this James Bowes business. No, Mr. Storm I wouldn't be surprised if that bastard ends up dangling at the end of a rope."

"Good Lord, Captain. I really don't understand. What did Freddy have to do with Jamie's death? That was an accident...?" Roger was about to add a 'surely' but on reflection decided not to. He felt extremely nervous. There was a gleam in the policeman's eye that made him believe he was about to hear something else about Freddy that he couldn't possibly ever have imagined.

"An accident you say? I don't believe it for a minute, and I am going to tell you why."

"I have a horrible feeling I'm going to need a drink. Can I offer you one, Captain?

"You can indeed. I will have a large brandy." He pointed at the bottle on the drinks cart. "And in case you are wondering if I am allowed to drink while on the job, of course I am."

Roger wasn't sure he believed him, but poured him a large brandy over ice. He handed the glass to van der Westhuizen, who didn't even wait for a 'cheers' before he gulped most of it down and held the glass out to Roger for a refill.

"I asked you how long you'd known Frederick Blank, Mr. Storm," he leaned forward and his face twisted into an ugly grin, "because I have known him for the exact same amount of time."

"You have?" Roger felt his paranoia getting the better of him. He was convinced he'd be implicated in whatever was going on.

"Oh yes, I was the investigating officer when he burned half the school down, and as I recall from your file you were at the school that day. Your first day at the school."

"My file?"

"Please, Mr. Storm. You don't think we have a file on all you people? I know everything about you. I know you were a big protester at the University and I know your liberal views now and how you'd like to see the end of Apartheid, and the black man in power. Trust me Mr. Storm you are very close to crossing that line between a cozy home and filthy jail cell."

Roger couldn't speak he was so terrified. It was at this point that Carol jumped in and Roger's love for her increased a million-fold.

"Look Captain van der Westhuizen, I am not sure what you're getting at here. You came to see us about the accident involving Jamie Bowes, who had dinner at our house that night, and left shortly afterwards. That's all we know. And I am not sure what crap you have on my husband, but he's done nothing wrong. So get to the damn point before I call your superiors."

To both Roger and Carol's surprise van der Westhuizen sat back and smiled. He'd never been spoken to that way by a woman before, let alone one of the faith he detested. He made a mental note that when they were finally able to round up all the Jews, he'd seek out Carol and teach her a thing or two about respect.

"You are quite right, Mrs. Storm. This is not about your husband. So let me tell you what we know about what happened that night and the next day. And believe me when you hear them you will understand how stupid you people all are to believe the pack of lies that seems to be constantly spewing from the bastard Blank's mouth like venom from a mamba."

That night, after van der Westhuizen had left, wobbling slightly from the copious amounts of brandy swilled during the telling of the stranger than fiction story, Roger and Carol had to admit the evidence of foul play was pretty overwhelming.

"For a start," van der Westhuizen had begun, "Frederick Blank and James Bowes took out five-million-pound insurance policies on each other's lives a few days before they'd left London. They did the same when they got to Johannesburg before renting a car from Avis. While this in itself is not unusual for people from a foreign country visiting what I believe the Brits call the 'dark continent', it is unusual that they'd made each other the beneficiary when, as far as anyone knew, they were just friends and they both had families. If you ask me their relationship was more than just that of friends. They were engaged in acts for which the bible recommends stoning, burning or castration." There was spit forming at the corner of his mouth.

Roger shuddered at what he knew in his heart was deteriorating into utter madness.

"Your friend, Mr. Storm, is either the most stupid man in the world - and therefore the luckiest because he has escaped major punishment so far - or the unluckiest man in the world because the Lord has spared him up to now for the hangman."

"I'm not sure I understand your reasoning entirely. Aren't you jumping to conclusions, Captain, if you don't mind me saying so?"

Van der Westhuizen looked at him in amazement.

"I do mind you saying so because you are not in the least bit qualified to question my methods. The second piece of evidence, less damning but more puzzling, was how James Bowes ended up on a stretch of road nowhere near either Mrs. Blank-Goldman's apartment or the Radium Hotel where he allegedly met the mysterious women that no one has been able to trace. And of course we know that is bullshit because they are raving homosexuals.

"Third," van der Westhuizen said, holding up his glass for a refill, "the car according to the experts could not have been traveling fast enough for any mistake to have been made that was not deliberate." He sucked on an ice cube. "And this Mr. and Mrs. Storm is even more mysterious. There was a hole in the window on the passenger side that was made from the inside..."

"Well, wouldn't Jamie's head have hit the windshield pretty hard?"

"Clearly you are confused Mr. Storm. I said," and he slammed the glass down with such force that the brandy shot out onto his face, "the hole was on the passenger side, not the windshield. And the driver, whoever the driver may have been, still had his seatbelt on."

"I'm sorry, said Roger, "I am confused. What do you mean by 'whoever the driver may have been'?"

"Did you identify the body, Mr. Storm?"

"No, I told the policemen at the Goldman's place that Freddy's brother Monty, who is a doctor, said he would."

"Very convenient I must say. There is no way Dr. Montgomery Blank who specializes in toe-nail surgery, so hardly a doctor, could have identified the body because he'd never seen James Bowes. He was in Cape Town until late the night of the murder and yes, I am calling it a murder." Van der Westhuizen began to slap his hand as he rattled off what he knew. "Even convenientier, the autopsy was never carried out because both Dr. Blank and the city pathologist Dr. Segal – yet another Jew by the way – decided that there was no need for one and released the body to a funeral home that cremated said body the next day. You can imagine the shit Segal and the funeral home are in."

"So what you're saying," said Carol, "is that you suspect the body in the car was not Jamie, and everyone was involved in a conspiracy."

"Very clever Mrs. Storm. That is exactly what I am saying and I have one week to prove it before the inquest. And I will prove it you can be sure of that. I will prove beyond a shadow of doubt that the body in the car was not that of James Bowes but rather of some unknown person carrying Bowes' identity documents. He was killed, then strapped into the front seat of the car beside a very live person who steered the car slowly into the dam, broke the window and swam to safety. Blank then contacted his brother the doctor, who more than conveniently identified the body and talked that other moron pathologist into letting it go before an autopsy could be done. At which stage the body was illegally cremated destroying any way to identify the remains. In the meantime, James Bowes, with fake identity documents slips out of the country to places unknown. At this point, Frederick Blank, criminal not-so-mastermind, will collect the millions in insurance money. Except that he won't. Because Mr. and Mrs. Storm I am the mastermind, and I can assure you that within a week, I will have that fat bastard in my iron grip absolutely finally and forever, or my name isn't Fanus Pieter Joubert van der Westhuizen."

He stood up and staggered to the door.

"By the way, Captain van der Westhuizen," said Carol as she was about to shut the door behind him, "are you a bigot and an anti-Semite? Because you certainly sound like one."

"Of course I'm not a bigot nor an anti-Semite. I am a good Christian. I just hate Jews, blacks and gay people like everyone else does. Anyway, you have been of no help at all Mr. and Mrs. Storm, but I am sure you will be well grilled at the inquest."

As it turned out, neither Roger nor Carol testified at the inquest. Captain van der Westhuizen did, proving that he was not exactly the mastermind he believed himself to be, and with absolutely no way to substantiate his case, foul play was ruled out – though the pathologist and funeral home were reprimanded for breaking protocol – and van der Westhuizen returned to police headquarters to face the wrath of his nemesis, the chief of police.

"You asked to see me, sir," said van der Westhuizen, narrowly dodging a coffee mug as it whizzed by and smashed to pieces on the metal doorframe behind him. Though he hadn't expected a warm welcome, he hadn't anticipated being assailed by drinking paraphernalia either.

"Well, 'asked to see you' is not quite how I put it van der Westhuizen. I reluctantly demanded to see you by throwing the heavy glass ashtray my mother-in-law gave me as a Christmas present – even though she knows I gave up smoking – at the prisoner who was cleaning my private toilet. We'll put his death down to 'slipped in the bathroom,' don't you agree?"

He laughed and van der Westhuizen who failed to see the irony hesitantly joined in.

"What are you laughing at van Der Westhuizen? You are responsible for that poor man's death."

"I don't understand, sir?"

"Your incompetence and total inability to convict one man over a period of twenty years, of either arson, fraud, robbery, diamond smuggling or murder - one man who has not just spat but pissed in the face of the law, and will in the future, unless I am very much mistaken, evoke a type of chaos on a scale that is unprecedented in the history of the world - caused me to lose my temper.

"Now, when I lose my temper, van Der Westhuizen, which is not that often I might add, my blood begins to boil. And when my blood begins to boil I tend to lose control of my emotions and I tend to throw things.

"And van der Westhuizen, just the sight of your large red and extremely unattractive face is causing me to lose my temper now, but as I now have nothing left to physically throw at you I am rather going to throw you out of the police force. I am demoting you with immediate effect to corporal so that your pension will be reduced and in your misery and poverty you will see the face of Frederick Blank and you will think about how a bloody Jew got the better of us, God's chosen people."

Somewhere in the deep recess of van der Westhuizen's brain something began to throb unbearably. The throbbing brought up all sorts of strange memories. He opened his mouth to tell the chief that to the best of his knowledge the Jews saw themselves as God's chosen people, but all that came out was a senseless babble. Much to the chief's horror, van der Westhuizen lurched forward with his hands out. His fingers found the jowly folds of the police chief's neck and began to tighten. The chief gasped for breath and tried to pummel his attacker. Then the fingers loosened and van der Westhuizen crumpled to his knees as the aneurism erupted, killing him instantly. The chief staggered backwards and fell onto his desk where the only remaining object of any substance, a six-inch spike attached to a weighted stand for impaling notes, found its way into his right kidney. He died six days later from complications when his dialysis machine went haywire. No one saw the young black man, who'd trained in electronics at Moscow University, and whose brother had been killed in police custody after 'slipping in the toilet' leave the room.

Chapter 18

In which Roger enjoys a delicious meal with the rest of the team

London, England
About a year ago

"How are you, Roger?" said Jamie, sticking out his hand.

Roger took it and squeezed harder than he should have.

"You don't have to break my hand," Jamie laughed. "I am not a ghost. In fact I'm very much alive. You look well, Roger. Older for sure but then aren't we all?"

Roger looked at Jamie in wonder. He didn't seem to have aged at all. His face was free of wrinkles and though Roger looked pretty hard, he didn't see any evidence of grey in Jamie's long blond hair.

"Eyes off him Roger, he's mine." Freddy grabbed Jamie and kissed him full on the lips. "I'm kidding you Roger. I know you're strictly hetero, but Jamie is hard to resist isn't he? Happens when you're born again, not in the religious sense of course, but as in returning from the dead. Although, come to think of it, so did I. But little good it did my looks."

Conchita came up to Roger and took his arm. "Let's go in to the dining room and eat and talk and laugh."

The dining room was decked out for a formal dinner though none of them had dressed for the occasion.

"Why don't you sit at the head, Ishea, as you're the lone wolf. I'll sit next to Roger and Jamie and Freddy will sit together," said Conchita taking control of the situation.

Roger's heart began to thump. What did she mean by referring to Ishea as the "lone wolf"? Did the seating arrangements mean that she had some feeling for Roger?

"We have a surprise for you, Roger," Freddy positively beamed.

"I have a feeling you're going to like the main course a lot, but first, alongside this excellent Chablis, some of the best oysters you've ever had followed by a poached lobster salad."

"Please tell me they're Limfjord oysters and that you have a lot of them. I've been dying for those beauties"

"Yes, they are, Jamie. Flown in from Jutland this morning," replied Conchita as Zecheriah and Alfons, whom Roger had come to admire from the delicious meals he'd prepared for him in Freddy and Conchita's absence, wheeled in a platter the size of a small landing strip, piled with big juicy oysters.

If there was any doubt in Roger's mind that the party, though small in numbers, could possibly swallow oysters by the tub, it vanished about as quickly as the oysters, though with less noise.

"My God but you guys eat well," he said, trying to grab whatever was left on the platter but failing miserably as Ishea's giant hand snatched up the remaining two oysters.

"We certainly do here," Freddy said. "Mostly to make up for what we have to eat when we're on a mission. Wouldn't you agree Ishea?"

The giant who'd said very little up to this point, looked up.

"Trust me, Freddy, what we eat on our missions is fucking luxury compared to what Zech and I had to eat when we fought in the Congo. You should try eating a monkey that's been dead for three weeks."

"Never have and never will, that I can promise you." Freddy stopped as he noticed Roger's puzzled expression. "Ah, I see you picked up on the fact that Ishea and Zech fought together. Why don't you at least fill him in on that aspect, Ishea?"

Ishea forked a large chunk of lobster into his mouth and chewed for a minute. Then he put his fork down and looked at Roger.

"Well, okay. As you've probably guessed, Roger, I'm also from the states."

"I can hear that, but I can't tell where from exactly. You have a slight accent. Possibly Hispanic?"

"You have a good ear. My father was Puerto Rican and my mother is Lakota Sioux. I grew up in Rosebud, South Dakota with my mother's people after my father was killed in a car crash. I joined the Marines when I was eighteen and became Special Forces when I was twenty-one. Zech, on the other hand, is ex-SAS. We first met in Iraq when the Brits and Americans teamed up on a few missions. We got on really well and decided we both wanted to make real money. So, we handed in our papers and joined Sandline International. Not sure if you know who they were...?"

Roger shook his head.

"Basically a legitimate company that hired out mercenaries Although that's not exactly how they marketed themselves. Anyway, we fought for them in a few places around the world, and when they shut their doors in 2004 we went to work at another organization for a few years - which I am sure you're going to hear all about - and then for Freddy and Conchita."

"Ishea is nothing if not concise," said Conchita taking a sip of wine.

"I prefer to think of it as being efficient rather than concise Conchita, my love. I told Roger all that is necessary to answer Freddy's question."

I'm not so sure you did, Roger thought. You just called her *my love*. He was totally confused.

Conchita laughed. "That's why you and I could never be together, Ishea. I like people who display a little more emotion." She put her hand on Roger's hand and squeezed.

He couldn't breath for a second, and he felt himself turning as red as the lobster shell on his plate. Was she merely toying with him? He couldn't believe that someone so beautiful could have any feeling for someone who was a total wreck. Whatever was going on got put on hold as Zecheriah and Alfons brought in the main course.

"Ta da," said Freddy raising his glass. "Be prepared to taste the best roast chicken you've ever eaten. Just to make up for what you missed in Paris."

And it was. The skin was crisp and the meat inside moist and tender with just enough juice to seep into the mashed potatoes as Roger cut into it. But as wonderful as the food was, and as reckless and carefree as the wine, of which he'd drank quite a lot, made him feel, he knew the light and shallow conversation would inevitably lead to exactly what it was that PaloMar was planning, and what they wanted of him. That crux came just after his second mouthful of mango and sticky rice. A truly delicious desert which is better enjoyed when one is not about to be told that one is off on some mad lark that will either get one killed or left to rot in some jail in an African country, full of people one would rather read about than meet.

Chapter 19

IN WHICH INSPECTORS BUNTER AND DARMSTAEDTER COME TO AN INTERESTING CONCLUSION

~

Munich, Germany
Around the same time

B unter and Darmstaedter had said very little to each other on their return trip to Munich, before checking into their hotel and agreeing to meet in the restaurant at 20:00 for a working dinner. Bunter arrived first and ordered a gin and tonic from the elderly waiter who had a hard time understanding him. He'd changed from his standard blue serge suit into a blazer and jeans. He had the pictures provided by Mrs Heidenreich in a Manila folder which he kept closed purposefully, hesitant to look at the photos without his colleague present. He'd taken a quick look in the elevator and had felt disturbed. It had been like looking at porn - not that he was averse to porn, but he preferred his sans flabby, elderly transvestites. As Bunter's drink arrived, Darmstaedter slid onto the bench opposite him in the private booth Bunter had requested.

They made small talk as they both ordered the schnitzel and a bottle of fairly decent Riesling. The folder of photographs lay in the middle of the table. Both were reluctant to open it. Finally, Darmstaedter slid his hand across and took it.

"This case gets more bizarre by the day, Matthew."

He opened the folder and stared at one of the photos that showed Heidenreich dressed in a schoolgirl uniform, lying across the lap of an older, severe-looking woman, his skirt hiked up to his waist, revealing a particularly fleshy backside. The woman who clearly was meant to be a teacher, had her hand raised as if about to deliver a spanking.

"Heidenreich was not a very attractive schoolgirl, that's for sure Constantin."

"I must agree with you, Matthew." Darmstaedter examined the photo closely. "What made his ugly ass attractive to that hippo is beyond my imagination." He shook his head sadly.

Bunter took out his glasses to take a closer look, and then screwed up his face. "Something is seriously weird here. And I don't just mean Heidenreich's buttocks." He studied the photos for a few minutes without elaborating on his precise objection to the goings-on. Then he looked up in astonishment.

"You've found something, Matthew?"

"I think so. Yes, for sure. I recognize a number of these people. Here take a look."

Darmstaedter laid the photos across the table, much to the distress of the waiter arriving at that very moment with their schnitzels. "You're right. There are some very familiar faces."

Bunter picked up one of the photos that showed a group of 'schoolgirls' frolicking in their gym slips. "There's Leonard Bonniface, one of the most successful venture capitalists in London, and if I'm not mistaken that's Francois Stern who owns La Bonte, the supermarket chain in France?"

"Ja, that's him. You know, I can understand maybe why these people want to dress up as schoolgirls. But why they would do so in front of each other?"

"Did you say you *do* understand why people want to dress as schoolgirls?" Bunter looked at his friend with a startled expression on his face. Darmstaedter, who had always been uncertain of Bunter's sexual orientation thought he may finally have hit a raw nerve and decided to have some fun.

"Of course, it's a very popular fetish in some parts of the world. I myself love to put on a short skirt and big bloomers and play games with my wife."

Bunter, who had very little sense of humor, choked on a piece of schnitzel and had a violent coughing fit until the elderly waiter, who was passing by, hit him hard on the back and informed him that pictures like the one he had in front of him would cause any decent person to choke.

Darmstaedter, in the meantime, was laughing hysterically. "My God, I was just kidding.."

"Sorry Constantin," said Bunter who had recovered sufficiently to take a sip of wine. "Of course I knew you were joking. Ha, the idea of you in a short skirt and knickers…very droll."

He was not very convincing, but Darmstaedter let it pass. "My real question is why do they do it in front of each other? Surely that is extremely dangerous?"

"I think I can answer that. Though once again this is simply opinion based on stuff I read, not scientific fact. I did a little research and it appears that over the years there have been many instances of wealthy, upper-class men getting together in clubs or at brothels and indulging in all sorts of strange behavior. London, especially in Bloomsbury and Fitzrovia, used to be full of them. Berlin was too before the war and I would imagine there are even more today. The reasoning is 'if I know your darkest secrets and you know mine, there is nothing we can hold over each other.' It's a collective guilt syndrome."

"Ja, I think I understand that." Darmstaedter wasn't sure he did comprehend the idea of shared secrets. In his experience someone always talked. "Anyway, I know Frau Heidenreich asked her private detective to mainly take pictures of her husband, so we are lucky to be able to get a glimpse of these few other people. But none of them that I can see, other than Heidenreich, are the victims of the hunting crimes. I mean, we can get them blown up and enhanced to be sure. In fact I will arrange for that first thing in the morning."

"We should most definitely do that, but I have something else I've been thinking about that I want to bounce off you this evening.

"I'm listening..."

"I have a feeling, Constantin, that this is just a diversion. This whole sex club. Look, I'm sure that a lot of people in powerful positions have strange outlets - although dressing up as schoolgirls may take the cake - but my gut tells me something else rather than spanking linked our victims. So let me ask you this: what do rich people have more of than anyone else?"

"Money, obviously."

"Correct, and what do rich people want more than anything else?"

"I would assume more money."

"And I would agree. I am asking this because something has been bothering me for a while."

"And...?" Darmstaedter waved his hand impatiently.

"So far we know that none of the deaths have made headlines. While we know wealthy families can keep stories out of the local press or TV news, none of them could keep incidents like these from international news groups. You agree?"

"Of course."

"So it would have to be more than just wealthy families or sex-clubs. It would have to be an organization with incredible power and tentacles deep into various governments. And the amount of money involved in whatever schemes or business they are in would have to be so prodigious that nothing, not even such heinous crimes, could get in the way."

"It would have to be so enormous that..." Darmstaedter couldn't finish the sentence before Bunter slammed his fist down on the table in excitement.

"Yes, yes, it would! The amount of money must be so big and there has to be so much at stake. They can't risk anything. They can afford no sensational publicity to expose something that could - and again I'm being dramatic - change the world. I know this is almost theatrical but I feel this, Constantin, I feel it right in here." Bunter tapped his head with his wine glass, spilling Riesling down the side of his face

Darmstaedter raised his glass. "I feel it too my friend. But there is just one thing I will add. There must be another organization involved. Equally powerful, or a good deal smarter. The one who is taking out the hunters."

Bunter looked as if he were contemplating some metaphysical problem on the nature of existence. He harrumphed once, tapped his nose with his fingers and then smiled.

"My God, Constantin, I told you that big head of yours contained a big brain. You're exactly right, my friend. So now perhaps we have to look in a different place. And I think I know just the person who may be able to help us. That is if she will go back on her promise to never talk to me again."

Chapter 20

IN WHICH ROGER LEARNS MORE OF THE PLAN AND BEGINS TO THINK CONCHITA MAY ACTUALLY HAVE FEELINGS FOR HIM

London, England
Same time

"This is it, Roger. This is where we reveal all to you, and after tonight if the other side gets you and tortures you, you will unfortunately tell them everything about us, which will jolly well spoil our whole operation and so we can't let that happen."

Roger swallowed the last morsel of the mango and sticky rice pudding. He had the distinct feeling he'd lose his appetite completely in a few minutes. "In the movies you'd at least ask me if I'm in or out."

"Unfortunately, this isn't the movies and you are in whether you like it or not." Ishea put his hand on Roger's shoulder. Roger didn't think he was joking.

"Perhaps," Conchita interrupted, "we should let our new marketing expert summarize for us what he has learned over the past ten days. Roger, if you don't mind, tell us what you understand so far."

Roger wanted to say that he most definitely wan't an expert, and he'd heard nothing, and if they could just get him back to his safe little apartment in Chicago he'd drink enough to forget the whole thing. But he didn't. As scared as he was at that moment, he also felt that the hopelessness and depression that had pervaded his soul for the last few years was lifting. He couldn't see where he was heading, but more than anything, he had a sudden desire to go there. And it wasn't just the thought, no matter how flimsy, of what could happen with Conchita that drove him. For the first time in months he actually felt alive. Even if it was in the company of supposedly-dead people.

He sat back, looked up at the ceiling and tried to organize his thoughts as best he could. Then he leaned forward, took another sip of wine and began to talk. "Ok, I've thought about who you say you are, who you could be and what I understand you're doing. But I can't say I know enough to accept anything at this stage as facts, so this is still just conjecture on my part. Freddy, Conchita and I assume, Jamie, you own, or owned, an international arms dealership called PaloMar Industries. Ishea and Zecheriah work for you. Though, I can't imagine Zecheriah is just a butler. For some reason you have had a change of heart and now instead of supplying arms to dictators in Africa to kill hundreds of thousands of people, you are going to use the money to help these same people drive out the neocolonialists. These neocolonialists not only include countries like China and Saudi Arabia but also a mysterious organization whose members seem to be big game hunters. Saving the wildlife of Africa appears to play a crucial part in this plan and by killing the hunters you aim to also draw out this mysterious organization. How am I doing so far?"

"You've summed it up splendidly." Freddy clapped. "And you're right, Zech isn't just a butler."

"Maybe, Freddy. But it's what I don't know that worries me. The last I heard about you and Jamie was that you were both dead. I don't know how you transitioned from corpses to millionaire arms dealers. I don't know what it is this mysterious organization is really about or how you intend to stop them. I am totally for the animals by the way, and I'm thrilled to hear that you are trying to save them and of course I'd like to do that..."

"Good, so fill up your glass and sit back and we will try to fill in the gaps. I'm not going to waste time on how Jamie and I survived. Put it down to a lot of money and a lot of good contacts. But we can talk about that at any time. You at least know the basics of why we're doing what we're doing. At this point you need to understand who we're up against and how you fit in to the plan. Ishea, why don't you start off by telling Roger about Der Felsen."

Ishea took a deep breath as if thinking where to start. "Der Felsen basically means 'The Rock' in German. It's the organization that both Zecheriah and I worked for before we joined Freddy and Conchita and Jamie."

"What are they, who are they...?"

Ishea looked carefully at Roger. He said nothing but his startling blue eyes told Roger not to interrupt again. "Just after the Second World War ended, a group of Nazi officers aided by American intelligence formed a company to take advantage of the millions of defunct weapons that were in old armories or scattered across the battlefields of Europe. We're talking millions of weapons and stacks of ammunition that were for the most part owned by nobody and available for nothing. There were other guys doing the same thing but Der Felsen had the advantage of knowing where the secret stashes were - including rockets, by the way. V1's and V2's."

Jamie clearly was not intimidated by Ishea because he interrupted without a second thought.

"It's really important to understand Roger that the arms trade isn't about one or two powerful groups. It is a huge collusion between governments, bankers, arms manufacturers, ordinary business people who invest in deals like they do in Lloyd's of London for insurance, and intelligence organizations looking to fund black ops. And while each one of these is as powerful as all hell, nothing happens without the dealers. We are the guys who bring everything together and engineer situations to create need. Most people have heard of Viktor Bout, the Russian arms dealer who is now serving a prison sentence in the US. Or Adnan Khashoggi the Saudi dealer who in the eighties earned over a hundred million dollars in a single year off commission from Lockheed. Perhaps you have read about the butcher of Sierra Leone, Charles Taylor, and the Israeli who supplied him arms, Leonid Minin?"

Ishea jumped back in before Roger could say he hadn't. "These guys are so wealthy that when they do deals with warlords they throw in the most popular weapon of all time, the AK-47, for free. And in case, Roger, you think we are talking about a handful of operations, know that we're not. This industry is worth billions and the most amazing part of it is that it is supported by governments. So the arms dealers, whether legal or illegal, for the most part get left to themselves. To do what they like. Sell to whomever they like. There is literally no limit and this is how Der Felsen got to be as big and as dangerous as it is today. But Der Felsen as you will come to understand, isn't just a weapons supply company."

The big man stopped and cracked his knuckles. No one said anything, Roger imagined because they were waiting for him to ask the obvious question.

"So what makes PaloMar different from, say, Victor Bout's organization or Der Felsen?"

"PaloMar began as a small operation selling excess and outdated armaments from Israel to South American guerrilla groups," Conchita said. "Freddy and Jamie gave me the initial money which they got from the insurance when Jamie 'died' in South Africa."

"How did you get the weapons?"

"I seem to remember that Freddy mentioned to you that my mother was Israeli and my father Columbian? What you don't know is that my mother was a Mossad agent who was on assignment to the CIA and was able to penetrate FARC, where she met my father, one of the original leaders. He of course didn't know she was a Mossad agent. He thought she was just some young idealistic American. By the time he found out I was two years old and he was so in love with my mother that he chose to kill himself rather than betray her. My father had the true passion of a revolutionary. It was just that his cause changed."

"Your mother must have been a remarkable woman," said Roger, "if she could inspire such intense love."

Conchita smiled at him. "Thank you for saying that, Roger. And you're right, she was indeed one of the strongest, most intense people I ever met." She was lost in thought for a few seconds. "Anyway, I grew up in the foothills of Columbia where I learned to survive on the run and kill when necessary. But I moved to Israel with my mother when I was a teenager.

Roger didn't say anything, admittedly half listening to the details as the vision of what it must be like to make love to this mysterious woman bounced around his head like a billiard ball.

"During my time in the Israeli army I too was recruited by Mossad and trained to be an assassin. Yes, you were right about what I did from the first time you saw me." She laughed at Roger's expression.

Roger was pretty sure that men didn't swoon, but he thought at that moment he was about to violate the male code of conduct. He ran quickly through the women he'd dated in his life, and the only one he considered vaguely dangerous up to this point was a nurse who worked for a proctologist and had a nasty fascination with his anus.

"When I left Mossad," Conchita continued, ignoring Roger's decidedly grey pallor, "I had all the contacts in the world: arms manufacturers, dictators, mobsters, warlords. As Ishea said, all intelligence organizations help fund secret operations by selling arms. I was in the perfect position to be the middle man."

"And all dear Conchita needed," Freddy reached over and squeezed her hand, "was money. Which is where the two of us came in. We started small, buying up excess Uzis from a crooked general in Israel and selling them to a bunch of Shining Path guerrillas in Peru. That's how PaloMar began in March, 2002. Any questions so far?"

Roger had so many questions he had no idea where to begin. So he muttered something under his breath about the whole thing sounding far fetched, and regretted it immediately.

"Jesus Christ," said Ishea, "I hope to hell you'll have something better to add than your opinion as to whether things are real or not. You're supposed to be on our team. Act like it. You know, something about you worries me, man. Tell me I'm wrong, Freddy?"

Before Freddy could respond Roger jumped up. Something inside of him, stimulated by the wine and his growing lust for Conchita, spewed out.

"You know what, Ishea. I don't have anything to add at this stage. I have never killed anyone or done anything seriously illegal as far as I know. I never asked to be here, so don't threaten me or talk down to me."

When Ishea stood up, Roger knew he was going to be hit very hard and most likely killed. Ishea walked up to him and stared down, his eyes boring into Roger's skull. Roger would have moved had his legs not been frozen. Luckily his terrified breathing must have come across as bravado, because Ishea stopped.

"I'm going to be honest with you, Roger. I don't trust you. Not that I think you're working against us. But I'm worried about you working for us. You're weak and ineffectual and totally distracted at all times. But, and this is a really big *but,* Freddy believes you have value and clearly so does Conchita. That will have to be good enough for me at this stage. I'm going to watch you carefully, and if I see you begin to put anyone in danger I'm going to make sure you don't."

Roger couldn't really disagree with Ishea on any of those points. He was definitely weak and while he didn't know what he was supposed to do yet, and therefore felt being called 'ineffectual' was a little unfair, he was decidedly distracted by Conchita. So he just shrugged and sat down.

Conchita who'd sat quietly though the outburst, leaned forward. "Stop Ishea. You forget yourself" Her voice was controlled but frightening. "You will never do that again. Never threaten one of our guests."

Ishea looked at her as though she'd slapped him in the face. He sighed deeply and retreated to his seat. Roger could tell he'd made an enemy. He was grateful to Conchita and relieved that Ishea hadn't pounded his head into the table.

"The arms business unfortunately isn't and hasn't been the big earner that it was in the old days." Freddy had taken over the story as if nothing had happened. "Oh, there's still a ton of money in it, certainly enough to keep a company like ours successful for years to come if that's what we wanted to continue doing. But for Der Felsen it's a real issue. A lot of their old shareholders pulled out, and they desperately needed new ones and a new source of revenue."

"Not many legitimate businessmen are going to invest in the arms business," said Conchita, "so the owners of Der Felsen decided to get new shareholders using the old fashioned method of blackmail."

Roger stood up again. His back ached from stress. "I'm sorry but this doesn't get easier. In fact it gets more bizarre and unbelievable by the word."

"Perhaps," Conchita continued, pulling him back down, "but it's true. Many, very wealthy, very powerful business people have outlets that, let us say are not golf or sailing. Activities where they can totally lose themselves..."

"She's talking about weird sexual activity," laughed Jamie, "in case you weren't following."

"Precisely. All Der Felsen had to do was find out what these were, which they could do easily enough, and then use them to blackmail these people into joining their organization. So they set up a very specialized brothel in Berlin and made sure the people they wanted, visited. Not hard to do, I promise. Once there, the men were photographed in compromising positions, and invited to join Der Felsen as shareholders. When they agreed to join they were presented with a money-making scheme that was bigger than anything they could imagine: owning an entire continent."

"It sounds quite brilliant, I suppose. Almost like reverse blackmail. Instead of taking their money to keep quiet you actually make them money to keep quiet."

"It is brilliant," said Jamie. That's what makes Der Felsen so bloody dangerous."

"But I want to know what you're doing about the animals. That's the part that appeals to me."

"You need to understand that there are two kinds of people in Der Felsen," continued Jamie. "Those that are totally caught up in their 'private life' - Der Felsen takes care of that believe me - and a good number, most of them dangerous psychopaths, that take advantage of the other activity that Der Felsen offers."

"Big game hunting?"

"Yes, big game hunting. It's almost a bi-product of taking over the land as Freddy explained. You can't have elephants or lions or big herds of wildebeest on land that you intend to grow crops on."

"You said you give the animals a chance to fight back..."

"We do," said Jamie, "we send in someone to intercept the hunters. And we kill them."

Roger gulped.

"Yes we kill them with as much compassion as they kill the animals."

"You're serious?"

"Oh yes," said Jamie, slightly drunk but deadly serious. "The person we send in has no compassion for trophy hunters or poachers."

"So you play God?"

"Someone has to. God certainly isn't playing the all merciful, all powerful deity he's supposed to be."

"You think we're wrong, Roger?"

"I don't know. I don't really believe in God but I have to admit killing someone seems extreme."

"Really," said Freddy, Googling something on his phone. "Ah yes, here it is. Let me read you something by a big Washington lawyer, best friend of your late Supreme Court Justice Scalia and a member of a very exclusive hunting organization which isn't affiliated with Der Felsen in any way, except for perhaps the mentality of its members. Here we go...'I've also been pursuing my passion — killing things. I'm sure many of you have become mamby-pamby girly men and think that killing things is oh, so redneck and lower class. Well, you'll be delighted to know that I generally go killing things with Continental royalty and English nobility, and we look down on the rednecks just like you do.'

"He goes on, 'I am pleased to report that I've killed lots of elephants, lions, buffalo, leopards, kudu, deer and the last legally shot black rhinoceros, together with more than a hundred and fifty thousand birds of various species. When the last duck comes flying over with a sign around his neck reading "I am the last duck," I will shoot it.'

"Those are the people we kill because if there is a God he is thrilled that someone is doing it for him.

"You want to kill Harry Bones, Roger?"

"Yes, well...look I don't know. I've said it and I've thought about it but I can't. I don't know how and I couldn't do it anyway even if I knew how. I have to kill the thought of him. That's the best I can do."

"Well, I tell you what," Freddy said. "Let's get through this thing, and when it's all over we'll arrange for Harry Bones to go bye-bye. It's the least we can do."

"I don't know," Roger said somewhat in horror. "Please let's discuss that before you do anything. I've been thinking a lot about it. As much as I hate him, it's not really my call whether he lives or dies."

"Then whose is it?" Freddy asked. "You said you don't believe in God."

"Enough for tonight," Conchita said, standing up. "We've told this poor man more than he can possibly digest at one time. Let's all get some sleep and we can continue tomorrow."

She kissed Roger on the cheek and whispered in his ear. "You are a very unpredictable man, Mr. Storm. But I like that about you."

Roger wanted to say something, anything, but couldn't, so he trooped off to his bedroom and fell asleep.

Chapter 21

IN WHICH INSPECTOR DARMSTAEDTER
MEETS A MYSTERIOUS WOMAN
AND LEARNS SOMETHING NEW
ABOUT HIS PARTNER

Le Pain Quotidien, Wilton Road, London
The next morning

Constantin Darmstaedter was bored. He looked at the huge bowl of milky coffee in front of him. "I could float a small ship in this, Matthew."

Bunter did not respond. He was preoccupied wondering just what it was he'd say to Clare Montrose when or if she showed up. Her email response wasn't clear on much other than that he was a disgusting bastard.

Darmstaedter yawned - they'd caught a really early flight from Munich that morning to make the tentative appointment with the person Bunter assured him knew every rumor, and the source of every rumor about conspiracy involving big business. "I'm not sure she is coming my friend."

But at that moment a large figure plopped down at their table in the chair unoccupied by the policemen's briefcases.

"Good God, Clare," yelped Bunter, trying to stand up and smashing his knees into the table.

"Don't get up, Matthew. I won't be staying long. I just wanted to tell you how I really feel about you. Although that could take forever if I started with arsehole and ended with wanker or some other insult beginning with the letters x, y or z."

"Clare, look I am so sorry. I honestly didn't mean..."

Darmstaedter tried to follow the list of insults that spewed from Clare's mouth and the excuses thrown up by Bunter when he could get a word in, but his comprehension of British expletives wasn't good enough. One thing was clear, and that was that Clare and Bunter must have been romantically linked at some point. Darmstaedter was surprised. Bunter, in their years of working together, had never once mentioned a member of the opposite sex. At first he'd wondered if Matthew was perhaps gay, but now he thought that Bunter was in fact more like his insufferable hero, Sherlock Holmes, and believed women to be either unsolvable puzzles or distractions. And yet here was Clare. Was she perhaps Bunter's, 'Irene Adler?'

He studied her carefully. She had long blond curly hair piled up on her head and a face that while full, and rather red at this moment, showed a cute button nose and sensual lips. While Darmstaedter could not see her buttocks and legs under the table, he liked her breasts, which seemed as angry as her, threatening to burst out of her tight white shirt at any minute.

His reverie was interrupted by Bunter who was trying to make introductions.

"Claire Montrose, this is Chief Inspector Constantin Darmstaedter from a special division of the German police in Wiesbaden. He and I are working on the case together."

Claire seemed to have calmed down slightly. "I'm pleased to meet you Constantin, and I am sorry you had to witness a little unpleasant unfinished business between Matthew and I."

Darmstaedter held up his hands as if to dismiss any issues. "It is my honor to meet you Miss Montrose. Matthew said you know the inside and outside of global business intrigue better than anyone."

"Well I like to think so. My ability to troll the dark web gets me more stuff than you can even imagine. The problem is how much of it is true? That part I don't know, and my clients don't expect me to."

"Who are your clients?"

Bunter answered for Clare, who'd taken a deep breath. "Seriously Constantin, you don't really expect Clare to answer that do you?"

"I am sorry, Clare. May I call you Clare, if you please?" He didn't wait for her to answer. "I honestly didn't mean to ask your exact clients."

"I am certainly not prepared to tell you anything about them, exact or inexact, specific or general. I wish to make that clear. Matthew slept with me for a year and I never told him a thing."

Darmstaedter was slightly taken aback. As familiar as he was with criminals who refused to cooperate, he didn't expect them to be sleeping with senior investigators at Interpol.

"Anyway," said Bunter, "it's not important who she works for or even how she goes about her business. We just need, if you are willing, Clare, to try to understand what we are up against."

"I'll try Matthew, on one condition."

"And that is?"

"That you promise never to walk in on me again, and that you take me out for an expensive dinner. Actually that's two conditions but that's the only way I'll help you.

Bunter agreed with a kiss to her pudgy hand and Darmstaedter wondered whether his comprehension of the English language had tripped him up yet again because he thought most people walked out rather than in on other people.

"Now," said Clare, "tell me everything you know about the people you're looking for." She listened attentively as Bunter explained to her what had happened leaving, much to Darmstaedter's surprise, nothing out. He trusted his partner but felt deeply suspicious of the mysterious Clare Montrose who drank her coffee without asking a single question or taking one note. Finally she put her coffee cup down and googled something on her phone.

"I'm assuming you've considered the International Order of St. Hubertus?"

"We haven't, and I don't have a clue as to who they are. Do you Constantin?"

"Ja, as a matter of fact I do, because my father-in-law is a member, though I fail to understand his reasoning for it. It is an international order of hunters founded in the 17th century by some Bohemian nobleman whose name I cannot remember. I do know King Juan Carlos of Spain is involved and a couple of old Austrian Hapsburg princes are at the top."

"That's basically right," said Clare. "People think of them as a secret society but they're not really. Just a bunch of old aristocrats and would-be-aristocrats who go to each other's estates and blow the shit out of animals. I can't imagine it's them. They're all so interbred they couldn't organize a piss-up in a brewery. But it's worth a look. Give me a couple of hours to see if I can access some overlay networks and I'll get back to you. Let's meet at 1:30 at the Ebury Wine Bar. It's ten minutes' walk from here. Look it up."

She took one last sip of coffee from the two-handed bowl and left.

Darmstaedter looked concerned. "My friend, you know I trust you completely but that woman seems very mysterious. Maybe even criminal, if you don't mind me saying so."

"No, I don't mind you saying that. She is mysterious but she's no criminal. Though she may have done some questionable stuff as a hacker. I take it you understand the dark web?"

"Of course, it is an enormous source of worry for us - child pornography, drugs, illegal finance and black-market weapons.

"Exactly, so earlier last year Interpol began to offer a dedicated dark web training program and Clare was one of the people we recruited to help us. She and I worked very closely for a while... please don't snigger, it's demeaning. Clare is one of the most technically competent hackers in the UK. I don't know who else she does work for but she convinced us that it wasn't some foreign government and it didn't involve pedophilia."

"And?"

"And she helps us enormously."

"Ja, but?"

"But, what?"

"But you were fucking her?"

Bunter's mustache bristled. "Good lord, Constantin. That's a little personal, don't you think?"

"I'm sorry, Matthew. But between you and me there can be no secrets. You've never talked about your romantic life before, whereas I have told you everything about mine, including things about my wife and my mistress."

"Yes, you have, and I have to say there are certain aspects that I wish you hadn't." Matthew shuddered, thinking of Darmstaedter's description of his mistress' tattoo. "But we're different that way. You look at any woman and find something attractive to fantasize about. I don't think of women that way."

"So you're not gay. I wasn't sure, but I am happy you are open about this now."

"No, I'm not gay...what the hell's the matter with you? Why would you think I'm gay? Just because I don't try to jump everything in a skirt, like you."

Darmstaedter looked aghast. "That is hardly true. I look at women the way a collector looks at a painting."

"Maybe, but most collectors don't try to fuck their paintings."

Darmstaedter could not argue with that.

"Anyway, I've always tried to separate my private life and my work, and in truth there isn't a lot to tell. I've never had much time for romance. Too busy being a copper to go out on dates. Then I met Clare, and something just clicked."

Darmstaedter sipped his coffee and looked at his friend. He was glad Bunter was opening up a little. It was the one thing, other than the stupid mustache and obsession with Sherlock Holmes, that upset him about his partner.

"It was all perfectly above board you understand," said Bunter. "Technically we didn't work in the same place. She was just a service provider."

"Really, ha!" laughed Darmstaedter. I bet she provided you with some special services. Come on Matthew, tell me."

The joke, as juvenile as it was, made Bunter laugh. "Not a chance, mate. Anyway, it all ended when I walked in on her as she was looking at something that I shouldn't have seen, a Bitcoin account that showed she was worth about twenty million pounds. She refused to divulge where the money came from, and when I insisted she told me she didn't want to see me again."

"It appears she is open once again to your company."

"Maybe, we'll see. Anyway, I've got some calls I need to make and emails to do. I'm sure you have the same. Why don't we just meet at the Ebury at 1:30."

Clare arrived late and immediately ordered a glass of Domaine des Pourthie, which she bolted back as if it were water.

"I take it you found something."

"I don't know," she said signaling to the waiter for another glass.

"But I think I did. First I'm not sure who the group is that's killing these people, the hunters. I actually can't find anything on them whoever they may be. But I believe the organization that the hunters who were killed belonged to, may be

Der Felsen. Nothing to do with the Order of St. Hubertus."

"My God," said Darmstaedter. "I know Der Felsen. And, if it is them, I am not sure what we can do about it. They may be untouchable."

"He's right," Clare said reaching over and taking a fry off Bunter's plate even though she had her own in front of her. "A lot of what they do is funded by governments. Black ops stuff, you know the kind. Killing drug kingpins, kidnapping someone's political opponent.

"And you know this from hacking into their files?"

"Actually I know this from looking at various government files. I can see some of Der Felsen's stuff, but I can't hack into their main system. They're so powerful and their resources so incredible that the encryptions are virtually impossible to crack."

Bunter bit his lip. "How do you know them, Constantin?"

Darmstaedter thought back to the first time he'd come across Der Felsen when a well-known radical Islamic cleric in Hamburg suddenly disappeared. The police couldn't find a trace of him. After two months of looking and questioning hundreds of people, one of their informants told them he suspected Der Felsen, an organization that no-one in authority seemed to know, had taken care of the cleric in the worst possible sense of the phrase. The Hamburg police had turned the case over to the BDA in Wiesbaden and Darmstaedter had gotten the file. He'd searched the databases for Der Felsen and found only one file that was accessible. He'd just begun to read it when his computer screen went blank and a warning notice came up letting him know that the files were off limits. When he questioned his superior he'd been told to drop the whole thing. Darmstaedter, who'd never been into doing more than he needed to, complied, but he'd read enough to give Bunter a small insight.

"Der Felsen was started by two high-ranking Nazis at the end of the war. One was Heinz Lammerding, who was wanted both in Germany and France for one of the worst civilian massacres in French history. After the war it is believed the British helped him escape. The second was Kurt Blome, who was a scientist specializing in biological agents like plague and cholera, using them on prisoners at Auschwitz. At his trial, he was acquitted by the Americans supposedly in exchange for providing information on germ warfare." Darmstaedter paused to take a bite of his rapidly cooling roast duck breast. "Obviously there's a lot more to Der Felsen, but most of the information is not available to us."

"So we don't know where Der Felsen is or what they do today. This is ridiculous. You have to know more, Constantin."

"I don't Matthew, and I don't think we should pursue this."

"Bloody hell mate. We've put too much into this to stop right now. What are they going to do, fire us?

"That's probably the least that would happen," said Clare who'd wolfed down her burger and was dipping her remaining fries in ketchup. "I can tell you a little more but not much and I'm not sure how you are going to take this further."

Bunter, not convinced of anything, sat back and let Clare continue.

"Der Felsen began as an international arms dealer. I don't know exactly how those two individuals had access to Nazi arms stashes but there must have been others involved. With the help of allied intelligence agencies, and of course none of this is really documented, they began to sell stockpiles of weapons, including V1 and V2 rockets to Chiang Kai-shek and other Chinese warlords in their battle against the Maoists in 1946. They made millions, and moved operations to other continents where wars were being waged too. They diversified obviously into drug smuggling from dictators who could only pay them in opium, and eventually into mercenary armies.

"Jesus," said Bunter leaning forward. "But how are people like Heidenreich involved?"

"I don't know exactly. I do know they have outside shareholders. Perhaps he was one of them."

"Well we have to find out who the others are. I'm sure if I checked some of the Interpol databases I'd find something."

"You won't," said Clare, "I already tried that. There's only one file and that contains the information I just gave you. Anything after 1952 is either gone or put into some file that I can't find."

"So we're stymied?"

"I am unfamiliar with the word 'stymied,'" said Darmstaedter. "But if it means 'screwed' then, yes, I have a bad feeling that we will be if we start to look into Der Felsen."

"Good God, man. We're high-ranking officers and we're going to do our jobs. We have to look further. This is very frustrating. What are you worried about Constantin? Reprisals from your bosses at BKA?"

"I am insulted, Matthew. Der Bundeskriminalamt is in no way corrupt. That I will swear to. There may be politicians that Der Felsen has in their pockets, but my worry is that organizations of this nature do not take kindly to anyone snooping about their business. Even high ranking policemen. And before you ask me if I am afraid, I am not. I will do my job but I think we should be aware of the danger involved. These are not normal criminals."

Bunter could see that his colleague was extremely upset.

"Look Constantin, we've know each other for five years and we've always worked really well together. I would never question anything to do with your commitment or character. Believe me, I know this is going to be extremely dangerous. In fact it might be a good idea to report in to both of our superiors at this stage to let them know what we're up against. Probably sooner rather than later.

"Ja, that's a good idea. We are going to need resources. I'll fly back to Wiesbaden this afternoon and call you later.

"I tell you what", Clare said. "Why don't you stay in London, Matthew. You can take me out for that dinner tonight and then come back to my place and we can try to find out something more. Because I know there's something. I just don't know exactly how to find it."

"Fine", said Bunter, "I'll pick you up at 8.00."

Darmstaedter winked at him and made an obscene gesture that Bunter hoped Clare hadn't seen.

Chapter 22

IN WHICH ROGER HEARS ABOUT HIS ROLE
IN THE PLAN AND A MYTHICAL BEING

London, England
The next day

When Roger walked in to breakfast the next morning he was surprised to see Zecheriah sitting at the table with the others who'd clearly got up much earlier than him. They glanced up briefly and nodded before going back to studying what looked like topographical maps spread over the table. Roger helped himself to kippers and eggs from the large chaffing dishes on the sideboard and joined them.

"For Christ's sake, watch out, man." Zecheriah quickly pulled a map from next to Roger's plate. "Don't spill your damn food on these maps. They're really hard to get."

All signs of the servile butler had vanished.

"He's right," said Freddy, the only one with a grin on his face. "We had to buy them from a contact we have at NASA. Impossible to get on-line in case you're wondering. These Roger, are maps of the Omo River Valley in Southwest Ethiopia. To be more specific the Omo National Park about eight-hundred clicks from Addis Ababa and near the border with Kenya. Very remote, very hard to get to and home to some tribes that are virtually stone age. We're heading there this evening.

"We?"

"Yes, 'we' includes you."

If they were expecting Roger to protest or whine and whinge and refuse to go, he surprised them.

"Fine by me. Just let me know what you expect me to do."

"You're joking".

"No I'm not."

"Then you're being facetious," said Jamie, "which we don't have time for."

"On the contrary. Last night you - all of you - asked me whether I was in or out. Before I had a chance to reply Ishea said I was in whether I liked it or not. I'm not saying I like this whole bloody thing or that I am doing anything of my own free will but here I am. So tell me, are we going to kill some hunters? Because I am ready."

Zecheriah looked up. "Who told you about killing hunters? We haven't done that for a while."

For a minute Roger looked confused. That was the only thing he liked about the operation. He was about to ask for an explanation when Conchita laughed. "You see, we have woken up the spirit in our timid friend, excellent."

"Yes, we have," Freddy said with a broad grin on his face." But Zech's right. We are not going to kill hunters on this trip. Unless of course we come across a few that we don't know about, in which case you may do the honors. What we are going to do is to meet a man, a very special man, who is going to help us organize the expulsion of the neocolonialists and return that part of Africa to its rightful state."

"Gun running and negotiations with armed mobs aren't exactly my forte, but what the hell." Roger paused. "Though, with all due respect, maybe before you tell me what I'm going to be doing you should tell me precisely what the plan is and why you're really doing this. I mean what's in it for you? And please don't say you're doing it for humanitarian reasons because I'm not going to believe that."

"There is no need to be petulant, Roger," said Conchita. "Sit down, drink your tea and let us tell you the plan. Then perhaps you will understand."

Roger looked down at Conchita. Even sitting at a table with a plate of half eaten scrambled eggs in front of her, she was intimidating. Beautiful and deadly, he decided. Either he was still in the middle of a booze- infused nightmare from which he'd awake any minute with a godawful headache or these people, no matter how insane and delusional they might seem, were for real. So he sat down and listened.

"I'm going to tell you what we need from you first so you can listen to the rest with that in mind." Freddy said. "What we require from you is a slogan or rallying cry, something that sums up what we're doing in a very simple but stirring way. You know what we mean, exactly what you used to do."

"Look, I came up with 'slogans' as you call them, for toilet bowl cleaners and insurance companies. Not dictators or wars."

"Well, you have a pretty good reputation amongst your colleagues as, how do you say it...a reductionist? You summed up the situation perfectly last night. You took random thoughts and strung them together. That's precisely what we need. Someone who can get what we're trying to offer the people into a simple, easy to comprehend message. Yes, this is bigger than toilet bowl cleaners and insurance companies. We are looking to market a revolution.

"That's important to understand. This is not about arms. As we told you, we're not selling guns or rockets anymore. We are selling a man and a movement. He is a remarkable man as you will soon see. Quite unlike anyone you have ever met. Close to a Gandhi or Mandela, I suppose. And the task ahead of him is as large as theirs were."

"If this mysterious person is as good as you say," Roger said, "why would he need a slogan? Mandela and Gandhi - as far as I know - didn't have slogans. And why me? Okay, maybe I am quite good at getting people to understand the importance of focus. But in truth there are a lot of people who are better at it than me, or certainly more well-known than I am. If you want a political rallying cry find the guy who really masterminded what happened in Egypt. I assume 'well-known' would be an advantage in terms of credibility. I worked for a mediocre organization and in the end even they didn't value me."

"You underestimate yourself Roger. I spoke to a lot of people who felt you were really, really good, especially with a more global audience. And that's precisely the problem. Gandhi, Mandela were trying to unite single – though admittedly diverse - countries. But here we're talking about a continent, with hundreds of different tribes and groups. We need to understand what it is that will get them fired up as one. That's the only way we can succeed. You're right that we could have gotten someone with more of a reputation, but in the end I know you - despite the fact that we haven't seen each other in years - and I have always trusted you. We don't want someone who is a public figure. Too many issues. Too many questions. We aren't going to have the advantage of Twitter and the Internet. Most of the people we'll be targeting can hardly feed themselves and their families let alone access information online. It's better for us to have someone who's a little more obscure. In any case it will be great to be together again."

"So what you're saying is you need someone who, if he disappears, no one will really miss."

"You are right in a way, my dear," Conchita said, the smile returning to her face. "But as you said earlier you were probably going to kill yourself anyway, so at least with us you will be dying for a good cause."

"She's joking," said Freddy leaning back in his chair and putting his palms together like a fat bishop offering up a prayer. "Roger, how much do you know about the royal dynasty in Ethiopia?"

"Not a hell of a lot. I know Haile Selassie was the last emperor and he was deposed in about 1975 when the communists took over."

"1974 to be precise. Yes, Haile Selassie was the last Emperor of Ethiopia but not the last of the Solomonic Dynasty. Jamie, you're more of the expert on this. Why don't you tell Roger about the House of Solomon."

"Well, ok. But trying to understand the complexities and lines and cadet branches would drive you nuts, so I'll give you the basics. You've probably heard of the legend that the Queen of Sheba went to Israel and had a dalliance with King Solomon?"

"I've heard about it but I'm not sure how much I believe."

"Oh, it's true alright. We've done enough research on the subject to feel more than eighty percent confident. Sheba and Solomon had a son, Menelik, who returned to Ethiopia and founded the Aksumite Kingdom. Apparently Solomon gave Menelik the Ark of the Covenant. That part we have no evidence for, but the Ethiopian Orthodox Church says it's in a small chapel in the monastery of Saint Mary of Zion. It may be there for all we know, but that is probably not important at this stage."

Jamie had an almost hypnotic quality to his voice, and Roger leaned forward, drawn to this fascinating figure as if he were part of the legend itself.

"What is important is that over the course of the hundreds of years from Menelik to Haile Selassie, different branches of the family have been fighting one another. By the latter half of the 19th century, the last uninterrupted direct descendants from the male line of Solomon and Sheba were supposedly Menelik II and his daughter Zewditu, who was the first female emperor. Well, that's what everyone thought. But in fact the Solomonic line is very much alive today, and the man we are going to see is the proof. What Wikipedia or any books on the history of Ethiopia do not record is that Menelik II also had a son. This son married a Somali princess who in turn bore him a son, the great-grandfather of the man who should be Menelik III. That is if Ethiopia was still an empire and his great-great grandmother Zewditu hadn't murdered her brother a week before his coronation."

"So you're saying Menelik III is the guy we're going to visit?"

"Exactly," Freddy said. "In 1974 the communists killed or jailed most of the royals who hadn't been able to leave the country. They eventually let the survivors out of jail after the regime fell, but by then most of the true claimants to the throne were dead. Except for Menelik."

"How did he escape?" To Roger the whole thing was beginning to sound like a boy's adventure tale.

"He didn't from the communists," said Jamie. "He'd been living in obscurity in the Omo Valley amongst the Mursi people, probably one of the most primitive tribes left in Africa, so no one really bothered with him. In fact none of the royals at the time of Selassie were that aware of Menelik's great grandfather's existence because the family went to live amongst the Falashas once Zewditu had murdered her brother."

"And the Falashas are?" The word was familiar to Roger but he couldn't recall what it meant.

"The original Jews of Ethiopia who supposedly came to Ethiopia when Menelik 1 returned from Jerusalem."

"I appreciate you telling me all of this," Roger said taking a final bite of his toast, "but it's getting quite hard to connect everything with so much legend and conspiracy rolled into one."

"He's right," said Ishea, who hadn't even looked as if he were listening. "Look, all you need to know is that the guy we are going to meet is a pretty special person with an incredible heritage.

He's Oxford educated and has a presence that both Zec and I, who are not easily impressed, can feel. If anyone can unite the tribes, and that's still a big if in my mind, it's him."

"Just wait till you meet him, Roger. He can fill in everything you're not getting," Freddy said, standing up and bringing the breakfast to a timely end. "We leave for the airport in about six hours so let's make sure you have everything you need. It's not going to be an easy journey."

Chapter 23

IN WHICH INSPECTOR BUNTER
GETS SOME ESSENTIAL INFORMATION
AND HAS VERY KINKY SEX FOR A
CONSERVATIVE BRITISH COPPER
❧

London, England
That evening

M atthew Bunter, wearing only his lobster-
print boxers, stood behind Clare as she
sat naked at her desk, staring at the computer
monitor. He was slightly drunk and still extremely
horny. They'd already had excellent sex, after
they'd returned to Clare's apartment, but looking
at Clare, perched like some exotic parrot on the
big inflatable ball that served as her desk chair,
excited him enormously. After washing down the
Tandoori prawns with mango salad and the mixed
grilled fish with a couple of bottles of Picpoul de
Pinet at J. Sheeky's, she'd invited him back to
delve into the world of hacking, where her mind
was presently, despite the constant prodding of
Bunter's erection and roaming hands.

"Stop that Matthew," she said slapping at the bulge in his boxers.

"Ow, Christ. You can't smack a man in his tackle."

"Get your mind off your tackle for God's sake and stop trying to squeeze my tits for a moment. Look, I'm trying to find something to help you. So either pull up a chair and help me read through this or go lie down on the couch and I'll wake you when I find something."

As Bunter could see no spare chair to pull up, and realizing there wasn't much he could add and his hopes of getting a quickie were almost nil, he lay on the couch and was soon snoring gently.

He was in the midst of a slightly erotic dream involving Clare and her big rubber ball when she shook him rather violently. "Wake up Matthew, I think I've found something."

He groggily followed her over to the screen and looked at what appeared to be an email chain.

"What is it?"

"Well, as I told you, trying to hack into Der Felsen is almost impossible. So what I focused on was trying to see if I could find anything that connected some of the dead hunters, and I think I have."

"Christ, Clare. That's brilliant. Let's take a look."

"Here," she said, pointing at the screen. "I hacked into Heidenreich's Gmail account. This is an exchange between Heidenreich and Donald Brink Jr, whom I don't recall you mentioning."

"I probably didn't. He was an American property tycoon killed a few weeks ago in Zimbabwe while hunting elephants."

"Well clearly, as you can see they knew each other and had a connection."

Bunter started to read an email from Heidenreich to Brink.

Donald, as you know our friends have arranged for me to shoot a hippo in Botswana in a few weeks - probably the one animal I have not had the pleasure of killing. However, this morning I received an anonymous note at my home telling me not to go on the hunt and to warn anyone else in our group to give up trophy hunting. I put in a call to Geoffrey but he has not responded. I know you are going to Zimbabwe to hunt elephant soon. I think we should speak.

There was a response from Brink.

Hi Dieter. Yes, I got a similar note a few days ago. I did tell Geoffrey but he said it was probably just some PETA crazies. He's probably right. I'd like him to organize a trip to shoot some of those bastards. Let's talk. I will get my assistant to set up a call tomorrow.

"Is that all you can find?"

"Have you any idea, Matthew how difficult it was to pull this up? I hacked into Heidenreich's private email for Christ's sake." Clare was pissed.

"I'm sorry, I just meant, is there anything else you found?"

"Not a lot, but I think I know who the Geoffrey is they're referring to. Geoffrey-Philippe van der Borrekens."

Bunter tried to sit on the ball with Clare with little success, and so had to continue leaning over her shoulder. "Who is he? I'm unfamiliar with that name."

"The reason I know who he is, or let's say the reason I'm pretty sure I know who he is, is because he is the head of Der Felsen."

"I thought you said you couldn't get any information on Der Felsen?"

"I'm having a really hard time, but there are a couple of files you can access that mention Der Felsen and Geoffrey. They're mostly by authors of books on conspiracy theories. You know the ones...?"

"All too well, dear Clare, all too well. Most of them are bloody crazy."

Bunter leaned forward and nuzzled her neck. Much to his surprise she put her hand up and pulled his head round so she could kiss him. Bunter fell forward onto her and within minutes he was happily bouncing up and down on the big rubber ball with Clare on his lap. It was far better than the dream.

Half an hour later, when they'd got into bed, Clare turned to him. "The hard part Matthew will be getting hold of van der Borrekens. I'm not sure how we do that."

"I'm sure Constantin can think of something. He's the brains." Matthew promptly fell asleep.

Chapter 24

In which jobs change hands at Burg Waldengraf

Thuringia, Germany
About the same time

F inding the leak in the organization had been relatively simple, thought Rudi, and in his opinion that proved just how stupid people could be. Although he shouldn't have been surprised, most mercenaries aren't typically the brightest individuals on the planet.

"How did you identify him so easily?" Geoffrey poured himself a glass of Dalmore 64 Trinitas.

He thought of offering Rudi a glass too, but the Trinitas was a gift from a very grateful dictator in West Africa and cost a hundred and fifty thousand dollars a bottle. Geoffrey appreciated what Rudi had done, but not to that extent.

Rudi watched as Geoffrey sniffed the whiskey as if he were a connoisseur rather than a jumped-up killer who would not be in the position he was in were it not for his uncle, who'd basically knocked off anyone opposed to his nephew taking over Der Felsen.

"I simply asked Demetri to ask who'd been closest to Corn and Payamps. Two names kept coming up: McPherson and Bejelica, the Montenegran. I questioned both, and while neither radiates enormous intelligence, I decided to focus on McPherson."

"And your reasoning?" Geoffrey took a small sip of the Scotch and rolled it round his mouth.

"Bejelica is quite shrewd. He would not have survived this long if he wasn't. He has an animal instinct for survival and while he has almost a reverence for Corn, he hates Payamps. So I focused on McPherson."

"I assume he has told you everything?"

"Everything we need to know. And you were right, he passed on the names of the hunters and the dates of their hunts to Payamps, with whom he had a special friendship. And of course for a considerable amount of money."

Geoffrey looked at his number two. He really despised everything about him. His shiny bald head with his long grey side whiskers. His dark eyes that seemed to dart about like those of a cobra seeking out a rat. Most of all he hated him because he knew Rudi hated him more. And there was nothing either one could do about the other. Der Felsen had always been run, since its inception, by both brains and brawn. It could not survive with the absence of either. Companies that operated in the shadow world, as Der Felsen did, needed strong men at the top, and shortly after it was formed the van de Borrekens family had been signed on to provided the muscle. His grandfather had been a colonel in the Wallonie, the French speaking Belgian Nazi collaborators who became part of the Waffen-SS unit that fought against the Soviet Union in Eastern Europe. He'd disappeared after the war to escape retribution at the hands of his fellow Belgians and joined up with Heinz Lammerding in Egypt, where the co-founder of Der Felsen was soliciting money from King Farouk.

Geoffrey's father had died when he was a young boy, and he'd been sent to live with his uncle Henricus who'd begun his own training as a soldier in the army of Jean "Black Jack" Schramme, the notorious Belgian mercenary commander who fought in the Congo shortly after independence. When Geoffrey graduated from the Royal Military College in Canada, Henrickus had arranged for him to join DynCorp International, a private military company that provided "security" for officials in Bosnia, Somalia, Kosovo, Libya and Angola. Geoffrey did well there and had soon earned a reputation for being an efficient leader, but with a brutal streak that made him a risk to his unit. Geoffrey was, thought Henricus, the perfect person to take over the management of Der Felsen when he retired. Of course not all of the directors agreed at first. Their collective position was that

Geoffrey-Philippe was a dangerous lunatic. After one or two vanished mysteriously, they all came around, and two years later, after a stint in Asia, Geoffrey-Philippe van de Borrekens was made Chief Executive of Der Felsen.

"Are you okay, Geoffrey?"

"Yes, yes I am. I apologize, Rudi. I was just thinking about what to do about PaloMar."

"Clearly we need to send them a message."

"No, Rudi. I disagree. This time I want to send them more than a message. This time I want to wipe them off the face of the earth. We've tried to send them messages but we have not succeeded. We have tried to buy them out and we have failed. We have tried to kill a few of them but they are still alive. They know what our ultimate goal is because we were unable to stop Payamps and Corn from leaving our organization. For that I will take the blame."

"Geoffrey," said Rudi, picking up the bottle of Dalmore and pouring himself a generous glassful.

Geoffrey opened his mouth to say something but he couldn't speak. His hands flailed around for a weapon but he was almost paralyzed by the anger he felt at Rudi's sheer and unbelievable arrogance at drinking his Scotch.

If Rudi realized what he'd done, he was totally ignoring it. "You mustn't blame yourself," he continued. "Understanding the mind of a mercenary is beyond anything that either you or I are capable of. I know you used to be one but your case was different. You knew that your uncle wanted you simply to gain experience before taking over Der Felsen. These men we hire are scum. They are misfits. People who cannot live in a normal world. They kill people and yet, as we have discovered, some of them have a soft spot for animals. They have a fierce loyalty to each other and yet betray the people who pay them. No, do not blame yourself my friend. Rather let us focus on how we will go about destroying PaloMar. I have a thought."

Geoffrey, having found the Smith & Wesson he had frantically been searching for, slowed his breathing. He picked up the revolver and slowly raised it till it was just about pointing at Rudi's large forehead. Only then did he lower it.

"Rudi, I want to hear your proposal, but first I need to kill something."

"Why not kill McPherson? He is still tied to a chair in the cellar and Demetri left plenty of him for you to work on."

"That's exactly what I will do. And when I return you will tell me your plan. And Rudi, as much as we need you, if you ever touch that whiskey again I will kill you."

After Geoffrey had gotten up and with a deliberate slow step, walked out his office, Rudi smiled to himself and poured another glass of the Scotch. A few minutes later he heard the sound of a shot followed by a scream. After a silence, the door to Geoffrey's office opened and Rudi watched in fascination as Geoffrey, ashen faced, staggered back in leaning heavily on the huge shoulders of Der Felsen's head of security, Demetri Guria.

"Ricochet," said Demetri without waiting for Rudi to ask. "Went right through Mc Pherson's head, hit the wall and lodged in Geoffrey's buttocks".

Rudi poured Geoffrey what was left of his scotch.

Later that evening after a medic had removed the bullet and sewn up the six centimeter rip in Geoffrey's gluteus maximus, and once he was, with the help of pain killers and Ambien, fast asleep, Rudi met with Demetri in his own office.

He pulled out a bottle of The Macallan Fine and Rare 1926 Scotch which had been a gift to him from the same dictator who'd given Geoffrey the Dalmore. At seventy-five thousand dollars a bottle it was certainly less expensive than the Dalmore but the flavor, to Rudi's mind, was far more concentrated.

"Demetri, this talk has been coming for a while and I can think of no better time than the present."

"You mean with Mr. Van de Borrekens shot in the ass?"

"Precisely, I've always thought that's where his brains were..."

If he had expected a smile from Demetri he didn't now get it.

"... and so this is the opportunity that you and I, and of course some of the others, need to use to decide on our future."

Demetri sat down on the couch opposite Rudi. He took a sip of the scotch and swirled it round his mouth, enjoying the note of licorice. He looked around the office comparing it to Geoffrey's. It was similar in size but it was the office of an adult. There were diplomas from both the University of Vienna and Oxford, and paintings by Schiele, Hundertwasser, Kokoschka and a landscape by Adolf Hitler which had always made Demetri a little uncomfortable. Geoffrey's office, on the other hand, looked like an expensive dorm room. While the furniture was modern there were animal heads - mostly blown to shreds - on the wall, and photos of Geoffrey in his mercenary days, posing with the ears he'd lopped off the people he'd killed. It wasn't the violence itself that upset Demetri. It was the lack of refinement with which the violence was carried out. Demetri had killed many people. Some fast, some slow. But he had killed them like a master-craftsman and hated people who didn't respect the art. Rudi, on the other hand, was an artist of manipulation and Demetri was comforted by that. The question in his mind was whether Rudi was in the process of manipulating him.

"I know you do not approve of Mr. Van der Borrekens' style, Rudi, and you know I'm not all that impressed with it either. But he is the head of our company and loyalty is paramount to me."

"Yes, yes, I understand that," replied Rudi brushing off Demetri's attempt to stay neutral. "But your loyalty is to the organization, is it not?"

"Of course, but until the organization decides to replace Mr. van der Borrekens, he represents the organization."

"How very noble and dutiful you are Demetri. I think we all appreciate that but the organization is reassessing much of what it has done in the past and Geoffrey-Philippe van der Borrekens is not really part of that process. You, on the other hand, are. Very much so. Here, let me pour you another drink and I will explain."

Rudi knew he was in dangerous territory. If he couldn't convince Demetri of what he intended to do then he was finished. His brains, alongside McPherson's, would no doubt be splattered on the walls of the cellar. He was watching Demetri carefully for any signs of doubt, but as usual the Bulgarian showed absolutely no emotion.

"You know the history of the organization and how it was founded and how it has made its money over the years?"

"Of course."

"Up until a few years ago those businesses were a perfect way to make a lot of money. But they aren't anymore, for numerous reasons. Too many cheap weapons in circulation from the conflicts in Iraq and Afghanistan and, of course, Syria. And we don't want to compete with the Mexican cartels either. They're too crazy. So two years ago Der Felsen began looking for a new source of revenue, and that, my dear Demetri, was in real estate."

"I'm not sure I understand."

"You would not have heard of this until now, and that is probably one of the reasons why Der Felsen has been so successful. Most of what we do is on what the American's call a 'need to know basis,' so let me fill you in. As I said, two years ago I brought a proposal to the board that involved buying up huge tracts of land in Africa. Land that stretches from Zimbabwe up through the Democratic Republic of the Congo to Ethiopia and then west of there to Chad and Niger. Land we could procure on behalf of individual shareholders that would solve some of the most pressing issues today and in the future."

Demetri said nothing and Rudi worried he'd lost him.

"Is this clear, Demetri?"

"What you have told me is clear, Rudi, but I don't yet understand the motivation or goal here."

"Of course, of course. Well, the end goal is to grow crops and farm livestock in the most efficient manner possible to feed countries that cannot provide for their own people. Countries like India, Pakistan, China and the gulf states."

"I'm not sure why those countries cannot buy up the land themselves."

"A good point. They can and they do where possible. But there are places where countries cannot afford to be seen to buy up land because it involves the forceful removal of people and the destruction of all wildlife. That is where we come in. We buy up the land from various dictators and warlords that we've been able to help stay in power and we sell it to various groups of investors who 'manage' the land on behalf of those countries."

"And our mercenaries help get the people to vacate the land?"

"Yes, we of course offer the people a small amount of money to leave, but unfortunately most don't really want the money and so they have to be forcefully removed. It's not pleasant, I know, but at the same time it's a hungry world and it has to be fed, and those who do not understand have to be eliminated."

Demetri closed his eyes and pictured the scene that Rudi had painted. He had over the years, working as a killer and torturer, become devoid of sympathy and feeling. This was simply a job. One he enjoyed even more than the sex he had at the company owned brothel in Berlin, and he had no desire to change that.

"I appreciate that Rudi, but as yet you haven't explained to me why Mr van der Borrekens needs to go."

"Ah, well, another drink perhaps?"

Demetri shook his head.

"Mr van der Borrekens, as you so formally refer to him, and to put it bluntly, is an unpredictable imbecile. His actions, allowing some of our shareholders to hunt on the lands we are trying to secure, has led to our whole operation being put in jeopardy. It was unnecessary and childish. We know for a fact now that PaloMar was involved in the killings of these prominent men - thanks to your interrogation- and we also know that both Interpol and the German police are trying to investigate us. No, Demetri I'm afraid the board has spoken. Mr van der Borrekens can no longer be in charge of this company."

"I see, and who will take over?"

"Why, me of course. And you, my dear Demetri, will be my number two. What do you say?"

Rudi knew this was the moment of truth. Demetri stood up and walked over to him and for a brief few seconds Rudi thought he would attack him. Then Demetri held out his glass for Rudi to refill. The two men clinked glasses and shook hands.

"I'd better take care of Geoffrey," said Demetri as he walked out Rudi's office. "As you say, he did blow his brains out."

Rudi breathed a sigh of relief. And now it was time to put an end to PaloMar once and for all. But he wouldn't do it the way that uncouth bastard Geoffrey would have done it. He would simply dry up their resources. He would cripple them financially. He thought about the lesson his father had taught him the first time he gave him an allowance.

"Money accomplishes a lot. A lot of money accomplishes everything. But no money accomplishes nothing."

That's when his father had snatched the money back out of his hand. The fucker.

Chapter 25

In which Roger gets to make love to Conchita

The cabin of a Falcon 7X on the way to Addis Ababa
The same evening

Roger had never been on a private jet, unless one counted his unconscious flight between Paris and London a week or so before, when he'd been shanghaied by Freddy and Conchita from Chez Daphne.

"The wonderful part of the 7X," said Freddy, as he ate another piece of sushi from the large and mostly depleted platter on the table between him and Jamie on the one side and Roger and Conchita on the other, "is that it can fly nearly six thousand nautical miles at a speed close to Mach 1."

They'd been flying for an hour and a half and Roger still couldn't get over how luxurious the interior of the plane was. While the dark wood and gold finish gave it a slightly gaudy look, there were six white leather armchairs that were fully reclinable and extremely comfortable, judging by the forms of Zecheriah Corn and Ishea Payamps fast asleep in the front two seats. At that moment the flight attendant who'd brought out the food and sake half an hour earlier walked in from the small galley to clear up.

"Thank you Melissa," said Conchita to the young blond women, "and when you've cleared up please can you make up these beds for Freddy and Jamie. Roger and I will sleep in the back cabin."

She turned to Roger and gestured towards a door at the back.

"Why don't you go through, Roger, and get into bed. I have a few details I need to take care of."

Freddy smiled at Roger and nodded at the door as if to say, 'it's okay.'

"You'll find toothbrushes in the bathroom but no pajamas I'm afraid."

Once more Roger found himself in a haze, his head buzzing at all the possibilities. Was she actually going to sleep with him? As thunderous and momentous as the thought was, he was terrified.

The 'back bedroom' had a large queen-size bed with a big soft- looking duvet and large white pillows on which, to his amazement, were two chocolates. He sat on the bed and ate one. Then he began to panic. Should he get into bed with his clothes on, or should he get naked? He went through precisely what Conchita had said and decided it did not overtly imply sex. In the end he took off his clothes, brushed his teeth and got under the duvet wearing his boxers.

His heart clattered against his ribcage. Conchita turned him on more than any other women he'd known but he couldn't get over the fact that he was, in the league of men who measured up to her, a poor specimen. He reached through his boxers and felt his penis. It seemed to have withdrawn into the same dark place as his brain. Perhaps it would be best if he just pretended to be asleep and saved them both considerable embarrassment.

Roger closed his eyes, and must have drifted off because a few minutes later he felt something soft and warm snuggle up next to him. There was no use pretending as he turned to look onto the face of the most beautiful women he'd ever seen. She leaned forward and kissed him. He tried to say something but she put her finger over his lips. She kissed him again, and this time he responded. Whatever he lacked in practice or prowess he made up for in enthusiasm, and while she must have realized just how nervous he was she ignored it, and any doubts he'd had about his inability to perform dissolved in a melee of bum, belly, breasts and sweat. Though he didn't last too long, when they were done, he lay back feeling better about life than he had in as long as he could remember. He turned towards Conchita, who was looking at him with a big smile on her face.

"Thank you, Conchita. That was...I mean you are the most beautiful..."

"Shhhh Roger...say nothing, my love. It is time for sleep. We have only a few hours before we land."

Roger fell into a dreamless sleep and was woken up a few hours later by Melissa proffering an awful looking green energy drink on a tray. He took one sip and spat it back into the glass.

"Jesus. I'm sorry, but what is this?"

"It's one of Mr Payamps' concoctions sir. He whips it up in the galley. If it's any comfort no one else likes it either, but he insisted I give it to you. Here, I'll pour it down the bathroom sink."

He stood up not realizing his boxers were somewhere at the bottom of the bed. Melissa just laughed.

"You'll need to get up now, Mr. Storm and join the others. We land in Addis in thirty minutes."

"When Roger walked out he had a rather sheepish grin on his face. Zecheriah and Adrian were still asleep. Ishea was deep in conversation with Freddy and Conchita who both looked up and smiled when they saw him. Ishea scowled.

"I don't even know what we're doing when we land," Roger said trying to get some reaction from the women who'd just saved him thousands in therapist fees.

"Well," replied Freddy, "we land at Bole International Airport in about fifteen minutes and once we've cleared customs we're going to check in to a hotel and relax for a while. At lunch you'll be meeting some of the others who'll be traveling to the Omo Valley with us. That's about all you need to know at this stage. I don't mean that in a rude way Roger but we're going to be in danger from the moment we land. You're going to have to stick with us and trust us."

"We are pretty certain that Der Felsen has been tracking us," Conchita continued. "It's not surprising seeing as they were involved in helping to remove the Surma tribe from their ancestral lands so someone could plant sugar. It's very close to where we're going and we suspect the jungle telegraph has been at work."

Roger let go of his normal impulse to demand more of an explanation and decided rather that the less he knew the less he would have to worry. So he sat back in one of the chairs and looked out the window at the land below. Brown arid plains shimmering in the heat gave way to farmlands and finally shanties and the outskirts of the city. It was both beautiful and petrifying, as he knew the most deadly things usually were. He had a sudden panic attack when they landed, realizing he had no idea where his passport was. The last he'd seen of it was in his room at the Lancaster Hotel in Paris. But like everything else, that too had been taken care of by the PaloMar machine, and his passport along with the others was handed over to a tall customs officer who came right aboard the plane and, sitting in one of the chairs, simply opened each and stamped them.

"Thanks Captain Mulugeta," said Zecheriah. "We appreciate you doing this."

"It's no problem, Zech. We appreciate all you have done for us. I hope your stay in Ethiopia is a good one. I will no doubt see you at some time on this trip." With that he got up and left.

No one spoke again until they were in the big black SUV heading towards the center of Addis, at which point Jamie, who was sitting in the front passenger seat next to Zecheriah who was driving, turned to Roger and said, "Just for the record, Roger, you will see we get a tremendous amount of respect and service here, and it has nothing to do with bribery or arms dealing, I assure you. We have funded orphanages and hospitals here for years and the present government appreciates that."

"Though that may not be the case after we visit the Omo valley," said Freddy.

Roger had nothing to ask nor add, so once more he sat in silence and stared out the window at the sprawling city until they reached the Sheraton Hotel. He wasn't sure what to expect from Addis. He'd been to quite a few capital cities in Africa over the years but there was definitely something magical about being in Ethiopia. The ride was relatively short and the city was modern, but being in Africa always made him feel different, more connected to the earth maybe. Someone once told him it was because when you set foot in Africa it was like returning to the place where mankind was born. Maybe they were right because while he should have been worried sick about where they were going and what they were doing, all he could think about were Conchita's breasts. He glanced over at her but she was engrossed in her emails.

Instead of pulling into the main entrance when they reached the Sheraton, they turned onto a side street where the manager and a slew of porters were waiting at a gated entrance to check them into one of the villas. It was probably the most opulent hotel Roger had ever been in. Conchita explained that the villas were big enough to sleep ten people and they'd have armed guards in case anyone was planning anything at all. Roger was less interested in those details as he was with whether or not he'd be sleeping with her again that night. He hung back as the bell hops carried their stuff into the villa and sat down in the living room while Freddy and Jamie walked into one of the bedrooms.

"Are you interested in where we're sleeping, Roger?"

Conchita was standing at the door to one of the other suites in the villa. At first Roger hesitated, but when Conchita laughed, he grabbed her round the waist and tried to pull her onto the bed.

"Relax, my dear. We will have plenty of time. But now we have people to meet, so take a shower and come out to the patio, where we will eat and talk."

Thirty minutes later they were sitting at a large glass table on the poolside patio eating injera, spicy goat and lentils with four dangerous looking individuals, discussing how they were going to get to Menelik and what they were going to do when they found him.

Chapter 26

IN WHICH THE TWO INSPECTORS GET CLOSE TO THE TRUTH AND THE ROLES AT DER FELSEN ARE ONCE AGAIN SWITCHED

Lyon, France and Thuringia, Germany
All around the same time frame

Interpol HQ on the banks of the Rhone is a huge edifice surrounded by checkpoints and high fences. Matthew Bunter had an office on one of the top floors overlooking the atrium. It wasn't exactly a cubby hole, but Darmstaedter felt a little embarrassed for his friend when he compared it to the size of his own office back in Wiesbaden.

"Are you surprised at the cooperation we're getting?" asked Bunter as he picked up a folder from his small glass-topped desk.

"Ja, I am actually. I imagined my talks with my superiors would have been, I'm not sure what the English expression is, but let's say more hostile or vague, maybe?"

"Same here. After our London discussion I wasn't sure what to expect either. Everyone's been overly nice and cooperative. So unlike anything I'm used to. Do you have the feeling that something isn't quite right? Like we're being set up?"

"I do. I have precisely that feeling. But I am not so sure it is, as you say, a set up. I think rather they are hoping we will fail and this whole thing will go away."

"Well, let's be a little on our guard. Hopefully we're wrong, because if we are this is exactly what we need to begin to solve this thing. Both your superiors and mine in perfect agreement, and a meeting with my director in a few minutes. I don't have water or coffee but I do have a bottle of single malt in my drawer if you'd like a quick fix?"

"Thank you, my friend, but I think we should not go in smelling in any way of liquor."

"Perhaps you're right, but I'm having one anyway."

Bunter took a swig of the scotch and gestured to the door.

Darmstaedter followed Bunter to the elevator, passing people of all nationalities who were scurrying about like giant mice as they made their way through different parts of the building. The director's office was on the top floor and about twenty times as large as Bunter's. They were ushered in by an efficient young man who told them to sit at the boardroom table that occupied one side of the office. The director was on the phone yelling at someone, which Darmstaedter felt did not bode well for their conversation, but when the call was done he walked over and shook both their hands. Darmstaedter was surprised that the director was American.

"What the hell have you guys been up to?" he said with a broad grin on his face. "You have a whole bunch of people in one heck of a tizzy. So sit down and let's talk."

Both Bunter and Darmstaedter sat down while the director opened his cabinet and took out a bottle of Maker's Mark.

"I'm having a drink, boys. You want one? You've earned it."

Bunter answered with a "yes, please," but Darmstaedter who, though not averse to imbibing, felt it was a little inappropriate to be drinking at this time of the morning, and that English speakers were probably all raging alcoholics. He hesitated before nodding his head.

"Herr Director," said Darmstaedter after he'd pretended to take a sip of what he decided was a vile liquid, "I'm not entirely sure what it is we have done to earn 'it', as you put it."

"I'll tell you precisely what, Inspector Darmstaedter. You have opened up a door - a very small opening maybe, but a door nevertheless - into Der Felsen. You may not know, although I'm sure Bunter does, that at one point Interpol was actually run by the damn Nazis. In fact - and you may know this, Darmstaedter, because he first worked in your organization - in 1968 the president of Interpol was one Paul Dickopf, who'd been an active member of the SS during World War Two. Am I mistaken that Dickopf translates as Dick Head?"

"You are mistaken Herr Director. It is just a name that sounds like that. But yes, he was very controversial in how he handled ex-Nazis when he was in charge of the German Federal Criminal Police before he came to Interpol. Something my department is not proud of and has worked hard to expunge, if that is an acceptable word."

"Yes, that's a perfectly good word, but I am more surprised Dickopf doesn't mean Dick Head."

"Well, Dick Head in German would be Schwanz Kopf"

"Schwantz Kopf, hmm, interesting. I'm going to make a note of that if you don't mind, this language thing still bamboozles the hell out of me every day." He wrote it down on in his notebook and poured himself another drink.

"Anyway, as I was saying, we are pretty convinced that Dick Head, or Schwantz Kopf as you call him, helped protect Der Felsen by making it almost impossible to get any information. And I, between you and me, suspect someone in our organization is still helping them. That's why *your* boss, Hans Marenholtz, and I decided to get personally involved. Does that answer your question?"

Darmstaedter was so totally confused by the whole Dick Head discussions that he'd forgotten what his question even was.

"Perfectly, Sir," said Bunter, desperate to move on. "You said we'd opened a narrow door..?"

"Yes," responded the director, taking another large swig of Maker's Mark. "Though I'm not too certain about the size of the door itself, I was referring to the narrow opening."

Darmstaedter was more convinced than ever that the director had been hitting the sauce pretty heavily before their meeting, and hoped this would lead somewhere productive eventually.

"Look boys, we've been trying to understand exactly what it is that Der Felsen has been up to these last few years. We know they've moved out of arms dealing for the most part, like all the other big traders - too many arms, not enough money - into something that involves unlawful and illegal land grabbing for mining, deforestation, and agriculture. What we don't know is who their shareholders are - other than those hunters who were killed - nor how they're going about doing it."

"And do you have any leads as to who would be trying to sabotage them by killing the hunters, Sir?" asked Bunter. "The two of us have hit a brick wall."

"Not really, son. But the brick wall you hit may also have the doorway with the narrow opening that I mentioned. That's where we need you two to visit Der Felsen and speak to the head guy, Geoffrey-Philippe van der Borrekens."

"To be honest Herr Director we haven't even been able to establish where Der Felsen is situated. We appear to be blocked every time we attempt to find out."

"I know, my friend. That's been deliberate on the part of my predecessors and your old bosses. But Hans Marenholz and I are not the old school assholes that they were. We know each other well and we're determined to get rid of the hidden agendas and red-tape bullshit flowing through the halls of criminal investigation organizations like sperm from a donkey's penis."

The metaphor was almost too much for Darmstaedter who took a huge sip of his drink and almost drained the glass. The director quickly poured him another as he continued to talk.

"So Chief Marenholz and I got hold of your minister of the interior, and together with the attorney general, he gave us permission to access anything you need. But most importantly you have an appointment with that van der Borrekens son-of-a-bitch at their headquarters in Thuringia tomorrow at ten. It's not that easy to get to - deliberately, I imagine - and I'm warning you, you may be in for some hiking."

At nine-forty the next morning, having abandoned their rental vehicle where the road from Suhl abruptly ended, Bunter and Darmstaedter found themselves on a goat path leading to what they hoped was Burg Waldengraf. In the distance they could just make out some rather ominous gates on what seemed to be close to the summit of Grosser Beerberg.

"Jesus," panted Bunter feeling as if he'd just had a four hour session with Clare on her giant rubber ball. "How high is the Grosser Beerberg anyway? It feels like we've ascended Everest."

"Hardly my friend. The Beerberg is only nine hundred and eighty-three meters tall and as you can see, we are not even above the tree line of the Thuringian forest."

"Speaking of Beerberg I could use a cold pint right about now."

"What is it with you English speakers and your direct translations? The 'Beer' in Beerberg has nothing to do with beer. Do you know there is a place in the Czech Republic called Bendova? Or a town in Turkey called Arcelik Sokak? Do you believe any of those activities are prevalent in those places?"

"Probably not, but more interesting is how you know about them."

"I read a lot and I store everything." Darmstaedter tapped his head and Bunter once more marveled at its size. Darmstaedter grimaced in dismay at the illogical minds of non-German speakers. "Well, we are here now and maybe Mr. Van der Borrekens will give you a cold beer. I on the other hand am more interested in why the road ended a kilometer ago. How do they get here? I am sure they don't hike like this."

As they approached the gate, two guards appeared armed with Heckler & Koch HK416 assault rifles.

"Those are special forces only rifles," whispered Darmstaedter . "These people are serious."

Darmstaedter spoke to the guards in German, and while they appeared to have a hard time understanding exactly what he was saying, they had clearly been expecting them, and one of the guards opened the gate and told them to wait at the guardhouse. A few minutes later they heard the sound of a small motorized vehicle approaching, and then out of the trees appeared a golf car with tank treads.

"You will please to get on," said the guard obviously favoring the universal language of broken English.

The path to the castle itself led directly through the forest for about fifteen minutes. At first it was eerily quiet, and then all of a sudden they heard the distinct sound of heavy machine gun fire and mortar explosions.

"Jesus Christ!" yelled Bunter. "Take cover."

The golf cart driver, who'd said nothing up to this point, turned to them and with a heavy Hispanic accent said, "Do not worry. These are just training sessions."

"For what, "shouted Bunter over the noise, "taking over a small country?"

"No," laughed the driver. "Just small parts of a big country." He must have realized he'd said too much as he immediately shut up and accelerated along the path.

"What the hell is going on here, Constantin? I really don't like it."

"Too late for that, Matthew. We are about to enter the devil's *arschloch*."

Bunter may not have understood German, but Darmstaedter's meaning became only too clear as the golf cart passed beneath a low dark arch that narrowed before it opened up onto a wide cobbled courtyard. It certainly felt like they'd passed through a demonic asshole. He shivered as the cart made its way to the surprisingly modern steel doors set in the front of the castle. The cart stopped and the doors slid open automatically as the two policemen walked up the front steps.

"Good morning, gentlemen, please come in."

Their greeter was a young woman with fiery red hair dressed in a short blue skirt and cream blouse. As professional as Bunter and Darmstaedter were trying to be, neither of them could take their eyes off the stunningly beautiful woman who simply smiled as if she were used to every man ogling her. Which of course she probably was because they probably did.

"Please come this way inspectors, and I will take you to Mr Fleisser's office."

"Umm, excuse me, ma'am," said Bunter, "but we actually have an appointment with Mr. van der Borrekens."

"Yes, I know. Unfortunately Mr. van der Borrekens was called away unexpectedly and won't be back for a few weeks. Mr. Rudi Fleisser is the acting CEO of Der Felsen. The board is set to approve his promotion next week. He will of course explain. And my name's not 'ma'am', it's Mab."

Darmstaedter was desperately trying to place her accent. Her looks certainly fit an Irish or Scots stereotype, but her voice had an American lilt to it. His mind soon drifted off with names and accents as they followed her along the brightly lit and very modern corridor, antithetical to what one would have expected in a castle, and he fixated on her bottom as it bounced along merrily with every step. He missed his wife a lot. And his mistress even more.

"You can wait here, inspectors," said Mab, indicating a particularly uncomfortable looking couch that rested against a stone wall, and next to a door that both policemen suspected must be Rudi Fleisser's office. Both sat down and looked around at the rather dreary reception area. It certainly didn't seem like the headquarters of a successful company. Mab wished them well and walked off to another part of the castle.

"This looks more like some cheap warehouse in a dockyard than a stately old castle."

"Ja, it seems such a waste of a magnificent building. Although I must admit Mab added some elegance."

"Jesus, Constantin. Have you ever met a woman you didn't find attractive?"

"Not yet, and not while I still have the ability to admire such a magnificent derrière. You should start, it will loosen you up."

Before Bunter could respond, the door opened and a small hideous gnome-like creature in a black business dress and sporting a large bandage on the end of her nose walked out. Much to Bunter's horror, Darmstaedter began to study the gnome. Then he smiled at Bunter and shook his head.

"Guten morgen, meine herren. Herr Fleisser will see you now." Her contempt for the two men could not have been clearer and Bunter could have sworn she snarled at them like an angry badger as they walked into the office.

If the outside was austere, Rudi Fleisser's office was magnificent. The walls were covered in light grey silk wallpaper, the floors strewn with Persian carpets, and while neither Bunter nor Darmstaedter knew much about art, they recognized the quality of the work on display. Rudi, who'd been sitting behind his large mahogany desk, stood up to greet them. Darmstaedter looked at him in amazement. He knew he'd seen him before, but he had no idea where. He quickly recovered as he shook Rudi's hand and then watched as Rudi walked over to

Bunter, who had wandered over to one of the paintings.

"I notice you are looking at that landscape, Inspector Bunter," Rudi said. "It is by Adolf Hitler and was given to one of our founders by the man itself."

If he'd meant to shock both men, he succeeded admirably.

"Oh, I'm sorry. I realize that is probably non-PC as the Americans say. But we have never denied our roots, and I am sure you gentlemen have already done enough research to know exactly what I am talking about."

"Yes of course, Herr Fleisser," said Darmstaedter. "We have had access to your history, but history is not why we are here. We are interested in the present."

"Of course, of course, my dear inspector. I was merely giving you a little context. Please sit down and I will ask Liebmut to get us some coffee."

As if on cue, the horrid little gnome appeared and, once given their coffee orders, stormed back out. Rudi must have noticed Bunter's frown.

"Ach, don't mind Liebmut. She has been here for forty years and she is unused to outsiders, especially the police. And she is also in pain after an unfortunate incident that took off the tip of her nose. Which of course, brings me to your visit. We do not normally grant interviews, but I was asked by a rather impressive person in the German Bundestag to be of help to you."

"Thank you, Mr. Fleisser. We appreciate your time. Our visit is important because we are investigating a number of murders of prominent men who seem to be tied in some way to your organization."

"I'm afraid you have me at a disadvantage."

"Why so, sir?"

"I am not aware of anyone in my organization being murdered..."

"Herr Fleisser," said Darmstaedter taking out a small notepad. "We know that Dieter Heidenreich and Donald Brink Jr. were shareholders of Der Felsen. We also believe," he consulted his notepad, "that Major General Mohammed Al Rahim of Dubai, who also ran a company called Otterlo Business Corporation was possibly a shareholder..."

"Gentleman," said Rudi standing up and walking over to a filing cabinet. If Darmstaedter and Bunter had any expectation that Rudi might open it and disclose some of its contents, they were wrong. He stood next to it like a German Shepherd guarding a bunker. "I cannot and will not disclose our shareholders. That would be completely unethical."

Bunter, who was still tired from his hike and a little thrown by the angry gnome, couldn't help himself. "I was unaware, sir, that ethics entered into your business model at all."

Rudi drew himself to his full five foot six, his black eyes seeming to flash. "You forget yourself

Inspector Bunter. I am talking to you at the request
of someone who would be extremely unhappy if I
disclosed your rude behavior. Now I think perhaps
this interview is over, ja?"

All off a sudden Darmstaedter knew exactly
where he'd seen Rudi before.

"I apologize for my colleague's remark," he
interjected, causing Bunter to give him the evil
eye. "He is English and therefore very direct. If
you cannot disclose your shareholders, and I
understand why, please would you explain to us
exactly what business you are in?"

Rudi seemed to relax and, turning from the still
fuming Bunter he spoke to Darmstaedter. "That I
can tell you. As you know I am sure, we began as a
legitimate arms dealer trading in the international
markets. By the way with the cooperation of a
number of governments including yours, Inspector
Bunter. This was up until a few years ago when
the company was still run by the uncle of the late
Mr. van der Borrekens."

"The late Mr. van der Borrekens? The young
lady who showed us in said he was called away,
not that he was dead..."

"Did I say 'late Mr. van der Borrekens'? Oh dear,
I meant the late uncle of Mr. van derBorrekens,
who of course was also a van der Borrekens. He
used his noble title, Ridder. So Ridder Henrickus
van der Borrekens is dead, but Geoffrey-Philippe
van der Borrekens is very much alive. Confusing
is it not when you have families in the business?

Anyway unfortunately Geoffrey-Philippe, who is very much alive, as I said, is visiting one of our clients in Ethiopia."

Rudi knew he'd slipped up. He hoped to hell Demetri had disposed of Geoffrey's corpse properly. He should never have agreed to 'help the police with some enquiries' as the German minister had asked him. Damn these two meddling cops.

"You were saying you are no longer in the arms business?" Bunter asked.

"Ja, ja, yes indeed I was," Rudy replied, recovering his composure. "No, today I can say that we are in the real estate business."

"Really, how interesting," said Darmstaedter. "So you buy up real estate in countries like Ethiopia?"

"Exactly, Inspector Darmstaedter. Ethiopia and other countries in Africa. Real estate for development."

"I don't understand," said Bunter standing up and walking towards a window that overlooked the large forested estate. "If you are no longer in the arms business, why do you need mercenaries and why would one of your mercenaries have said you used them to take over land abroad?"

If Rudi had been confused before, he was enraged now - and both policemen knew it.

"Look," said Bunter, "To be honest we aren't that interested in what you're doing. That's someone else's problem. We're working on a very specific case where a number of extremely rich and prominent people who may have been shareholders of Der Felsen were killed in what the news media reported as mysterious hunting accidents."

"We are not after you, we are after their murderers," said Darmstaedter.

Rudi closed his eyes tightly and breathed out a number of times. He could feel one of his panic attacks coming on. He walked over to his desk and sat on the edge so he was higher than the two policemen.

"You have said things that are pure speculation. You have asked questions that are both rude and arrogant. You are putting me in a very awkward position in that I would like to help you with your enquiries but I do not know the answers. We have numerous shareholders who are all rich and prominent as you put it, but this is not a public company and therefore our records are unavailable You cannot get a court order because we are registered in Lichtenstein. Now I really must ask you to leave."

"Of course and our apologies for any misunderstanding, Herr Fleisser."

Bunter looked at Darmstaedter and wondered where he was going with his apology.

"But before we leave," Darmstaedter added, I just want one question answered?"

"What is it?"

"Did you know Herr Heidenreich on a social level?"

"I have no recollection of ever meeting him. I am not sure I would even recognize him if I saw him at a social event."

"How about his buttocks? Would you recognize those?"

"What are you implying, you filthy swine?" Fleisser looked as if he was about to burst, and even Bunter's mustache bristled in confusion. Darmstaedter opened his briefcase and extracted a photograph from a folder. "What a pretty Schulerin - schoolgirl - you are, and how excited you look to see the teacher spank Heidenreich's pimply bottom?"

Half an hour later the two policemen were in their rental car returning to Suhl.

"Good God, Consantin. You were quite spectacular. I had no idea where you were going with that."

"Thank you, Matthew, I don't know what we would have achieved if I hadn't recognized him from Frau Heidenreich's photos. And to be honest I wasn't sure he wasn't going to have us killed then and there and then deny we'd ever been to the castle."

"I agree and I suspect when he finally recovers he may well want to have us killed. What I don't understand is how someone like him can be in charge of an organization like that? He seems like a nervous nelly, a complete idiot, but I suppose we got what we needed out of him."

He thought back to Rudi breathing in and out of a paper bag trying to recover from his anxiety attack. When he could once again speak clearly, he reluctantly told them about PaloMar and how he suspected that they were behind the killings. Beyond that, and swearing he'd only been to the 'Naughty School Girl' club once, he would say no more.

Back in the castle Rudi had managed, with the aid of a large scotch, to calm down. He thought carefully about the situation, and decided he'd better call Demetri in Ethiopia and warn him that the police were now involved. He dialed his number and much to his surprise Demetri answered on the first ring.

"Demetri, it's Rudi."

"Yes, I know, Rudi. Your name came up on my phone."

"Good, well I'm afraid we have a bit of a problem. I have just had a visit from two policemen who know about PaloMar and the murders."

"Hold on one second, Rudi. I just have to load my gun..."

"Mein Gott, who are you about to shoot?"

He was surprised to see the door open and Demetri come in followed by a supposedly dead Geoffrey. His surprise was short lived and so was he, as Demetri swiftly shot him in the head with a single 9mm bullet from his new Maxim 9 with its built-in silencer.

"I like that gun, Demetri," said Geoffrey-Philippe as he hobbled over to take a look at the glassy eyed corpse of Rudi. "Well, now that's out of the way let's get our force together and finally go and finish those bastards."

Chapter 27

IN WHICH ROGER MEETS THE REMAINING MEMBERS OF THE EXPEDITION AND A POTENTIAL ISSUE POPS UP

Addis Ababa, Ethiopia
Within a day of current events

"Ah, here he is," said Freddy. He beamed as if he was welcoming Roger to a meeting of the glee club. "This is Roger Storm."

As Roger walked up to the table, he raised his hand in what he hoped was a masculine enough gesture to the bunch of clearly hardened mercenaries. There were three men and one woman. The woman, Enku Melgiste, a stunning Ethiopian, spoke several tribal languages and would serve, Freddy explained, as their interpreter once they got wherever they were going.

No one seemed to be talking business as they ate and so Roger, after helping himself to the food on the side table, sat down in the only open chair between two of the other mercenaries.

The three men, Paulus Mhlangu, Abel Letsoko and Khosan Belezi introduced themselves briefly and then began to laugh with Ishea and Zech.

"Like Freddy you are originally from South Africa?" asked Khosan, who finally turned to Roger.

"Yes we grew up together. But I lived and he died." Roger said it as a joke, but Khosan didn't smile.

"Freddy has died many times," he responded as if he was revealing a mystery, "and no doubt he will die again"

"You mean he's faked his death many times?"

"Yes, it is a good thing to be able to do in our business. In truth, we have all died. We are all new men and citizens of many countries but our own."

"Where are you from originally?"

Like you and Freddy, we are also from South Africa. We worked for Executive Outcomes..."

"I remember reading about them after I saw that movie *Blood Diamond*. Weren't they a private military contractor? Started when apartheid ended and those special units were disbanded?"

"Yes, you're right. The three of us were recruited from 32 Battalion, and we fought in Angola and Sierra Leone before we ended up in Papua New Guinea with some of the Sandline soldiers. That's where we met Ishea and Zech."

"But they weren't working for Freddy and Conchita yet..?"

"No. In 1998 we became outlaws when the South African government passed a law banning foreign military assistance. We had no family, no home and nowhere to turn. We were living in a refugee camp in Zambia when Zech and Ishea found us and offered us a job with PaloMar. And that's how we got to know Freddy, Jamie and Conchita. Our job was to help train the armies of the people we sold our weapons to...and to assist Ishea on Freddy's side project." He laughed.

"What's that?"

"You know, discouraging big game hunters or helping them to die in 'hunting accidents'."

"I thought you'd stopped that."

Khosan looked confused. "Not really. I helped Ishea take some people out a week ago."

"Really? Zech told me you hadn't killed anyone for a while."

"Well," replied Khosan looking over at Zech who was in a heavy conversation with Enku, "Zech doesn't really feel the same way about hunting as we do. So maybe they just don't tell him anymore. It's an obsession for Freddy and we help him." He turned back to Ishea who was explaining something to do with security and Roger's thoughts turned to Freddy and his obsession with saving wildlife. He couldn't remember Freddy ever being preoccupied with it before. Perhaps that was just another side of Freddy's that Roger didn't know. He'd have to find out more.

Once lunch was over, the group got down to business. The same maps Roger had seen in London were unfurled on the table and everyone stood up and listened to Ishea as he pointed out the route they'd be taking to the Omo Valley, consulting their translator, Enku, every few minutes. Roger stood as well so as not to look too out of place and feigned interest, but no one asked his opinion and he had none to offer. His mind was totally focused on Conchita who was leaning over the table making suggestions every now and then that had Ishea and Jamie nodding. Freddy stood to the side, having a rather animated conversation on his cell phone that Roger couldn't quite hear. Conchita looked up, caught him staring at her and smiled.

"Hold on, ladies and gentlemen." Freddy walked up to the table and put his phone down. "We have a slight problem."

Everyone stopped what they were doing and gave him their full attention. "That was Eduardo - our operations manager in London, Roger. He said he had a visit from two police officers yesterday asking what PaoloMar's relationship with Der Felsen was."

"British police?" asked Adrian.

"Apparently one from Interpol and the other from some branch of the German police. They're working together on a series of murders and wanted to speak to a Mr Ramsey Sinclair."

"Who's that?" Roger asked.

"That's me," replied Freddy. "I probably should have told you that both Jamie and I had to change our names when we applied for residency visas in the UK after we'd 'died'."

It made as much sense to Roger as everything else, and so he didn't even bother to question it.

"Anyway, this is a slight problem because Eduardo told them we were in Ethiopia somewhere, buildings schools, and he doesn't think that'll be the end of it."

"It damn well isn't going to be the end of it," said Jamie. "How the fuck did they even connect us to Der Felsen unless Der Felsen told them? Zecheriah can you see if you can get hold of your contact. Check if he knows anything."

"Sure, Jamie," replied the big Englishman, who took out his cell phone and walked into the villa.

"I don't like it at all," said Jamie. He stared directly at Roger who didn't quite know where to look. "I trust everyone of us except Roger. But he doesn't know anything and I'm pretty sure he wouldn't have a clue how to contact anyone regardless."

Everyone else looked at Roger, who opened his mouth like a fish that's just been taken off a hook.

"It's not us," Conchita jumped in, saving Roger yet again. "And it certainly isn't Roger. Jamie. I'm surprised at you. What a ridiculous suggestion. Let's see what Zech says after he speaks to his friend. This is not the time to panic."

"No one is panicking Conchita,"said Ishea, "and please don't get defensive about your boyfriend. Whatever Zech finds out. I think we can safely say that the only way the cops could have gotten to us is through someone at Der Felsen."

So that was it, Roger thought. Ishea must have really had feelings for Conchita at some point. He was jealous, the big fucker. Roger looked at Ishea and smiled. He experienced a sense of satisfaction he hadn't felt in years. Ishea stared back at him, his blue eyes intense and hooded. Roger should have felt terrified but he didn't. He felt great. He almost gave Ishea the finger, but then thought better of it.

"First," said Freddy, who'd kept quiet up to this point, "Roger is someone I asked to come on this trip for a very specific purpose. Whether you like that or not, Ishea and Jamie, I don't care. I trust him and Conchita does too, as much as we trust you. And you know we trust you with our lives. So that conversation is over. Second, Ishea's right. Someone at Der Felsen suggested we'd been involved in killing their shareholders. There's nothing else it can be. The good news is there's no evidence to connect us and there is no way Der Felsen could know about Menelik yet. We're the only ones who do."

At that moment Zecheriah returned. He didn't look happy.

"Not good news, I'm afraid to say. He's not answering."

"Maybe he's in a meeting," suggested Jamie.

"No, we have a texting signal. Even if he was in a meeting he would have sent me a signal in return."

"Well it's not conclusive," Jamie said, even though one look at Zecheriah suggested something different. "Maybe he doesn't have his phone on him."

Before they'd even had time to speculate further, Enku, who was looking out the window, said, "The police are here and they don't look happy."

Two minutes later, the same officer who'd stamped their passports on the plane walked onto the patio. Enku was right, he certainly didn't look happy.

Zecheriah pulled out a chair for him.

"I'm sorry to intrude," said Captain Mulugeta, "but there are a couple of things you should know."

"Some lunch Captain?" said Freddy, indicating towards the remains of their lunch.

The policeman didn't even acknowledge the gesture. "Look, we know you do a lot of good things for us, so we try to help you out as much as possible. But there are a few things going on that I don't like and I don't think anybody above me is going to like either."

"I'm not sure what you mean, Captain," Jamie said rather unconvincingly.

"I'm not naïve, Jamie. I know what you really do, and I'm sure people in my country have benefited over the years, but I don't know what you have planned now and I can't imagine that this group," he pointed at the mercenaries, "is here to help build hospitals or clinics." Jamie started to protest but the policemen held his hand up to stop him.

"Whatever it is you have planned there is another group who seems to know about it"

"What do you mean?" asked Ishea.

"I mean shortly after you got to the hotel, a Boeing Business Jet landed with twelve people aboard. People who clearly are not here to build hospitals either. On their customs forms they claim to be property developers who are here to scope out large leases of land in the western regions. I'm sure you may recognize the name of the group's leader, Geoffrey-Philippe van der Borrekens. Ring a bell?"

"Fuck." It was the first time Roger had heard Conchita swear. "Yes, of course we know him Captain. His company and ours are rivals in certain fields."

"That I know, Miss Palomino. What I do not know is why you are both in Abbis at the same time. I have to have your word that you are not here to sell arms to any groups in Ethiopia..?"

"I can assure you we are not," replied Conchita. "Captain, we have always been honest with you and you have always been very supportive of us. I promise you that we are on a humanitarian mission. Not to build hospitals, as you have rightly surmised, but to meet with a man who needs our financial assistance to help people in your country and others in the region. These men," she pointed at the soldiers, "are here for our protection, that is all."

"Look," said Captain Mulugeta, "I have not had any reason to doubt your intentions in the past and I accept your word today. But when two rival international arms traders arrive in Ethiopia at the same time with men who are clearly soldiers, I begin to worry."

"And we do too, Captain, "said Freddy, "but our mission is a peaceful one. We'll do whatever we need to avoid trouble, I promise you."

"In which case you won't mind if my men search this place and your equipment for weapons of any sort? Not that I don't trust you, but I will have to have that in my report."

"Of course not, you go right ahead," replied Freddy. "You're free to look wherever you like."

Roger watched in horror as the Captain and five of his men who'd been hanging about outside began to look through their rooms and luggage and finally their cars. He was totally convinced they'd be pulling out sub machine guns and pistols and whatever else he imagined mercenaries carried on missions. To his amazement, however, they uncovered nothing and after a brief chat about staying safe and keeping in contact, Zecheriah walked Captain Mulugeta back to his vehicle. Roger watched through the window as he and Zecheriah got into a pretty animated conversation. Then to Roger's surprise Zecheriah pushed an envelope into the captain's pocket just before he drove away. He was about to ask Freddy what was going on. If they didn't give bribes why had Zech seemingly handed one to the captain? At that moment Zecheriah came back into the room.

He's worried that we're going to cause a great deal of trouble for him. I tried to assure him we're not."

No one breathed a sigh of relief. In fact, the tension in the room was palpable.

"How in God's name did we fuck this up so badly?" asked Jamie.

"We didn't fuck up," responded Ishea sharply. "We planned everything to the nth degree. You know as well as I do that every mission, no matter how well thought through, has a certain degree of risk. None of us know what happened at Der Felsen when the cops arrived."

"I think I can build a scenario."

"And what's that, Freddy?" Ishea asked.

"I've begun to suspect for some time that there was something going on between Geoffrey and Rudi Fleisser."

"They never liked each other, even when we were there. It's nothing new," said Jamie.

"I understand but at that point they needed each other, whether they disliked each other or not. Der Felsen always had a strongman and a business man side by side at the top. But I don't think that's necessarily the case anymore. If they are officially in the land- grabbing business, despite needing some forces to help negotiate people off their ancestral ground, why does Der Felsen, and especially Rudi, have use any longer for a hot-headed psychopath like Geoffrey, whose only use is devising awful ways to kill people?"

"That makes sense," Jamie said. "I mean, I remember exactly what was going on in the room when we refused to sell to them. Rudi would have kept trying to negotiate but Geoffrey wanted us dead. So more than likely Rudi is trying to get rid of Geoffrey by setting him up."

"And that means one thing," Conchita said, standing up and moving to the window. "Geoffrey is in Ethiopia to kill us."

None of the others, Paulus, Abel, Khosan, Enku or Roger had said anything at all during this discussion. Excluding Enku, whom Roger imagined worked in a slightly different capacity for PaloMar, they were soldiers who knew their place wasn't to question but simply obey. Roger, on the other hand, hadn't contributed anything because a) he couldn't, and b) his original fear of being in the company of homicidal lunatics (Conchita being the exception, because horny people will overlook anything) had made him start to tremble in an alarming manner.

So far no one had mentioned the one thing he thought needed serious mentioning.

"So, I'm assuming the operation is off?"

"Don't be bloody daft, Roger," said Zech. "This means we get to kill two birds with one stone, man. Show some backbone. I promise you you're going to need it."

"Yes, if we handle this correctly," agreed Freddy, "we could take out Geoffrey and still get to Menelik. Perfect!"

Roger was about to ask about the fact that they had no weapons and a lot less manpower, but on realizing that their previously rather grumpy group had lightened up considerably at the prospect of eliminating Geoffrey (whoever he may have been) he decided to postpone his concern. As it turned out he needn't have worried about the weaponery but the larger numbers in the Der Felsen contingency would soon prove to be an issue.

Chapter 28

In which the two Inspectors and Clare realize that they're too late to stop anything

London, England

The bar at Dukes Hotel on St James's Place in London makes some of the best Martinis in the world. It's pretty crowded at five in the evening, but the two inspectors and Clare had managed to get a table and order Martinis made with Sipsmith gin, which the waiter had not recommended for Clare because 'women find it too dry.' This did not sit well with Clare who promptly told him to fuck off and very nearly got them booted out before Bunter intervened by pulling out his Interpol ID.

As they sipped the ridiculously expensive drinks Clare had promised to pay for, Bunter rather dejectedly brought up their meeting with Eduardo de Mello, PaloMar's head of operations.

"All we got from the bugger was that the three principles, Ramsey Sinclair, Alan Lomax and their partner Conchita Palomino, which sounds like a totally made-up name if you ask me, were somewhere in Ethiopia building schools."

"And you don't believe it?" asked Clare

"No, we do not," replied Darmstaedter, who'd decided after his first sip that he was more of a wine or beer man than a Martini drinker. "On the contrary my dear Clare, when you have two of the biggest arms dealers in the world together in one place, one claiming to be building schools and the other buying up real estate, then something stinks, do you not agree?

"The problem," Bunter said, pulling an olive from his Martini, "is that there isn't much we can do at this stage."

"And why's that?" asked Clare as she signaled the waiter to bring over the Martini cart for a refill. He pretended not to see her.

"We have absolutely no proof that the PaloMar people actually killed any of those hunters. All we have is the suggestion from that wimpy little fucker, Rudi."

"I believe him," said Darmstaedter. "He was not in a position to lie to us. But Matthew is right Clare, we have absolutely no proof. No evidence, no witnesses. Just the ramblings of an Austrian who likes to dress as a schoolgirl."

"But surely you can get them in Ethiopia...catch them doing some massive arms deal or something like that?"

"Again, unfortunately not. My counterpart in Addis Ababa says that they only operate above board over there. PaloMar has built numerous schools and clinics, and Der Felsen has been instrumental in buying huge tracts of land for agriculture. But, as Constantin says, the whole thing stinks. There's no question in either of our minds that someone associated with PaloMar murdered a whole bunch of hunters who were all shareholders in Der Felsen."

"Well, that puts them way up there in my book. I'm for anyone who bags a few hunters."

"Yes, but Constantin and I cannot take the same attitude. Our job is not to take into account why people do what they do.."

"Oh pooh, Matthew. You're so up-tight about things. So let's have another Martini and then you and Constantin can tell me about Rudi dressing up as a schoolgirl and perhaps I can find out about the place he goes to. Sounds more fun. Now, where is that blasted man who walks around pushing the drinks trolley like a transvestite French maid? Hoi you, over here."

The poor waiter took one look in her direction and promptly disappeared into the kitchen.

Chapter 29

IN WHICH ROGER GETS A GUN
AND MEETS A RASTA

Addis Ababa and the road to Omo, Ethiopia
Same time

L ater that afternoon, after a rather hurried
but strangely satisfying love-making session
involving techniques Conchita must have
learned while interrogating prisoners in Mossad
headquarters, Roger and she lay together on the
bed pretending to sleep so as not to have to discuss
all that had transpired after lunch. He could hear
Conchita breathing heavily, but he knew she was
far from being asleep as was he. Finally, he put out
his hand and clutched hers tightly.

"Are you worried, Roger?" she asked.

"Look, Conchita. This whole thing has been
bizarre from the moment I met you and Freddy
in Paris."

She stiffened slightly.

"Except for falling madly in love with you, of
course," he hastily added. "These things, your

world, mercenaries, arms dealing...they are so far from anything I've ever imagined."

"I know, my darling," she put her head on his shoulder, "but they exist, and while I feel awful that you are caught up in this, you're going to have to trust us to get you through it."

"I want to, believe me. But I don't know the first thing about fighting. I've never even held a gun let alone fired it at someone."

"That's not surprising. You are, as you say, in a world you didn't even know existed. I would probably feel the same way in your world and I doubt if I would last as long as you have in ours. So believe me I do understand. Let me explain where we hope to go with this. I realize we've told you some of this but I also know it's hard to understand at first. That Africa, or at least this part of Africa is being exploited by the West once again is obvious. We can't fight China and Korea and India, who are at the core of the situation, because they're too powerful. But we can fight the one organization that has allowed them to gain control of such enormous pieces of land at the expense of the people and animals who inhabit it."

"Der Felsen and Geoffrey?"

"Yes, precisely. A number of years ago, as we said at lunch, when we met with Geoffrey and his number two, Rudi Fleisser, they were trying to buy us out. They told us precisely what business they were moving into, and it was something we felt we had to try to stop. We had enough money to last several lifetimes. None of us had families or dependents, and I suppose we were sick of selling weapons to people who killed other people out of greed. Freddy said it to you in London. I can't make excuses for what we did back then. Perhaps if there is a God he will punish me for those transgressions when I die, but the very least we can do now is try to help. We may not succeed, but no one in the history of the world ever has without trying. Menelik, when you meet him, and I hope you will see this, has an aura and a presence that exists in few people I've ever met. In fact no one I've ever met. He is unique, Roger. If anyone can inspire people to rise up and overthrow their oppressors, it's Menelik. Plus he has the lineage."

"Which may just be myth, you know that?"

"Perhaps, but in Africa it is impossible to separate myth and legend from fact and reality. So, in essence it's true even if it isn't. One thing we can see in black and white though, is that his ancestors were the only rulers in Africa ever to have won against the colonialists. That alone is epic, something that will have power in every country around Ethiopia."

"Still today? That was a long time ago."

"Africa has a long memory. It doesn't forget easily, and it never forgives. We have to try this, we have to try to give people back what was taken or there is no hope at all. And as for the hunters... well they are not at the core of our operation, but they do play an integral part. Ever since I met him and we started to work in Africa, Freddy has had a love affair with the animals. And it's grown over the years. He has always hated people who come over here to kill these beautiful creatures so they can mount the heads on their walls. He sees that as an offense against the universe. And Africa without its herds is not a whole continent."

"I agree. Killing hunters seems extreme but personally I don't really have any qualms. Although I'm glad you've given up selling guns. That was harder for me to stomach."

"Well until we realized that Der Felsen was arranging the hunts as part of their shareholder agreement, we tried not to kill the hunters. We mostly tried to scare them, warning them beforehand with an anonymous letter, though that hardly ever worked. There is a natural arrogance in people who cannot see why destroying beautiful creatures for their own pleasure is wrong. The letters certainly never worked with Der Felsen shareholders. So we started killing the hunters the way they killed the animals. It may be brutal, but judging by the reaction of Der Felsen, it is effective. And it's proved to be pivotal. But now the police suspect PaloMar and that's not good. I'm not sure how long we have until they get to us, so we have to move fast. We can't let anyone stop this mission before its begun."

"Okay, I get all that but it's still so far from what I know that I can't believe I am going to be of any help. I can't imagine what I can do. I am just being honest."

"No, my darling. You are being...how do you say it...self- deprecating? You will help Menelik, you'll see. He says so many brilliant things. What you will do is find that one thing that matters most and then it will be our job to get him and his message to the people.But enough for now."

Roger was about to explain the difference between self- deprecating and knowingly useless when she reached down and grabbed his penis which much to his surprise seemed un-phased by their impending doom as it rose up rather smartly. He grabbed a handful of her generous buttocks and heaved to as a friend of his from the navy used to say. Afterwards, when they'd dressed and made their way out to the patio to enjoy cocktails with the others and talk excitedly about the trip the next morning, as if it was an outing to a church picnic, Roger realized that whatever happened he was more in love than he'd ever been, as cliched and short sighted as that may have seemed.

"Have a drink, Roger," said Jamie handing him a beer. "They won't attack us here."

His words were hardly comforting.

The next morning they left Addis just after dawn and Roger found himself sitting in the back seat of a three-car caravan of tan-colored Toyota Land Cruisers.

"We haven't really had a one-on-one discussion about everything Roger," said Freddy, who was sitting next to him. "I'm sorry about that. I do owe you an explanation about what happened after Jamie's mock-funeral and my suicide."

Roger thought about it for a few seconds and decided that nothing Freddy told him would make any more comprehensible this entire theater of the absurd, for which he seemed the only member of the audience.

"You know what, Freddy. It doesn't really matter. I really am glad you're alive and that you're doing things that could potentially change the world. I think Brian will be too if we make it through this alive and are able to tell him. You and he were always my best friends, and I've never met anyone since that could ever replace you two. When I thought I'd lost you I honestly felt like someone had ripped out a huge part of my heart. I got over it eventually, but all the same I could never really stop thinking of you and all the amazing things you introduced me to when we were kids. In a way, this isn't that much different. It's a continent burning, rather than a school burning."

Freddy just looked at Roger without saying anything.

"I also, though this is weirder than everything else I've been through in the last two weeks, have fallen in love with the most beautiful woman imaginable, and I suspect she has some feeling for me."

"Why do you think that's so weird?"

"Well for a start I'm such a damn fuck-up compared to everyone else she'd probably ever met. I just can't imagine why she'd fall for me."

"Good Christ, man," said Zecheriah who'd been listening to the whole conversation. "That's precisely why. You're everything we're not."

"Yes," agreed Paulus, "you are probably the only nice guy she's ever met.

"Or the only one who hasn't been shot or shot someone," laughed Freddy. "Look Roger, jokes aside I do realize that you find this whole situation beyond belief, but if we can achieve anything at all I hope one day you will be able to look back and acknowledge that you were, be it in a small way, part of giving Africa back to the people to whom it belongs."

It wasn't the cheeriest of situations but somehow Roger's mood improved. He was in this whether he liked it or not and he decided to make the best of it.

"Zech, when are we stopping?"

"The coffee farm's another few kilometers, Freddy. So about ten minutes."

"Why are we going to a coffee farm?" Roger asked.

"We're picking up a few supplies for the trip. And the coffee is excellent."

Up until that point in time the ride had been pretty uneventful. It began on a fairly decent road and the few villages they passed through looked like villages anywhere in Africa with goats and donkey carts. A kilometer past the town of Shashemene the convoy turned left at a small sign that read simply 'coffee estate'. The condition of the road became suddenly deplorable and they bounced over the corrugations and potholes till the road finally ran out at an iron gate with a guard house. As they approached a tall man with Rastafarian dreadlocks emerged with a huge grin and what looked like a sub-machine gun.

He knew everyone and everyone other than Roger knew him.

'Roger, this is Hondo" said Jamie who seemed most at home with the Rasta.

"Wa Ghana, mon?" said Hondo shaking Roger's hand.

"You almost sound Jamaican," Roger said, hoping he wasn't being rude.

"Very good mon," said Hondo, his grin getting even broader. "Yes, my family came here from Jamaica years ago to settle in Shashemene."

"There are still about two hundred Rastas here," added Jamie. "They were originally invited to Ethiopia by the Emperor Haile Sellasie."

"By way, Jamie mon, my Empress she says dat bad bredren dey pass through Shashemene early dis morning."

Roger had no idea what the hell Hondo was saying, but Jamie did because he turned to the others and said, "Hondo says his wife told him that some bad guys came through Shashemene earlier. Could only have been Geoffrey and his crew."

"We have to expect trouble at some point before we hit Arba Minch. Let's get the equipment loaded. I want everyone in full battle gear," Ishea said, going into command-mode.

Hondo opened the gates, and they drove another half kilometer to a farmhouse where a few more Rastafarians were standing next to large metal boxes. There was a table with a large coffee pot and mugs which the Rastafarians poured and handed round. Freddy was right, the coffee was amazing, though there wasn't time for a second cup before the mercenaries moved towards the boxes. Ishea and Zecheriah opened them and Roger saw that they contained weapons of all shapes and sizes. They began to examine them carefully until they were satisfied everything worked.

"I'm happy to help but I don't know exactly what to do," Roger said to Conchita who had picked up a flak jacket and an odd looking rifle.

"The experts are handling this. You have to do nothing but wait here. I will get everything for you."

Freddy and Jamie joined Roger and they watched the mercenaries and Enku, who was obviously not just a translator, suit and arm up with an array of both handguns and rifles.

"What are we going to be doing?" Roger asked.

"Whatever Ishea tells us to do. He's in charge from this point on."

"I'm at a bit of a loss. They last thing I fired was a Nerf gun. Have you guys shot stuff?"

"Of course," said Jamie, sounding slightly imperious. "We were arms traders. You don't think we tried out what we sold?"

"I don't have a clue what you did," responded Roger who was beginning to dislike Jamie almost as much as he disliked Ishea. "I haven't studied the day-to-day lives of arms traders. Not much help when you're trying to write a commercial for drain cleaner."

"It's okay Roger," said Freddy, once again trying to restore peace. "Yes both of us have fired weapons before though we've never really been in an actual combat situation."

"What do you mean you've never 'really' been in a combat situation?"

"Well," said Jamie, who seemed to be trying to make up for his rudeness, "we've obviously been in conflict zones when we meet our clients but not in a situation where people have actually shot at us. Look, I'm sure Conchita will get you a handgun and body armor. The chances of you having to use the gun are pretty slim, so don't worry."

"Whatever happens," Freddy put what he hoped was a reassuring hand on Roger's shoulder,"you couldn't be in better hands. Ishea, Zech, Paulus and the other guys are some of the most highly trained soldiers you will ever come across. And Conchita is better than all of them. She isn't going to let anyone harm you."

At that moment Conchita walked over to Roger with a flak jacket.

"Here, let me help you put this on the right way."

He assumed by now she realized that technicalities weren't his strong suit, and he would have no doubt had it on back to front.

"I want you to have a handgun as well," Conchita said, handing him a nasty looking pistol that he reluctantly took.

It was smaller than he imagined a handgun would be.

"This is a Beretta PX4. It what they call a sub-compact and it's very reliable."

"I'm sure it is, but I don't even know how to cock it."

"I will show you and you can shoot off a few rounds to get the feel. Watch out everyone'" she yelled, "Roger is going to shoot off a few rounds and they could go anywhere."

People wisely moved as far from him as they could, which proved to be sensible as his first few shots went wild. After six shots though he got the hang of it, or as close to the hang of shooting a handgun as one could possibly get after six shots. He clicked on the safety as Conchita had showed him and put it back in the holster that was strapped to the belt on his flak jacket. As scared as he may have been, he had enjoyed the feeling of power the gun gave him. He took the gun from its holster once more, pictured the grinning face of Harry Bones in front of him, and squeezed the trigger. The bullet ricocheted off the side of the farmhouse and narrowly missed Hondo who was smoking a joint and didn't seem to mind.

Roger stood by himself trying desperately not to overthink anything and watched as the others piled up what looked like enough weapons to equip a small country.

As he was about to get into one of the Land Cruisers an odd- looking truck rolled up from behind the farm house.

"This," said Freddy will be our transportation from now on. The Land Cruisers will stay here in the barn."

"I've never seen a truck like that," Roger remarked to no one in particular.

"It's a Unimog," said Khosan, who'd walked up to Roger. "We can't ride in the same vehicles we came here in. Too many people know we left Addis in the Land Cruisers, and no doubt some drone somewhere had eyes on them. This, my friend is one of PaloMar's best vehicles. It's got enough equipment to operate as a mobile headquarters and plenty of room for the ten of us to travel in.

And it can go anywhere."

"How the hell did you get all this stuff here? It doesn't seem legal, and judging by everything else I've seen and done I'm not sure any of it is."

"The Shadow World," Khosan said, "works very differently than the world you know. We don't operate within the law, and we don't operate above the law as many people would assume. We operate below the law, in the shadows where the things you don't want to think about and don't want to do, live. Roy and Conchita may not approve of me telling you this, but we have places, refuges in many countries where we can stay and hide if necessary. We have hundreds of soldiers we can call if we need them, and yes, we do have enough weapons at our disposal to equip a small army."

"Well, if Der Felsen has twelve mercenaries, we seem slightly undermanned." Roger must have thought this rather than said it because rather than respond, Khosan walked over to the Unimog and helped the others stash the gear.

Zecheriah, who seemed to be the designated driver, got into the front seat with Enku, and Ishea opened the side door for the rest of the group to shuffle through. There were four separate pilot-style chairs and a built-in table with two benches that didn't easily accommodate six large people. Nevertheless Freddy, Conchita, Jamie and the three South African mercenaries crowded onto the benches while Ishea stood at the head of the table. Roger sat in one of the captain's chairs, which looked and felt a damn side more comfortable.

There was a monitor over the table providing a feed to the cockpit of the Unimog so that Enku and Zech could hear what was going on in back. While most of the weapons were stored in a compartment under the vehicle there were also two cases below the benches with assault rifles and what looked like, from what Roger had seen in movies, RPG launchers.

"My gut feeling," said Ishea, "is that we won't be hit before we get to Arba Minch. This is a main road. Too many people around to call in the paramilitary guys. But after Arba, the road to Mago is pretty bad and isolated. Plenty of opportunities for them to launch an attack."

"Do you think an anti-tank mine?" asked Jamie.

"No, I don't think so. I don't believe Geoffrey wants us totally destroyed before he has a chance to personally kill us. Most likely a low-grade anti-personnel mine that will disable the vehicle. Then he'll come in with his forces."

"And therefore," added Roy cheerfully, "we'd better get him before he gets us. I can't imagine what horrors he'll dream up to send us on to the next life."

The others laughed and Roger once again nearly threw up.

Chapter 30

IN WHICH AN ATROCITY OCCURS

Debub Omo, Ethiopia
The next morning

Mago, a village in Debub Omo, one of the most sparsely populated administrative zones in Ethiopia, had a population of one hundred and fifty on the day Geoffrey-Philippe van der Borrekens, Demetri Guria and their ten hand-picked mercenaries rolled up at six o'clock in the morning in their specially-equipped Land Rovers. When they left an hour or so later the population had dropped to one, and it was doubtful he would last until the lunchtime. The only reason they'd left him alive was to deliver a message to the PaloMar party, which at the time was a few hours away, camped for the night in the Tama Wildlife Reserve.

The soon-to-be-deceased inhabitants of Mago had not been used to white people. One or two missionaries had passed through over the years, dispensing some strange religion that the villagers didn't understand at all. Sensing there wasn't much chance of getting anyone to believe in an alternative invisible white God, the missionaries had moved on to the next village where they met with equal ambivalence and the threat of violence. For this second encounter the people of Mago were curious about the new group of white people.

Geoffrey had signaled the others to remain in their vehicles while he approached the group of villagers. He purposefully left his pistol in the Land Rover so as not to alarm anyone before they needed alarming. Though of course he knew he'd be needing it soon enough.

"I am looking for Menelik," he said to an older man who seemed to be in charge.

The old man didn't appear to understand what Geoffrey was asking and after the third attempt started repeating 'Menelik, Menelik, Menelik' in a strange sing-song voice.

"Yes! Menelik, Menelik," yelled Geoffrey his voice beginning to go up a few octaves. "Where is Menelik?"

The old man kept up his sing-song and suddenly the crowd took up the chant. It sounded like a giant swarm of angry bees, and Geoffrey felt his head begin to throb worse than his injured buttocks.

"Shut up you bastards" he screamed, and returned to his Land Rover to reach through the open window for his pistol.

He pointed it at the old man and then shot him in the right foot. The old man fell down and began to moan as his foot, blown away by the heavy 9mm hollow-point round, began pumping blood at an alarming rate into the sand. But the crowd kept up the chanting, at which point the rest of the mercenaries armed with their assault weapons exited the car and pointed them at the villagers. They waited for Geoffrey's signal.

Before Geoffrey could react a man emerged from a nearby hut and in a voice that sounded like it should have been accompanied by a trio of celestial trumpets said, "Stop. I am Menelik."

The crowd parted and the man who called himself Menelik walked towards Geoffrey and the Der Felsen soldiers. Geoffrey, who was both a narcissist and psychopath, was discombobulated by Menelik's presence, and he felt himself begin to tremble.

Menelik was tall, perhaps six foot five. His skin was almost golden and his features more Semitic than African, and if it wasn't for the fact that he wore a simple linen robe and his feet were bare, he would have looked like some biblical prince. Ignoring Geoffrey and the soldiers, he knelt down in the bloody dirt next to the old man who lay whimpering quietly as his life bled from the shattered artery. Menelik cradled his head and the old man stopped crying and closed his eyes. Then Menelik stood and walked up to Geoffrey. He spoke in perfect English.

"Who are you that you come into our village and commit such a vile act?"

Geoffrey had said and done nothing while Menelik comforted the old man, but by now he'd recovered his swagger. He raised his pistol to within a few inches of Menelik's face and said, "It's irrelevant who we are. What is relevant is that you tell us precisely why Freddy Blank and Conchita Palomino and those other swine from PaloMar are coming to see you. And please don't deny it or I will shoot another villager." With that he turned the pistol on the nearest women and shot her in the head.

The crowd screamed and Menelik lunged forward. Geoffrey, who had been expecting that, took a step back and raised his pistol again, stopping Menelik in mid-stride.

"I'm sorry, my English is not that good. I meant I'd shoot another villager on top of the one I just shot."

Menelik lowered his shoulders and took a breath. "I am here to help these villagers develop farming methods that work in the world as it exists today, with little water and the little land that is left to them after the Western and Eastern nations once again stole so much. That is all."

Geoffrey smiled and nodded his head as if he understood, and then he shot the nearest man in the stomach. The crowd screamed again, and at that moment Menelik attacked him. He was quicker than anyone Geoffrey had ever encountered before, and far stronger. He grabbed Geoffrey's right hand with the pistol and bent it back until the barrel of the pistol almost disappeared into Geoffrey's left nostril. Geoffrey tried to punch Menelik in the kidneys with his left fist, but Menelik grabbed that too and began to squeeze Geoffrey's hand until Geoffrey squeaked in pain.

"Demetri, stop him for Christ's sake."

The other mercenaries, who'd up until this point done nothing but point their guns at the terrified villagers, rushed forward to aid their commander, but Demetri held up his hand to stop them.

"What do you want us to do Geoffrey? Should I shoot him?" he asked calmly.

"No, you idiot. We need him alive...yeow" His voice went up a few octaves as Menelik kneed him in the groin.

Then Geoffrey felt the pressure release as Menelik went suddenly limp. Demetri stood above him with a stun baton in his hand. Geoffrey scrambled to his feet and jumped up and down on his heels a few times to help his balls descend.

"What is wrong with you, Demetri? Why didn't you help me before?"

"You normally don't need help, Geoffrey."

"Yes, well he fought unfairly." He aimed a kick at Menelik's head. "My God, Demetri. You have never felt strength like that. This is more than a normal man." He stood staring at the still unconscious Menelik. "I need him securely tied up and then put him in the back with that other bastard. And then I need to send a message to those PaloMar swine."

Demetri pulled some nylon ties from his pockets and fixed them round Menelik's wrists and ankles.

Menelik was too large to carry so he dragged him over to the Land Rover and pushed him none too gently onto the floor of the vehicle next to the other prone figure. The villagers who had just stared in abject terror, began to wail again. Geoffrey tried to block his ears but the sound began to drive him more crazy than he already was, and after a second or two he turned to Demetri.

"Get rid of them. Everyone but that man over there. I need him to be alive for another few hours to give a message to PaloMar."

It took the mercenaries under four minutes to massacre the villagers. It wasn't that the kind of men Geoffrey hired enjoyed killing. They just didn't think about it. They shot the villagers mechanically and without concern for gender or age. When it was over they walked around administering coup de gras bullets to the heads of the few who hadn't died in the initial massacre.

If the man that Geoffrey had initially spared felt relief in any way at not being shot, it vanished as soon as Demetri pulled out his combat knife and stabbed him quickly in the liver. It happened so fast that the man didn't at first realize it. Then he clutched his upper abdomen and sank to the ground. Demetri picked him up and dragged him to the shade of the nearest hut. In what seemed like an act of kindness he put a blanket over the man and a full bottle of water next to him. There was, of course, no kindness anywhere in Demetri's soul. All he'd done was make sure the man had the two things he'd need to stay alive for a few hours as his life slowly left his body.

Geoffrey came up and looked at the dying man. "How long?"

"Four hours maybe a little longer. I didn't hit a major artery."

"Well you'd better be right. I need him to give Freddy and Conchita a message. Now where they fuck is that helicopter?"

Had any of the villagers survived besides the single man, who appeared to be lounging drunkenly against one of the huts, they would have been surprised to see another vehicle approaching their village two hours later. Despite Ishea's best attempts at saving the wounded man, he lasted only long enough to give the PaloMar party the short message that Geoffrey had prepared. There were too many bodies to bury so they left them for the vultures and hyenas with prayers from those who prayed and thoughts from those who didn't. Their desire for revenge was deep.

At that moment the Der Felsen soldiers together with Menelik and the other prisoner, had just landed their helicopter on Kunda Damo, less well-known than the much larger hilltop monastery, Debre Damo, but equally unassailable. Surprisingly enough, they didn't slaughter the fifteen monks who lived there, but herded them into a stone cell to be used as hostages if possible. They took the bound, but now conscious Menelik to the main temple and stuck him on the altar like an animal about to be sacrificed. No one said a word to him, nor he to them.. But they felt his presence very uneasily.

The other man was tied to a chair in what served as a kitchen for the monks. He was clearly terrified.

Chapter 31

IN WHICH ROGER REALIZES THAT THERE ARE SOME NIGHTMARES FROM WHICH YOU DON'T WAKE UP

❧

The Omo Valley area, Ethiopia
The previous night

No one had asked Roger to help when they settled into a clearing near a clump of trees about five hundred meters off the track that served as one of the roads in the Tama Wildlife Preserve. Roger hadn't pitched a tent for years but the others did it like it was second nature and soon had the camp set up and an electronic perimeter installed.

"It's not that effective really," Zech told Roger when he asked him how it worked. "If they have, and you can be sure they do, sniper rifles and grenade launchers, they can take us out from a kilometer away. But if they decide to sneak up on us to cut our throats, we'll at least know a few seconds before."

By that point Roger had become numb to threats or the potential of a bullet hitting him in the head, so he shrugged politely and walked over to where the others were preparing a meal. After they'd eaten something he didn't recognize and drank coffee - there was no booze - he climbed into his tent. Not that he had much choice in the wardrobe department, but other than taking off his boots, he decided it was probably just as well to stay fully clothed. He lay awake listening to the others talking and knew there was no way he was ever going to sleep. He went over his life, as he'd done just about every night since Paris, and realized that nothing he thought of or replayed or analyzed about his situation would make sense or give it the meaning he so desperately needed. He closed his eyes again, thought about Conchita and wished he had an Ambien.

The voices outside went quiet and all of a sudden he heard the zipper on his tent begin to open. Conchita came in.

"Can I sleep with you tonight?"

"Jesus. Of course, Conchita."

Roger held up the flap of the sleeping bag and she crawled in. As he put his arms around her he realized that other than the flak jacket, which she'd removed, she was also fully dressed.

"Just hold me tight," she said and he felt her tremble. "Are you scared, Roger?"

He thought about saying 'no' but deep down he realized she already knew how scared he was. "Yes, I'm very scared. I mean, I'm scared of what

Der Felsen could do, but I think I'm most scared of losing you now."

It sounded trite but he really meant it. She kissed him on the lips.

"I'm scared of that too, but whatever happens to us - to Freddy and Jamie and me and the mercenaries - I promise you that we will make sure you are okay. We dragged you into this, for all the right reasons, I know, but I think now it was unfair and that I have to get you out."

Roger wanted to tell her that a few minutes before being blown to pieces or being scalped or whatever horrific method Geoffrey had in mind for them was a little late to say that, when he'd been begging to get out from the beginning. But of course he didn't say that. Instead he held her face and said, "I don't care what happens to me, Conchita, I never want to be separated from you."

Surprisingly enough he was starting to get horny and instead of just holding her, he started to fumble for her breasts, which were straining against her khaki bush shirt. He was half-expecting her to tell him to get his paws off her top hamper, but Conchita proved to be as eager as mustard and after a rather sloppy attempt at removing their pants and pulling down their underwear, they were soon going at it like two stoats. The sounds of flesh slapping together might have been disturbing to anyone listening and Roger hoped to hell the others were asleep or patrolling the camp closer to the other tents. It didn't take either of them more than a few minutes to climax. Then Conchita, much to his horror rolled over, and with her perfectly formed bare bottom tucked into his groin, fell fast asleep. She was clearly not as worried about cleaning up as he was and seeing that the nearest cloth happened to be her shirt tail, he used that and hoped she wouldn't notice the stains when she woke up. He tried again to go to sleep but had an urge to pee, so he pulled up his pants, put on his boots and tried to be as quiet as he could exiting the tent. He almost jumped out of his skin as a large shape materialized in front of him. It was Zecheriah.

"Gotta pee, mate? Happens at your age," he whispered with a grin.

"As a matter of fact, I do," Roger replied not caring for Zech's tone one bit.

"Well, perfect timing, because I was just coming to get you in any case. You have first watch."

"What are you talking about? No one said anything about me taking watch. I don't know the first thing about it. I don't even have my gun."

"You don't need it. Just keep walking around the perimeter, and if you see or hear anything yell. None of us sleeps that deeply."

"Are you sure about this, Zech?" Something didn't feel right.

"Yes, while you and Conchita were rattling about in there, Jamie and I agreed you could take first watch. Half an hour and then Paulus will take over."

"I don't know. I thought Ishea was making those decisions."

"Well, he isn't. Now do what you're fucking well told."

Out of excuses, Roger nodded his head and walked over to a large tree to pee. Zech watched him for a few seconds before getting into his tent. It was a warm night, not boiling as Roger had imagined this part of Ethiopia to be, and very dark with just a sliver of moon trying it's best to hide behind a few clouds. Other than what sounded like a large herbivore ruminating over God knows what, the loudest sound was his pee hitting the ground.

He finished up and turned to do what he hoped was something in the region of "keeping watch" when a huge arm wrapped round his neck and the silver tip of a knife almost touched his right eyeball. He tried to scream but all that came out was a grunt as the arm tightened. He felt the blood running out of his head just before he blacked out.

When Roger awoke this time he was slung over the hump of a camel, which in his delirious state seemed odd until he thought of the ruminating sounds he'd heard earlier. They were going at a rather fast clip through the darkened bush and he must have jerked in panic and almost slipped off but whoever else was on the camel grabbed him with one hand. He heard a click and then a jab of pain as a needle went into his shoulder and then nothing until he woke up on the hard floor of a Land Rover next to a man who was also tied up.

Despite the pain in his head he tried to smile at the other captive but all he could do was crinkle his eyes behind the duct tape that covered his mouth. It was obvious that the other captive was in pain too but he crinkled his eyes in return and something about him made Roger feel less panicked. Whoever the other guy was he was clearly used to rough treatment or made of sterner stuff than Roger. He never uttered a sound, while Roger groaned and moaned until one of the men in the front turned round and kicked him in the head, which hurt like a son-of-a-bitch. After that he tried his best to moan silently until the Land Rover abruptly stopped.

The door at the back opened and the two prisoners were manhandled out. The landscape didn't look much different from anything Roger had seen in the past two days, except for the helicopter that stood, it's blades still spinning, in the middle of a clearing. He wasn't sure what type of helicopter it was, but it proved large enough to carry the two of them and the twelve Der Felsen mercenaries (that's who he assumed they were) across the bushveld towards a group of hills at the foot of a mountain range. On the hill they seemed to be flying towards, was a peculiar structure, almost like a stone castle.

One of the soldiers, the young man who appeared to be in charge, turned towards Roger and his trussed up companion and said, "Gentlemen, that is the monastery of Kunda Damo. It's where we will be staying for a day or two, and where we will slaughter both of you and your friends at PaloMar. It's beautiful from this view, is it not?"

Though they hadn't spoken a word, other than a grunt or two from Roger as they bumped into each other, Roger suddenly realized his companion was Menelik. He could feel the man's presence. Once again it calmed him and took his mind off the awful tortures he imagined would be coming. He looked down from the helicopter and saw they were hovering over the central courtyard of the monastery. Small figures were gathered there waving angrily at them, but they scattered as the helicopter landed and the mercenaries leapt out waving their assault rifles.

"Don't kill them yet, unless they attack us." Geoffrey shouted. "Stick them in a cell until we know how many they are and if they have any means of accessing the outside world. We may need them as hostages."

The monks were yelling and gesturing wildly but went meekly with three of the mercenaries who pushed and shoved them with the barrels of their rifles. Menelik and Roger lay on the ground where they'd been dumped, as it was impossible to stand with the ties round their ankles. Geoffrey said something to another brute of a man who nodded. He in turn yelled at the remaining mercenaries who went off to different parts of the structure. Two remained to help Geoffrey and the Brute grab both Menelik and he under their arms and drag them towards the main building.

The stone door opened onto the inside of a large church that could have been carved out of pure rock. The walls were covered in beautiful, almost Byzantine paintings of saints. Not that Roger had much time to admire them because at that point Menelik and he were separated. Roger was dragged down a short passage to a stone room that looked like a primitive kitchen and thrown onto the floor.

His bowels began to somersault and he cursed the day he met Freddy. He tried to imagine what they'd do to him and decided that he'd tell them everything before they began the torture. At that moment Geoffrey and the Brute entered the room and Roger froze in horror. The Brute, who he thought rivaled Ishea in size, carried a folding chair. He picked Roger up as if he were a rag doll and shoved him into the chair. Then he ripped the duct tape from Roger's mouth - together with what felt like a few feet of skin.

"Ow, fuck, that hurts!" Why are you doing this to me? Please, just let me go and I'll tell you everything.

"Why are you doing this to me...?" Geoffrey mocked Roger's whine. "You fool. You know exactly why we're doing this, and the only place you're going is hell. Starting in a few seconds..."

"Look, I'm nobody in this whole thing, please..."

"Not nobody," said Geoffrey, grabbing his hair. "You're the marketing 'genius' Roger Storm, who Freddy believes can capture the wisdom of Menelik III and turn it into a speech that will unite Africa."

"Ow, Jesus. I am not a 'genius'...."

Geoffrey slapped Roger viciously across the face and Roger screamed in pain

"Shut the fuck up, you sniveling little bastard. We don't need answers from you, in case you believed that would postpone the intense pain you're going to feel. We know everything about who you are and what you do. And just in case you're interested how we know, I will tell you. Mercenaries are loyal to no one but he who pays them the most, and those fools at PaloMar - yes, your big fat friend and the woman you are fucking, rather sloppily from what Zecheriah Corn has told us - are not paying Zecheriah half of what we are to keep us informed. Yes, Zecheriah is our mole. So now he will lead them to us - yes, to try to rescue you and Menelik - and then we will have a nice little butcher's party, and feed whatever is left of all of you to the vultures."

Roger's head was spinning from the slap, but everything Geoffrey said about Zecheriah suddenly made sense. His lack of knowledge of the recent killing of hunters, his interaction with Captain Mulugeta in Addis and his rather strange behavior in the camp. The horrible bastard.

"Don't worry, we won't kill you right away. But Demetri here is going to soften you up a little, because we need you to look quite damaged for the video, though you seem rather soft already." He prodded Roger on the cheek.

"Please, you don't need to do this. I'll do whatever you ask. I really don't want to be hurt."

"Oh you don't..." Geoffrey looked concerned. "Well why didn't you say so to begin with?" Then his face split in a horrible grin. "Maybe next time we get together I'll take that into account.. But unfortunately today we are really going to have to hurt you. Bad timing on your part. Any more questions before we begin?"

"Yes, Roger mumbled, "Was I on a camel?"

Roger wasn't sure why he asked that, but of all the things that were worrying him at the moment, the camel ride sprung to mind. Geoffrey looked at him for a second, slowly bunching his fist, but before he could punch Roger, Demetri stopped him.

"Yes, you were on a camel. When we grabbed you from the PaloMar camp we couldn't get the vehicle close enough without alerting the guards. So we sent one of our people in on a camel. There are lots of them around here in the villages."

Roger nodded his head in understanding and that's when Demetri hit him. He couldn't believe the explosion of pain, but through it he heard Geoffrey saying that he didn't want Roger too damaged, just bad enough to send a video to Freddy.

Only someone who's been beaten up badly by an expert can truly understand what it feels like. Roger, up and until that point had not, and so he had no clue as to what was happening besides that it hurt worse than anything he could have imagined. Perhaps if he'd been younger and in better shape he would have held up better. But he wasn't and he didn't and he could feel his insides breaking apart. Through the blood and vomit he begged Demetri to stop, and he tried desperately to pass out, but every time it felt as if he were falling into the black void of unconsciousness the pain took over, until he supposed his body released so many endorphins that he just heard the blows rather than felt them. Demetri had started on his face, first on his nose and then on his eyes and ears. After that he moved onto Roger's upper torso. The punches were quick, more like jabs than haymakers. Designed to cause pain rather than damage. Roger thought he was dying and he wished Demetri would just hit him so hard that his head would come off.

After what seemed like an eternity but was probably no more than a minute, he heard Geoffrey, who'd been filming the whole thing on his phone, tell Demetri to stop.

"Enough, Demetri. He looks bad enough. His ear looks like it will come off with one tug. Funny. Maybe rip his shirt away so I can show the blood and bruising on his upper body. Ah yes, look at that. Good, now let me hit him once more, just for luck."

"Don't try to do my job, Geoffrey," Demetri said, standing in front of Geoffrey. He reached out and grabbed Roger's splattered nose and pulled it back into shape so that he could breath.

"You're too sensitive," laughed Geoffrey. "Why waste a good nose on someone who won't be using it to breathe much longer? Now let's take him over to Menelik so we can get one shot together before I send it to Freddy and Conchita."

Demetri, much to the half-conscious Roger's surprise, picked him up rather gently and carried him, almost like a baby, back along the passage to the church where he and Geoffrey sat Menelik and Roger back to back on the floor. Roger thought he heard Demetri whisper that he was sorry, but he was so befuddled from the beating that Demetri could have said anything and he would have believed him. He tried to turn his head towards Menelik and though he couldn't tell much through his already swollen eyes, he thought Menelik looked unscathed.

"Smile for the camera, boys," said Geoffrey, laughing hysterically. "Perfect, perfect. Ah, Roger, they are going to be so sad to see you looking like this that I am sure they are going to throw all caution to the wind to get over here to help you. Especially the beautiful Conchita. Though, what she sees in you is beyond me. You know, perhaps before I cut her guts out I should fuck her, if only to show her what a real man is like."

If he'd been expecting a reaction from Roger, he got none. Geoffrey made an obscene gesture that resembled a dog humping a tree and then gave up.

Demetri who'd been standing by while the maniacal Geoffrey finished his photographic assignment and pressed 'send', came over to Roger and poured water into his mouth. He pulled the duct tape off Menelik's mouth and then did the same for him.

'You are such a sentimentalist Demetri," said Geoffrey. But let's leave these two alone and go organize ourselves. I have a feeling we won't be waiting long."

For a while neither Menelik nor Roger said anything to each other. Roger, because he wasn't sure he even could, and the pain which had moved from sharp to dull had numbed him to all feeling. He couldn't see Menelik all that well because they were still back to back, but he could sense him. While Roger knew it was in all probability purely psychological, he could feel a power emanating from Menelik. Not in some metaphysical way, but an intense warmth that somehow restored a crucial iota of life to his battered body. Suddenly Menelik spoke and Roger tried to listen because he knew that this was what Freddy and Conchita and Jamie had wanted him to hear.

"I'm truly sorry for what happened to you, Roger. It looks as if they beat you very badly, and though I'd like to say you will recover in time, I'm not sure that time will be given to us. I watched these people...I would say these animals, but I have never seen animals do what they did to the villagers...perform acts that I had hoped would never be seen in this world again. But I suppose that's too much to hope for. I know very little of human genetics - though I do know a thing or two about grapes - but I suspect that unless science can find and alter the evil gene, mankind will never stop killing and hurting and destroying. We enjoy violence too much and the sense of power it gives us over lesser beings. Do you believe in God, Roger?"

Roger wanted to say he hadn't up until this point but would start right now if it would get him out of this situation. He tried to move his mouth but it was too painful.

"I should believe in the one God," Menelik continued. "After all, my House is mentioned in the Bible and technically we are still the guardians of the sacred Ark of the Covenant. Which, by the way in case you are wondering, is just rubbish. It doesn't exist. It's just an empty stone chest guarded by some blind monks. Probably perfect for storing biscuits. But of course I can't believe in God the way Christians or Muslims or Jews do. Not an anthropomorphic God. I suppose I am more of a Pantheist than anything else, but my feeling is that God is simply an excuse to do things for some people and a reason things happen for others. Basically, I believe God is no more than a justification for not taking responsibility for your actions. It's either "God willing" or "God's will". That's what makes people reluctant to take action and opens them up to exploitation. That's what we have to overcome if we are to change how things are in this part of the world. We have to show the people that the power of their own destiny lies in their hands not in some mythical being or despicable warlord."

Despite the fact that Roger's ears were severely damaged and his brain felt like mashed potato, he listened as best he could to hear a theme or a thought that encapsulated Menelik's beliefs. Most of it made sense though Roger thought there were a few peculiar phrases about grapes and biscuits that seemed out of place.

"We are all part of the universe," Menelik droned on. "We are made of its elements. You are stardust, Roger. I am stardust. Different stars, maybe, but from the same part of the cosmos. I have often wondered which part of the cosmos. I suspect I am from somewhere near the Big Dipper. For some reason that feels like home. As if I am a big dipper in the well of life." Menelik paused as if he were contemplating the thought. "Or even a big tub of ice cream. Ah, yes. A big dipper in a big tub of ice cream. I love ice cream. I don't know why I'm thinking of ice cream at this moment."

Roger didn't either. He quite liked the "well of life" idea and felt he may be able to work with it, but he was also beginning to believe that perhaps Menelik had been given a drug that caused partial hallucination.

"Do you know who Karl Kraus was, Roger? He was a journalist and writer in Vienna at the end of the Austro Hungarian Empire. A brilliant man. He said, 'Improve yourself, it is the way to improve the world.' A simple statement with huge meaning. Think about it. Think about a single improvement multiplied by a billion. Do you not think the world would be better?"

Even if he could have nodded or grunted Roger didn't believe it would have stopped Menelik talking. He was getting more and more confused by what the man was saying. Bits appeared to be brilliant observations, but the rest sounded like pure gibberish.

"Which is why, Roger I do believe what Freddy and Jamie and Conchita want to do is a noble thing. Oh yes, to move from being merchants of death to restorers of life."

Roger tried to nod. He liked that phrase too. He wished he had a pen and paper with him to write it down together with the 'well of life', and then realized his hands were tied anyway.

"How beautiful and worthwhile. And the idea that you will be able to help me focus my thoughts into a single magnificent and compelling cry that penetrates the very souls of the oppressed to get them to rise up and drive out these new colonialists, these modern day versions of the western slave-owner, for that is what they are, Roger, simply slave owners. When you own the financial institutions that control the lives of the people then you are no more than a slave owner. You must agree, surely?"

Yes, yes, I agree, Roger wanted to shout. But at this moment please shut the fuck up and let's try to get out of here. Still, speech was impossible.

"I am the last of my line, the last son of the sons and daughters of Solomon and Sheba. My family ruled from Israel down to what is now Zimbabwe, and I shall do so again if these bastards don't kill me first. Not that they can of course because I am invincible."

Menelik's voice started to go up one octave at a time and the more Roger listened the more Menelik began to sound like a blithering idiot.

"Oh, no. Nothing can kill the son of Solomon. Neither spear nor scimitar shall stop me..."

Actually, an AK-47 would probably do the trick, Roger wanted to tell him.

"Come, Roger. Let us stand and we shall walk out of here together and I shall protect you from these swine and we, you and I, shall wipe them from the face of the earth..."

Menelik managed to stand up, but as he couldn't move his feet he tried to hop only to fall over in a heap on the floor. He began to ramble about mysterious powers and astral projection and descending in golden chariots from the sun and raising up the dead and other things that totally confirmed Roger's conclusion.

Please stop, Roger tried to say. You're supposed to be the strong one. But at this point Menelik adopted the fetal position and looked like he'd peed on the floor. If Roger could have panicked more than he already was, he would have. He knew now what any logical person would have thought at the beginning of the nightmare: there wan't one normal person in the bunch. His instincts had been right all along. They were all certifiably mad.

Once more he started to think that perhaps he was dreaming the whole thing and would wake up in his apartment in Chicago with an awful headache and an empty half-gallon of vodka. Suddenly he began to cry. The tears were not because of the pain but out of sheer desperation, and he knew then that the only escape was to do what he'd had wanted to do two weeks before.

And that was to die.

He had a feeling his wish was about to be granted when he heard what sounded like a shot in the distance followed by two explosions. The church door was open and he saw that it was dark outside. Through his half-closed and decidedly foggy eyes he thought he could see figures running, and then more shots and what sounded like someone screaming.

Roger stopped sniveling and tried to focus on how to get the hell out of there. The only way would be to role towards the open door, and so that's what he began to do. Every movement sent sharp pains through his chest from his bruised and no doubt broken ribs, but he forced himself to keep moving until he hit an obstacle. It with Menelik, still in the fetal position babbling quietly to himself. He looked at Roger and nodded his head like a bobble doll.

"Hello, Roger. Would you like some tea and cake? It's from a very old family recipe. Dates back to my great-great-great-great-great grandmother Sheba. Actually has dates in it, funnily enough."

This was, Roger thought, the Mad Hatter's Tea Party performed by the Marquis De Sade and other inmates of the asylum at Charenton. Not sure what he would have said if he'd had the ability to say anything, he nodded politely and kept on rolling towards the door. The frequency of the shots intensified. Then there was an explosion that would no doubt have deafened him, if Demetri's beating hadn't already left him a paid-up member of the hard-of-hearing club.

Smoke began to drift into the church, and through it he thought he saw a large shape coming towards him.

"Hello, Roger, me old mate," said Zecheriah Corn. "Don't try to speak, although you're probably not in the mood judging by the size of your swollen lips. Demetri did a good job on you... Jeez, that's got to hurt."

Roger looked at him with absolute hatred, fear having abandoned him a short while before.

Zecheriah pulled a nasty-looking combat knife from a scabbard attached to his ankle and kneeled down next to Roger. He forced Roger's head back and put the blade against his throat. At that point, Roger managed a small whimper which was at least progress.

"Oh, just in case you're wondering," Zecheriah said, pulling the blade away for a second, "I would imagine at this stage your mates Freddy, Conchita and Jamie and the other schmuks are pretty much mincemeat, or close to it. I led them right into the trap that Geoffrey set, and I have to tell you Roger, I am surprised they followed me. Personally I would have had my suspicions of me a long while ago, as I suspect you did in Addis. Oh yes, I saw how you looked at me after I gave the Captain that packet of money. But Freddy and Conchita, they're trusting people. They really believed I liked being a butler when we weren't in combat. All it did of course was allow me access to everything Der Felsen needed to know. Anyway, I'm just gonna cut your noggin off, shouldn't hurt more than you're hurting now."

He returned the blade to Roger's neck and began to cut into the flesh. The blood spurted out, mingling with whatever bodily fluids were already congealed on his shirt. Suddenly the blade was pulled away and Roger twisted his head to see what had happened. Zecheriah was staring at his arm, right about where his hand holding the knife should have been. The appendage in question was quivering on the floor a few feet away and Ishea Payamps stood over him with a large machete.

Roger thought of all the movies where the seriously disappendaged combatant simply roars in pain and then launches an attack on his de-limberer and realized those scenes were all wrong. Instead of bellowing in rage, Zecheriah looked at his stump for a few seconds before keeling over. Roger didn't know if he was dead from shock or whether he'd just passed out, and he didn't really care. He wanted to kick him in the face, and once Ishea cut the ties on his hands and legs he tried to, but couldn't manage to lift his leg. It was all he could do to walk in a straight line. Ishea handed him a cloth which he pushed against the wound in his neck but Zecheriah's cut wasn't deep and the blood slowed to a trickle.

Ishea cut Menelik's ties and Menelik gave him a broad grin and then walked back into the church muttering something about finding a tractor.

"Come," said Ishea, taking Rogers arm to steady him. "We have to get you out of here, I promised Conchita."

"Where?" was what Roger tried to say but had no idea what came out.

Ishea got his meaning. "I don't know," he said pulling Roger behind him. He'd sheathed the machete and produced a machine pistol. "All I can say, Roger, is that I hope they're okay. We didn't plan this assault properly. Freddy and Conchita pushed because they knew, after what we saw in

Mago, we had to get to you before Geoffrey killed you."

Ishea was breathing heavily, and Roger saw that there was blood on his thigh as he steered them down the side wall of the church towards the door. The gunfire had stopped, but the smoke was still there. Roger could hear someone moaning.

"There's a staircase the monks use to get up to the monastery," said Ishea. "We tried to create a diversion by flying a drone over before we launched smoke grenades so Freddy, Conchita, Jamie and Zecheriah could get up. Zech said he'd lead and the others followed him through the smoke. Even at that moment we didn't really know Zech had turned. I don't know, Roger. They could have made it, Conchita's been in worse situations.

"I don't want to lose her, Ishea. I really need her." Roger could hardly get the words out.

The big man squeezed his shoulder. "I know that. And I'm sorry if you thought I was jealous. I loved her too, but it was a long time ago." His voice broke but he recovered quickly. "They got Paulus and Abel, but Enku, Khosan and myself made it through. Come on and stay behind me. The others are outside. I think we killed eight of them but we don't know where Geoffrey and Demetri are holed up."

Roger followed him as best he could though he was unsteady and his whole body ached. They got to the door and Ishea looked out. It was already dark and the smoke made visibility almost impossible.

Ishea pulled Roger to a low stone wall where Erku and Khosan were crouching. Enku had an assault rifle and Khosan carried a much bigger gun with a huge drum of ammo. Shots were coming from the upper story of a building opposite the church and hitting the wall right in front of Roger. Khosan raised the strange-looking weapon and fired off three rounds in quick succession. There was a huge explosion and two bodies tumbled into the courtyard.

"That leaves two of them," whispered Enku. "But where we don't know."

They lay behind the wall for what felt like hours as the smoke slowly cleared and the courtyard and surroundings became more visible under the sliver of moon in an otherwise black, though stunningly beautiful star-studded sky. Erku had given Roger some painkillers which must have contained an opiate because as the pain vanished he began to feel quite high - and even asked Khosan if he had a spare gun. Khosan handed Roger a pistol.

At that moment, Geoffrey yelled from across the way. "I'm coming out we need to parley."

"Fuck you Geoffrey, you son-of-a-bitch" Roger yelled back and fired wildly at the place he thought Geoffrey must be standing.

"Jesus, Enku. What the hell did you give him?" said Ishea putting his huge hand over Roger's mouth. "What do you want to say Geoffrey? I'm not sure there is much parlaying to be had. There are only two of you and four of us."

"Ah," cackled Geoffrey like some demented witch doctor. "It sounds like Roger Storm's head is still attached to his body. I should have known that Zech was unreliable. You can't find a good mercenary for love or money these days. Anyway, I hope you aren't counting on him as your fourth, judging by his attempts to hit me, he's more likely to shoot his dick off.."

Roger couldn't move anyway with Ishea's arm round his neck so he remained silent. The sudden burst of bravado and anger had worn off. As much as he wanted to worry about Freddy and Conchita, especially Conchita, he suddenly couldn't. He was feeling like the biggest sucker in the world. He knew now that nothing that had been said to him was true, and that whatever noble reasons he might have had for what had happened or what was about to happen were no more than the sounds of birds' in flight. His pointless life that had for a brief moment acquired meaning was once again pointless. At least, he imagined, it would be over soon. He held the gun in his right hand and slowly brought it up to his temple as if he was practicing how he'd blow his brains out. He'd certainly end his life before he'd let Geoffrey and Demetri touch him again.

Then a shape appeared in the doorway of the opposite building. It was Geoffrey. Khosan leveled his weapon, but Ishea touched him on the shoulder to stand down.

"What do you want Geoffrey?"

"What I want is for all of us to go home. None of this has worked. Your plan with Menelik is done. It is over."

"That part perhaps," Ishea replied in a very calm voice. "But this whole thing can only be over when you are dead, Geoffrey." He leveled his rifle.

"I think not, Ishea, you traitorous bastard. If you kill me, then I kill her."

At that moment Demetri walked out pushing a battered and bloody Conchita ahead of him. He walked to the edge of the courtyard where the cliff began and held her at arms-length by the throat. The wind howled from the valley below whipping Conchita's hair about her face.

"Either you agree now, throw down your guns and go home, or she goes over the cliff."

Roger's heart began to race. He couldn't believe she was alive.

"Conchita," he managed a loud croak.

She looked at him and tried to say something, but Demetri strengthened his grip on her throat. Roger couldn't see clearly, but it seemed as if there were tears in her eyes. But it could just have been a reflection of the stars shimmering overhead, oblivious to the horror below. At that moment Roger's heart truly broke and to everyone's amazement he stood up and walked towards them.

"Let her go, please, please."

Ishea tried to reach for him but Roger managed to brush him off.

"Of course, Roger," said Geoffrey, "Oh, very brave and noble. Not at all what I was expecting. Yes, I will let her go. In fact I will let you both go. But not home, I'm afraid. We need some great romantic drama to end this story, don't you think? Something sensational. Yes, you can both go over the cliff." He lunged at Roger and his demonic laugh echoed through the night.

It happened so fast that none of them had time to react. There was an awful scream, and suddenly Menelik hurtled from the church doors and flung himself through the air at Demetri and Conchita. Menelik was not big in the sense that Ishea was big but he was tall and wirey and perfectly, so it appeared, suited to launch himself as a missile. He hit Demetri in the chest, and though Demetri could have, under normal circumstances, swatted him off like a fly, the momentum and his position on the cliff's edge worked to his disadvantage. He let go of Conchita to try to steady himself, but it was too late. He began to wobble, and then making one last ditch effort to save himself, he caught hold of Conchita's shirt. Roger put out his hand to grab her, but all he got was air. It was too late. She, Menelik and Demetri toppled over the cliff onto the rocks below. None of them screamed.

Roger could do nothing but peer into the darkness and cry out in helpless rage. The others who'd stood back in shock now moved forward. But before Roger could turn to them Geoffrey had his arm around him and the sharp point of a dagger once again touched his eye.

"Back off Ishea," Geoffrey said, the madness vanishing from his voice. "I'm walking away and I'm taking him with me..."

He didn't say anything more. There was a pop and Roger felt himself drenched in blood from the hole that appeared in Geoffrey's forehead from the silenced pistol in Enku's hand. He looked down at his arm and saw thick grey goo. That's funny. He thought as he passed out, it's the second time I've had someone's brains on my sleeve.

Chapter 32

IN WHICH ROGER GETS TO EXPLAIN THINGS TO THE TWO INSPECTORS AND FINALLY MAKES IT HOME

London, England
A few days later

"That's a pretty incredible story," Bunter said to Roger as he put his teacup down on the sitting room table.

"Almost too incredible," added Darmstaedter, who was pacing up and down the room as if he was getting his morning exercise. "There are questions to every answer you've provided."

The pale sun streamed through the windows of Freddy and Conchita's London house and in a way warmed whatever was left of Roger's heart. He leaned back in his chair and swallowed. He thought of his last sight of Conchita going over the cliff and realized his emotions had been so depleted over the past few days, that what remained was an almost empty void. There was virtually nothing left inside to let out.

"Inspector Darmstaedter's right. There are more questions and all of them begin with 'why'. Why did they approach you, for a start? Why did they go in on such a hair-brained scheme knowing it had virtually no chance of success?"

"I've thought about that a lot as you can imagine, and of course everything I can tell you is just speculation. So let me try to answer the second part first."

Darmstaedter sat down in the opposite chair to Roger and Sebastien the cat leapt onto his lap. He scratched the cat behind his ear and then pushed him off gently. Both policemen took out their notebooks.

"If I think back on everything Freddy got up to in life, all of the crazy schemes, none of them had an entirely satisfying conclusion for him. There was always something that went wrong at the last minute that ruined the elaborate plotting, or the lack-thereof I should say. His ideas were all pie-in-the-sky, so ludicrous, that any normal person would have given up before they began. But I don't think Freddy had the ability to give up. He saw an opportunity and refused to waste it. I imagine those are the sort of people who ultimately change the world, and perhaps one day, if Freddy is still alive, and God knows he may still be, he will. Was PaloMar real by the way?"

"How do you mean?" asked Bunter

"I mean was it a legitimate International arms company? As successful as they led me to believe?"

"Very real, Herr Storm," said Darmstaedter. "From what we understand, PaloMar was enormously successful, but it appears that Conchita and Jamie were the real business brains. Freddy was the visionary. He came up with the plans and the ideas and the others made them happen."

"That makes sense, I suppose. Freddy was a visionary for sure, but he also had the ability to get people to do things that went against everything they believed about themselves. You can't believe the trouble he got me into when I was a kid, and I am someone who avoids trouble at all costs."

"Except for the last two weeks," grunted Bunter.

"Yes, you're right, except for the last two weeks. Anyway, I'm not surprised he got Ishea and the others to help him kill big game hunters or go on this insane quest." He stared off into space.

"What are you thinking, Herr Storm?"

"I suppose two things still puzzle me."

"And those are?" asked Bunter.

"Well, I can't believe with all their experience and security that Zecheriah was able to act as a double agent for Der Felsen. I thought there was something weird about him when he said that they'd stopped killing hunters a while back. Khosan told me Zech didn't agree with it, so the others didn't involve him. But I'm telling you he didn't know they were still doing it. So clearly they didn't trust him with everything. The other question I have is why any of them thought Menelik could possibly have been the Ghandi or

Mandela of this age? It took me all of five minutes to realize he was a nutter of the first order. Maybe crazy people think other crazy people are sane and normal people are crazy?" Roger paused as if he was pondering the question.

Neither Darmstaedter nor Bunter knew the answer and so they kept quiet as Roger continued.

"And as to why Freddy chose me to accompany them I can only imagine he genuinely wanted to help me. He told me he'd been keeping tabs on Brian and me for a long time after his fake death. I bet he thought he could help me find my purpose again by getting me into something that was in his mind no different than what he got us into at school. And as always he'd be there to protect me. In that way Freddy was one of the greatest and most generous souls I have ever come across. And though I'm still so goddam sore from the beating, and so sad and emotionally drained at losing Conchita, who I know deep down could never really have loved me.

"Inspector Darmstaedter's more the expert in that particular field, Mr. Storm, but in my limited experience it sounds as if she definitely had strong feelings for you."

"Maybe you're right, inspector. I guess for a moment I did live, didn't I? And perhaps that's all we can ever hope for, to really be alive, if even for just a moment."

Darmstaedter understood, much more than Bunter, what Roger was going though. He gave

him a sympathetic smile. "The physical pain will
fade Herr Storm, I promise you that. The pain of
love unfortunately takes a little longer. But I wish
you could give us some idea of what became of
Ishea Payamps."

"I do too, Inspector. But I can't. Not because I
don't want to, believe me. I honestly don't know
what happened to he, Khosan and Enku after they
put me on the PaloMar plane in Addis. All he said
to me was goodbye and that he knew I'd be okay.
I did ask him what he was going to do and he said
that he and Khosan still had things to clean up. I
don't know what happened to Enku. Maybe she's
still in Addis."

"Unfortunately she isn't. We checked with our
contacts there. She too has vanished. And you say
you never saw Freddy or Jamie's bodies?"

"I didn't say anything because I didn't see
anything. I passed out, probably for the fifth time
in two days, and I'm surprised my brain still works
judging by the amount of blood that's rushed in
and out of it over the past few weeks. They must
have given me another knock-out something-
or-other because I only came around when the
Unimog was dropping us off in Addis."

"I do believe you," said Darmstaedter, "but the
strange thing is, and you will no doubt appreciate
this, another hunter, a very wealthy Spaniard, was
killed in Namibia after he'd shot a cheetah just a
few days ago. Someone tied him to the back of a
vehicle and dragged him behind at the exact speed

a cheetah sprints, until there was very little skin on his body. Then they tossed him over an ant hill. Just as a cheetah would do with it's prey."

"Sounds quite awful, but appropriate, and I'm glad in a way," Roger responded. "It certainly feels like Ishea is still in business. But I wonder who he works for. Do you think..?

"You never know," Bunter said, "all of your friends seem capable of multiple lives and deaths. Of course for us it means that part of the case is still open. People are being killed and it's law-enforcement's job to find those responsible and bring them to justice.

"I understand, but who brings justice to the thousands of animals killed every year for someone's enjoyment? Only people like Ishea and Khosan. To be honest, I hope you never find them."

"Well if it makes you feel any better, Herr Storm, we probably won't. Now that Freddy and Conchita and Jamie are supposedly dead, the case as far as we are concerned is closed. Any further murders will be a job for the local police."

"The other problem, Mr. Storm," Bunter, who secretly agreed with Roger but would never have said it, jumped in, "is that while you are free to go, everything to do with PaloMar has been seized. That includes, I'm afraid, this house. So you're going to need to move out in the next day or so."

"Well, at least whoever was running the office here before you shut it down left me a ticket back to Chicago for this afternoon. Unless of course that is also part of the seizure...?

"I suppose technically it is," said Darmstaedter, dislodging Sebastien, who'd jumped up on him, once again, "but I believe under the circumstances we can overlook that."

"Well, Mr. Storm," Bunter said handing Roger his card. "If you ever hear of anything please inform me. I do understand you won't want to do that, but for us this is murder, no matter how justified you may think it is. As Inspector Darmstaedter said, the case for us is closed, but personally I hate loose ends. Well, good luck and I hope your injuries heal."

"One last question if you don't mind me asking, inspectors?"

"Go ahead," replied Bunter.

"What happens to Der Felsen now that everyone seems to be dead?"

"Unfortunately it is still operating. They have a new CEO who claims Geoffrey had gone rogue and that his actions in Mago were not in any way sanctioned by Der Felsen."

"Evil doesn't die easily," added Darmstaedter. "But the good news is they will not come after you now. It would be too obvious."

With that the two inspectors stood up, shook Roger's hand and left. After Roger had walked them to the door he climbed the big staircase to his room. His suitcase with freshly laundered clothes lay open on his bed. He looked around for the last time and his eyes stopped on a particularly striking painting. He recognized it as a Jasper Johns and knew it had to be worth millions. For a moment he thought of taking it. He certainly felt he deserved some type of compensation after all he'd been through. It was the least he was due. He'd tried to hold up his end of the bargain, and yet as far as he knew Harry Bones still fouled the earth with each step he took. Evil indeed, did not die easily. He thought back to the moment he'd fired the gun at Geoffrey, hoping to kill him, and wondered what he would have done if it were Harry Bones instead who walked out the building at Khunda Damo. Maybe he had changed.

In the end he left the painting. Stealing something that was already stolen didn't feel right. So, taking his bag and thanking Alfons the chef, and the young assistant for taking care of him for the past two days, and ensuring the cats would be taken care of too, he walked out the door and hailed a cab.

He was back in his apartment in Chicago by nine o'clock that night.

Chapter 33

IN WHICH ROGER RECEIVES
A MYSTERIOUS LETTER

Chicago and Grand Cayman.
Soon after

Not much had changed. It was as if Roger had simply walked out the door to his apartment and down to the grocery store rather than gone on the most outlandish adventure imaginable. The bed was still unmade and the red wine - by now turned to vinegar - still standing on the kitchen counter. He opened his computer to check his emails. Besides the usual spam there was nothing but a note from his youngest son's wife asking him if he was okay as they hadn't heard from him for a few weeks. He sent a short but friendly response saying he was fine and that he hoped he could take them to dinner soon. He checked his bank balance and saw that there was enough to get him through for a month or so before he'd have to start drawing on his savings. After near maiming and death by ghastly individuals, money didn't seem all that important. It was late but he figured the liquor store down the block was still open. So he pulled on a sweater and went down in the elevator.

"Mr Storm!" He looked around in horror, half-expecting to see Geoffrey or Demetri, but it was just Frank the doormen. "This was delivered by hand for you this afternoon."

It was a thick Manila envelope with no postmarks or indication of who'd sent it. He took it from Frank and folded it in half and stuck it in his pocket. Then he walked to the liquor store to buy a bottle of vodka, the cheapest they had. Fifteen minutes later he was back in his apartment sitting on his couch with a full tumbler of vodka in his hand, thinking of everything, and thinking of nothing. He still hurt and his nose, while set, was still broken, and the stitches the doctor in Addis had used to reattach most of his ear just before they left the airport itched like crazy. He tried to picture Conchita, lying on top of him, telling him she loved him, and the emptiness which he'd begun to feel in London, and thoughts that had left him dry, returned. He'd cried a lot over the past few months but he couldn't do it anymore. Whether he'd truly changed as a person was yet to be seen. He certainly felt different but he'd need some outlet to prove it.

The Manila envelope lay in front of him and he opened it expecting to find some legal document from his ex-wife, or something else that would no doubt drop him further over the edge, but it was neither. It was another thick envelope with the address for the Cayman Island Bank and Trust Company embossed on the front.

He tore it open to find a letter with the name Archibald Rossiter, Private Banker, on the bottom.

Dear Mr Storm

Please do not read this letter in public nor allow it to be seen by anyone else but yourself, nor discuss its contents with anyone else but myself. Failure to adhere to these instructions will render what I have to tell you null and void.

You will find an electronic ticket waiting for you tomorrow morning at Cayman Airways check in - I believe the flight leaves O'Hare at 09:25 - for George Town. When you land you will be met by a representative who will bring you to the bank, where I will explain to you how to access and use your account that presently holds a substantial sum of money.

As proof of the veracity of these details, I was told to tell you that Freddy and Conchita want you to be happy.

My sincerest regards
Archibald Rossiter.

The office of Archibald Rossiter was rather formal compared to the cool, pastel Caribbeaness of the little bit of George Town Roger had seen on his way from the airport. Dark green silk covered walls were hung with antique maps and rather boring English landscapes. Heavy drapes blocked out most of the view and the only light came from two bronze sconces and an angle poise lamp on the big wooden desk. It could have been a banker's office in London or Zurich were it not for Archibald Rossiter himself. He was a short fat man with a rich dark skin and an anxious grin that did everything to make Roger feel even more apprehensive than he had about getting on the plane that morning.

Rossiter was dressed in long khaki shorts and a crisp white shirt and he leapt up from his red leather chair as if he been totally surprised by Roger's appearance.

"Oh my, yes indeed. Welcome Mr. Storm. Welcome, welcome.I hope the four hour flight from Chicago was not too uncomfortable. We sent you a first class ticket, I believe? Sit down, sit down."

"No, it was fine. Really easy, thank you but..."

"And this is your first time in Grand Cayman?"

"It is. I've never really…"

"No mind, no mind, I'm sure you are very curious as to what I have to tell you. By the way, I must say you look as if you've been in a prize fight. Are you in much pain? Would you like some aspirin?

Archibald was speaking so quickly and Roger, who was still jet-lagged, was having a tough time keeping up with the decidedly one-sided conversation.

"Um, no, not a fight. It's a long story, Mr. Rossiter..."

"Then let's get down to business because I intend to tell you something that is going to make all your pain go away, I promise." He laughed nervously.

"Okay, but I'm really confused as to..."

"Then I will enlighten you immediately. Just sign these papers on the appropriate pages." He pushed a stack of neatly labeled papers across the desk and sat back. Roger tried to read the first page but it was so full of abstruse legal terms that he couldn't make head or tail as to what it said. He stopped, took a deep breath, and looked at Archibald Rossiter who smiled expectantly at him from his large wing-backed chair.

"Mr. Rossiter, look. I have no idea what I'm about to sign or what I'm doing here, for that matter. Your letter mentioned two people with whom I just spent the most unspeakably horrific few weeks. It also said that I had a bank account with a lot of money in it, and you just confirmed that. But you're going so fast and I haven't totally recovered from my ordeal and my head's spinning."

Rossiter leaned back in his chair and sighed. "Mr. Storm, you're right and I apologize. I've had butterflies in my stomach all morning about this meeting.

"Why's that?"

"Well, to be absolutely honest with you, everyone I've ever dealt with that is somehow involved with PaloMar has looked as if they'd rather kill me than eat bacon and eggs for breakfast. You have no idea of the people I've met ever since I began to work for Mr. Blank and Miss Palomino. Not one I'd have taken home to meet the wife. But I get the feeling you're different. You're the first person that doesn't appear to have a stiletto strapped to his leg. In fact you seem quite nice."

"I don't know how nice I am," replied Roger warming to the little man, "but I assure you I have nothing strapped to either of my legs."

"Excellent," replied Rossiter relaxing a little. "Then let me explain the situation. Three days ago I received instructions to transfer the sum of fifty-five million dollars into a bank account for you. What do you think about that, hey?"

"You just said fifty-five million dollars?" Roger had heard him perfectly but the amount seemed so outrageously large that his brain demanded confirmation.

"Yes, that's precisely what I said. "Fifty-five million dollars."

"And this is from Freddy and Conchita? Who are both dead..?"

"Mr. Storm, I am not at liberty to say precisely who instructed me. All I was told is that, and I quote, 'Freddy and Conchita want you to be happy.' As to the current status of their corporeality, of that I have no actual knowledge."

"This is quite over-whelming Mr. Rossiter. I honestly don't know what to say. I am..."

"Then say nothing, Mr. Storm. That is my advice. In my experience anything you'd like to say is best left unsaid, and any questions you want to ask are best left unasked."

"But is this legal? I mean the police in London told me that all of PaloMar's assets were frozen."

"That's a perfect example of the type of question that is best left unasked. However I will allow it this time. "Yes, their assets were frozen but the money you will shortly receive comes from a separate company not actually tied to PaloMar. It is marked as payment for services rendered and will have tax implications for you in the United States. Though even after that you will still have a substantial fortune at your disposal.

For the next two hours Archibald Rossiter explained the terms of the account and precisely what Roger would need to do to use his new found wealth. After Roger had signed the papers, Rossiter invited him to dinner at one of the island's best jerk chicken restaurants where they ate and drank till late in the evening.

"Well Roger, I think your idea of how to use the money is quite wonderful and very appropriate, if you don't mind me saying so. And I'm sure if you set it up properly you can get a huge tax break. I have people in New York that I can put you in touch with who deal in this sort of stuff. Look, I know this has all happened rather quickly but when exactly do you intend to go to South Africa?"

"As soon as I can Archie. I want to discuss it with my sons. There is something I need to take care of, and they'll need to be prepared if anything should go horribly wrong. Now, I don't mind telling you I'm totally exhausted.

"Of course. Get some rest. I'll have a driver to take you to the airport first thing in the morning.

Chapter 34

IN WHICH THE STORY ENDS
AS IT BEGAN

Chicago
Very recently

H arry Bones sat in his office contemplating
the perfectly laid-out plate of sushi in front
of him. It all looked delicious, and he didn't know
where to start. He glanced over at the little mirror
on his table and raised his eyebrow in appreciation
at what he saw. Not a hair out of place on his
head or his eyebrows. Even the unruly ones in his
nostrils were safely tucked away for the moment.
Just about everything he'd set out to do in his life
had been done. He'd made more money than he
could possibly go through. He'd climbed over
the backs of anyone who had been above him in
his career and emotionally castrated anyone who
stood in his way. He felt neither remorse nor pity
for any of them. His therapist had tried to delve
into Harry's childhood to see if there were perhaps
some underlying parental issues that had made
Harry into one of the most devious and immoral

patients he'd ever had. He'd ultimately concluded that Harry was simply a cunt.

There was only one outstanding matter that still brought a frown to Harry's Botoxed brow. One of his acolytes in the office who'd retained a somewhat friendly relationship with Roger Storm, the person who he hated more than anyone else he'd ever met, told him that Roger had bought a private game reserve in South Africa for a great deal of money. Harry didn't get it. Where the hell had Roger got the money and how dare he be happy? In fact the thought of Roger being happy was almost more than Harry Bones could bear. He grabbed a piece of sashimi off the plate and, dipping it without his usual aplomb into the soy sauce, popped it into his mouth. He ate another few pieces and sat back to contemplate if there was anything in his files he could pull out to use against Roger. He'd like nothing more than to sue him for every penny he'd suddenly got. All of a sudden he was tingling all over, but he wasn't sure it was the familiar tingle of anger.

Fifteen minutes later his assistant knocked on the door to see if she could clear away the remnants of his meal. When she received no response she gingerly opened the door and peered in. Harry Bones was sitting in his chair staring at her. At first she thought he was dead, but she then could hear him struggling for breath. She screamed and rushed over to administer the Heimlich Maneuver, but nothing popped out of his quivering mouth.

Being as efficient an assistant as someone like Harry Bones demanded, she immediately called 911 and then watched as Harry Bones quaked once, soiled himself and died.

The autopsy revealed that Harry Bones had died from an excessive amount of tetrodotoxin, a poison found in the pufferfish and for which there is no antidote. The pufferfish, also known as fugu in Japan, is not illegal in the US, but very few restaurants serve it. The place where Harry got his take-outs was surely not one of them. The police checked the restaurant and found absolutely no evidence that they had or had ever had pufferfish in their kitchen, and concluded that it must have been added to Harry Bones's plate after it had been ordered. Suspicion fell on the delivery guy, but he had vanished.

The End.

CPSIA information can be obtained
at www.ICGtesting.com
Printed in the USA
LVOW03s2239200817
545702LV00017BB/774/P